AF095731

A TIMELESS Romance ANTHOLOGY

Silver BELLS

A TIMELESS Romance ANTHOLOGY

Silver BELLS

SIX HISTORICAL
CHRISTMAS NOVELLAS

LUCINDA BRANT
SARAH M. EDEN
HEATHER B. MOORE
LUANN BROBST STAHELI
ANNETTE LYON
BECCA WILHITE

Mirror Press

Copyright © 2015 by Mirror Press, LLC
E-book edition 2014
Paperback edition 2015
All rights reserved

No part of this book may be reproduced in any form whatsoever without prior written permission of the publisher, except in the case of brief passages embodied in critical reviews and articles.
This is a work of fiction. The characters, names, incidents, places, and dialogue are products of the authors' imagination and are not to be construed as real.

Interior Design by Heather Justesen
Edited by Annette Lyon, Melissa Marler, Cassidy Wadsworth, and Mindy Strunk

Cover design by Mirror Press, LLC

Published by Mirror Press, LLC
http://timelessromanceanthologies.blogspot.com

ISBN-10: 1941145620
ISBN-13: 978-1-941145-62-3

TABLE OF CONTENTS

Fairy Christmas
    by Lucinda Brant

A Christmas Promise
    by Sarah M. Eden

Twelve Months
    by Heather B. Moore

A Fezziwig Christmas
    by Lu Ann Brobst Staheli

A Taste of Home
    by Annette Lyon

My Modern Girl
    by Becca Wilhite

MORE TIMELESS ROMANCE ANTHOLOGIES

Winter Collection
Spring Vacation Collection
Summer Wedding Collection
Autumn Collection
European Collection
Love Letter Collection
Old West Collection
Summer in New York Collection
All Regency Collection
California Dreamin' Collection
Annette Lyon Collection
All Hallows' Eve Collection
Under the Mistletoe Collection
Sarah M. Eden British Isles Collection
Mail Order Bride Collection
Road Trip Collection
Blind Date Collection

Fairy Christmas
by Lucinda Brant

One

Salt Hendon, Wiltshire, England—1767

Christmastide was Kitty's favorite time of year. Since a small child, she'd looked forward to everything the season had to offer. The holiday scent of lavender and rose petals in bedchambers. Rosemary, laurel, cypress, and bay, fashioned into pungent, festive boughs with colored cord and hung in passageways. The mingled cooking odors of fresh bread, rich plum pudding, and gingerbread biscuits baking; of turkey, geese, and capon roasting on spits. And in the winter evenings, in the golden glow of candlelight, the inviting, bittersweet aroma of warm punch spiced with cinnamon, clove, and nutmeg, served up in little cups from a large porcelain bowl.

Public rooms were swept, dusted, and decorated with vibrant evergreens and red-berried garlands of holly, ivy, and mistletoe. Hearths crackled and radiated warmth, and beyond the partially frosted windows lay fields, fences, and hedgerows powdered white with snow, glistening under a diffuse sun.

It was a time for community, those low- and high-born, to come together at church, to commemorate the birth of the Son of God, and to pray in thanks for life's blessings. And it was a time for giving and helping those less fortunate, with small gifts and an open house that offered a hot meal to the needy. Most importantly, it was a time for family to gather and rejoice in one another's company.

But Miss Katherine "Kitty" Aldershot had not had a family, and thus a family Christmas, since her parents' death in a carriage accident when she was still in the schoolroom. The coach they were traveling in had overturned on a bridge and had fallen into a river. Her parents, along with three other unfortunates, had drowned, leaving Kitty and her elder brother orphans. He had promised to look after her and for a time had done just that, until he, too, died in an accident. He'd fallen from his horse, hitting his head and never opening his eyes again.

At eighteen years of age, Kitty found herself alone in the world. For her there was no London season attending routs, balls, or outings to Ranelagh Gardens and Drury Lane Theatre. With no expectation of a season and only a meager dowry, she had no hope of finding a husband, young or old, rich or titled. Yet each night when she said her prayers, she knew she had much for which to be thankful. She had been taken in by the wealthy and powerful Earl of Salt Hendon and his beautiful Countess, who had a young, growing family, and who already supported a handful of relatives with far more claim on the Salt Hendon largesse than did Kitty.

Kitty was given a room of her own, pretty clothes to wear, and never went cold or hungry. She was treated as one of the family, ate her meals at their table, and was included in all their plans. She did her best to repay the Salt Hendons their great kindness by helping to supervise their young children, providing companionship for the Earl's thirteen-year-old goddaughter, Merry, and being often at the beck and call of the Earl's eccentric aunt Alice, Lady Reanay.

Still, with her bedtime prayers said, tucked up in her four-poster bed, the chill taken off the sheets by the copper warming pan, Kitty sometimes found it impossible to stop the tears of self-pity running down her cheeks. It was alone in the quiet blackness of night that the stark reality of her existence became apparent and her future appeared most bleak. She would remain an indigent spinster for the rest of her life, relegated to family helper at best, social embarrassment at worst—which, according to the more acerbic of the Earl's friends and relatives, was more than Miss Aldershot deserved.

But Kitty was only eighteen and thus clung to the optimism of youth. She expected more from life—much more, particularly as she was a fair-haired, violet-eyed beauty. Her looking glass did not lie. She was confident she would make any man an attractive wife, and an accomplished one at that. She could sew, embroider, play the pianoforte, paint in watercolors, and was considered an able conversationalist, showing an interest in public affairs by reading the newssheets and being an attentive listener to the dinner table conversations between the Earl and his guests.

Yet, she did not want to be just any man's wife. She wanted to marry Mr. Tom Allenby. She had danced two dances with Mr. Allenby at the Salt Hendon masquerade ball, and from that night onward, she was as certain as morning followed night that he was the only man with whom she wished to spend the rest of her life. Such was her conviction; she had every expectation of receiving his proposal of marriage this Christmastide—and without ever exchanging a word or a letter on the subject with the gentleman in question.

Kitty refused to entertain any difficulties—most would suggest overwhelming odds—to the fulfillment of this expectation, not least the fact Mr. Allenby, as the brother of the Countess of Salt Hendon, was expected to make a great match. He was also a very wealthy young man, a Member of Parliament for Hendon. As such, he could have his pick during the Season of the flowering beauties who had a pedigree and dowry worthy of him.

None of this deterred Kitty. She might not have discussed the possibility of a shared future with Mr. Allenby—how could they, surrounded as they always were with family and friends?—but since the ball, they had been enough in each other's company to convince her there had developed between them a silent understanding of their feelings for each other.

Kitty believed that all that was required for matters to progress from this silent understanding to a mutual avowal of feelings was for her to have a moment alone with Mr. Allenby. This would allow him to declare himself, and she would accept his offer. To ensure this, she intended to orchestrate an occasion. It would require all her ingenuity and planning, not least because as a young, unmarried girl, she was never alone. Kitty might be the Earl's penniless dependent, but as the daughter of a baron, she was accorded all the protection and courtesy her birthright, and her guardian's preeminent position in Society, demanded. She had been assigned a chaperone, the eccentric Lady Reanay, in whose company she was expected to be at all times when not in the Nursery or her own room—making her, in effect, her ladyship's shadow.

Not only would she need to find an excuse to disengage herself from her ladyship's orbit, but a great deal would also depend on finding a quiet location within the Earl's Jacobean mansion for their meeting to occur. Her plan was becoming increasingly difficult, what with the mansion filling up with guests and family members staying for the holiday season, as well as with daily visits from local villagers, tenants, and owners of neighboring estates, all coming to partake of the Salt Hendons' festive generosity.

Undeterred, Kitty believed she might be able to use such yuletide comings and goings to her advantage. For while the Earl and Countess entertained family members and visitors alike, there would be enough distraction to coax Mr. Allenby to slip away with her to an appointed place and at an allocated time, with servants and family—particularly the beady-eyed Lady Reanay—none the wiser.

As the daylight hours grew shorter and the temperature dropped even further, the large wood-paneled public rooms filled with the laughter and chatter of a multitude of guests. Yet Kitty was more than ever convinced that the herculean task before her was within her powers to orchestrate.

And then into her life stepped a Prince.

Two

Prince Timur-Alexei Nikolai Mordvinov was a member of the Russian nobility. His Highness was part of a Russian trade delegation sent by Catherine the Great to negotiate terms of a treaty and learn all they could about England and its customs. England, or more precisely London, was the center of the consumer world. As such, the Russian nobility was obsessed with acquiring its wares. Her Imperial Majesty had supplied the Prince with a shopping list. He was to buy up all manner of porcelain and silverware, gold and gemstone trinkets, watches, mantel clocks, and fine furniture, and to send it all to St. Petersburg.

Prince Mordvinov was also commanded to provide Empress Catherine with detailed reports and drawings of everything that crossed his path, from the embroidered silks and velvets worn by great ladies to what went on behind the closed doors of the private gentlemen's clubs. The Empress and the Imperial Court wanted to know what type of tea leaf

A Fairy Christmas

was favored by society hostesses, the breed of dog walked by both sexes when promenading the Mall, the pattern on the silverware set on mahogany dining room tables, and the Chinoiserie wallpaper hanging in their boudoirs. Of equal fascination were the traditions of their noble counterparts.

And so His Highness was spending Christmastide as the honored guest of the Earl and Countess of Salt Hendon, with an Imperial sketch artist at his elbow. There was no better way to learn all there was to know about the customs and festivities of this most English of holydays than within the bosom of an English nobleman's family.

There was no better person to answer all the Prince's questions than the lovely Miss Aldershot. So said Lady Reanay, and the Earl and Countess agreed.

Once Kitty had recovered from her surprise at Lady Reanay's praise and the Earl's and Countess's faith in her ability to entertain a Russian prince, she was flattered and only too willing to be the Prince's guide. In Lady Reanay's considered opinion, no one entered into the spirit of the season more than Kitty, and she told the Prince so upon introducing Miss Aldershot. Clapping eyes on the pretty blonde, the Prince was clearly delighted with the arrangement.

Prince Mordvinov became Kitty's constant companion. From breakfast until dinner, he accompanied her everywhere, his sketch artist trotting behind them, hugging a blotter to his wool waistcoat and carrying over one shoulder a red leather satchel, gold-stamped with the Imperial coat of arms and heavy with the implements of his craft—graphite, paper, pastels, and ink.

The Prince directed Kitty to go about her tasks as if he were not there at all. In that way, he was free to observe, and she would, in time, not be overwhelmed by his presence. It helped Kitty's peace of mind that Lady Reanay was almost always in their company. Thus, whenever Kitty was caught up in the activity in the Nursery, be it helping the children construct and color paper Christmas decorations, joining in their games of Blind Man's Bluff, or busily engaged in supervising the maids' filling the small Christmas boxes with coins for the tradesmen and villagers who worked on the estate, Lady Reanay and the Prince retired to a quiet corner. There they drank tea and conversed in French—his preferred tongue, though he made the effort to speak English with Kitty and the rest of the household.

Kitty being Kitty, she might very well have found a way to incorporate the Prince into her plans for a clandestine meeting with Mr. Allenby. There was no better mechanism than a rival to shift a man into action to declare his true feelings. The household's foreign guest had impeccable manners and dress sense, and he was a prince. This alone should have worked to Kitty's advantage—had she decided that flirting with His Highness would prompt Mr. Allenby to act—but for two unalterable facts. First, Mr. Allenby was a young man of even temperament who saw the good in everyone. It was a quality Kitty much admired, but it also meant Mr. Allenby was unlikely to be aware of any cause for jealousy, least of all be roused by it. The second fact, and the most obvious, was that Prince Mordvinov, despite being a prince, was unlikely to be seen as a rival for Kitty's hand. The very idea was laughable.

It was not that the prince was ugly, fat, stooped, or with such hideous habits as to be abhorred. He was straight backed and had a pleasing countenance but for a long, thin nose. He wore the most exquisitely embroidered frockcoats and waistcoats, and his manners could not be faulted. He had bright, lively blue eyes and a smile that radiated friendliness. Despite his noble lineage, there was nothing haughty or conceited about his demeanor. Indeed, he went out of his way to put everyone at their ease and was so friendly and accommodating that within five minutes' conversation, Kitty liked him very well indeed.

Sadly, however, Prince Mordvinov was ancient, old

A Fairy Christmas

enough to be Kitty's grandfather, his face etched with the fine lines of time. She speculated that his powdered wig was not a wig at all but his own long white hair, dressed and tied at the nape with a large black satin bow. And she knew this to be so, as there were no telltale signs of hair powder on the upturned collar or shoulders of his frockcoat, which he changed twice daily. Kitty never saw him in the same ensemble twice.

It was little wonder the Prince and Lady Reanay spent their time drinking tea, leaving the sketch artist to follow Kitty around the room with his blotter. The elderly couple had much in common and were no doubt exchanging anecdotes about the aches and pains in their joints, various remedies for gout and toothache, and reminiscing about their lost youth. Kitty did not begrudge the couple their tea and conversation—it afforded her respite from the Prince's insatiable curiosity. His nonstop questions began with his first cup of tea in the breakfast room and ended with her curtsy to his bow of goodnight.

However, come Christmas Eve morning, the Prince did not show himself at breakfast. It was the first time in a sennight His Highness was absent. Kitty presumed he had gone out early with his noble host and the gentlemen of the household to observe the progress of the Yule log. Dragged by a team of oxen from the woodlot to the house, the seasoned log would be installed in the enormous hearth of the Gallery. This evening was the traditional time the Yule log was set alight, then kept burning for the twelve days of Christmas.

Thus, Kitty went up to the Nursery alone, only for the Prince to poke his white head into the playroom some hours later, looking for her. Dressed in a fitted frockcoat of richly embroidered red velvet, and leaning lightly on his Meissen-handled walking stick, his blue eyes were bright and his smile indulgent. A liveried footman went to announce his presence, but the Prince put a finger to his lips and shook his head as he advanced into the room. Kitty had her back to the doorway, helping thirteen-year-old Merry unpick a stitch in her sampler, which left it to the Earl's four-year-old son and heir, Ned, seated at his little drawing table, to blurt out his disappointment that it was not Uncle Tom come to fetch him away.

"He will be here soon enough, Ned," Kitty told the disgruntled little boy. "You won't miss the Yule log; that I promise you."

The little boy's pout and the sidelong glance of doubt that accompanied this assurance made Kitty smile. She kissed his chubby cheek, then rose and brushed her gossamer apron. Turning about, she discovered the Prince carefully making his way across an Oriental carpet strewn with toys.

"Good morning, Your Highness," she said buoyantly and curtsied. "I am sorry you had to find me. I presumed you were with the men observing the Yule log's progress. A servant could have been sent to fetch—"

"Please. Do not apologize, Miss Aldershot. It is most unnecessary," Prince Mordvinov replied with a smile and a quaint little nod. "I overslept. A rare thing. It was a novelty for me to find my own way here. In Petersburg always there are serfs around every corner, holding a candle, a handkerchief, or a snuffbox should you require it, to open a door, to close a door, to wipe your boots, to unbuckle a shoe, or simply to bow as you walk by. You English make better use of fewer servants . . . I do not even have Viktor as my shadow this morning. I sent him into the snow to sketch this big log of importance."

His gaze swept the half dozen nursery maids who had abruptly stopped their activities as soon as they realized there was a visitor; they bobbed a collective curtsy.

"But I have caused an unnecessary—*fuss*? Yes. Fuss, it is the right word for this intrusion?"

"You are correct about the term 'fuss,' Your Highness. But your presence is not an intrusion."

A Fairy Christmas

He saw her glance distractedly over his shoulder for a second time, and his smile widened. "Lady Reanay awaits us by the tea trolley. Are you able to come with me now before the tea goes cold, or must you wait for—er—*Uncle Tom*?"

"Oh! Yes, of course," Kitty replied, realizing the Prince thought she was expecting her ladyship to be at his shoulder, when in fact she had hoped to see Mr. Allenby—Ned's uncle Tom—and so she told the Prince, hoping her face was not flushed with a guilty blush. She bobbed another curtsy, saying in a rush, "If you will excuse me for one moment, Your Highness. I will then come with you."

When he made a gesture of acceptance, she quickly turned away to speak with Merry, and then to one of the nursery maids, who was sorting satin ribbons into colors to use as ties for wrapping the Christmas gifts for the servants.

"Uncle Tom! Uncle Tom!" Ned shouted and leapt up.

"Yes, Ned. Uncle Tom will be here very soon," Kitty said patiently, turning back to the little boy when Ned's chair hit the floor with a clatter.

And there, standing in the doorway, was Mr. Allenby.

Instantly, Kitty felt her cheeks grow hot. She took a step toward him but immediately stepped away again. "Oh! Mr.—Mr. Allenby! You—You are indeed come! How—how lovely to see you—*for all of us*—to see you!"

Three

"And how lovely to see you, Miss Aldershot," Mr. Tom Allenby replied with a smile, his gaze lingering on Kitty a moment longer than was polite. He thought her very pretty indeed in mint-green silk-striped petticoats and a red satin ribbon threaded through her blonde hair, which matched the color of her red silk shoes. "H-how lovely to see you *all* this fine Christmas Eve," he added with a polite nod to Prince Mordvinov before his gaze returned to Kitty.

A handsome man in his mid-twenties, Tom Allenby had a mop of auburn hair tied back with a black ribbon, soft brown eyes, a cleft to his square chin, and above that, a winning smile. He wore jockey boots and a greatcoat over his suit. Kitty surmised that he had just come indoors and, in his haste to fetch the children to see the Yule log, had not bothered to divest himself of his necessary winter apparel. It was only when Ned ran to greet him and was scooped up

A Fairy Christmas

that Tom and Kitty remembered their manners and broke eye contact.

"I trust I have not kept you all waiting too long?" he asked rhetorically as he rose to his full height, Ned in his arms. For want of something to fill the awkward silence, he picked up the drawing Ned had been busily engaged in creating.

"What's this you've been drawing, Ned? A lovely snow angel? She is *very* pretty."

Ned beamed at the compliment but shook his blond curls. "No! *No*, Uncle Tom! Not a—a *angel*. Guess again! Guess!"

Tom stared at the drawing with an overly dramatic quizzical stare, his bottom lip stuck out and eyebrows raised, and he shook his head slowly as if he had no idea, all to make his nephew giggle. Mentally, he was doing his best to decipher the squiggles and scrawls into something recognizable in the myriad of bright colorful lines, so as to not dampen his nephew's enthusiasm. His pronouncement that the drawing was an angel was a wild guess, but now as he really looked at it, he was not so sure he was wrong. It had two offset eyes, one larger than the other, with thick, black lashes and a mouth colored red. The eyes and mouth were drawn within the lines of a heart-shaped face, which filled the page. A collection of yellow squiggles with a thick red pastel line struck through them sat atop the head.

There was only one person it could be, and he announced confidently, "Why, Ned, she may not be an angel—though some would dispute that. 'Tis a likeness of Miss Aldershot, is it not?"

"Not Miss Alder—Miss Alder—It's Kitty," Ned stated. "It's Kitty Fairy Christmas!"

"Aah! *Fairy Christmas*. Of course! Kitty as Fairy Christmas," Tom Allenby repeated, then cleared his throat of a phantom obstruction; saying Miss Aldershot's Christian name suddenly made him parched. He dared not glance in her direction. "Look, there is the red ribbon in her hair." He held the drawing up for all to see. "Ned, you have captured Miss Aldershot's features perfectly, and you are quite the artist! Highness, what say you?"

The Prince inspected the drawing through his quizzing glass and pretended to ponder over it and to compare the drawing with its subject. He then nodded seriously and glanced at Kitty, who was blushing. "You are a very good drawer of portraits—Ned. And of Christmas fairies."

Ned grinned to be so praised and pointed at Kitty. "Give it to Kitty, Uncle Tom. P-l—*lease*."

Tom Allenby held out the drawing, and Kitty took it with a shy smile, quickly looking up at him when he did not immediately let go of the parchment.

Their eyes met.

He smiled at her.

Kitty smiled back. Such was the intensity of his gaze that she thought him about to say something. And when his lips parted, she was sure of it. She took a step closer, the drawing folding on itself, their fingers lightly touching, her violet eyes widening in expectation, her heart thudding in her chest. But he just stood there, smiling down at her, not saying a word.

Every time he was in her company, Kitty literally took his breath away. She was the most beautiful girl he had ever seen. This time she not only took his breath, but also his ability to form a coherent sentence. Since their two dances at the masquerade ball several months ago, they had met on several occasions, and with each it had become more and more difficult to be in her company and not get tongue-tied. And this time he had an important question to ask her. He had rehearsed his question many times while looking at his reflection in his dressing table looking glass, until he was confident in his delivery. But now, being in Miss Aldershot's presence again, the question dried on his tongue, and his mind went numb. So he just stood there, mesmerized, feeling a fool and wondering what had come over him. The last time he had been in such a state of stupefaction was when he'd been called upon to deliver his maiden speech in the House, and even that had not made him queasy!

It was Ned who moved time on, snatching the drawing and thrusting it at Kitty.

As if awakened from a dream, the young couple both fell back a step, and both looked at Ned. Kitty found her equilibrium and her voice first.

"Thank you, Ned," she said, mustering a bright smile. "I have never had my likeness drawn. And never as a Christmas Fairy." She looked at the drawing and then up at the little boy still with his arms about his uncle's neckcloth. "What a *lovely* drawing. You are a *very* clever boy."

Ned beamed with pleasure, then was suddenly bashful and turned his head into his uncle's shoulder, which made Kitty laugh.

Mr. Allenby chucked his nephew under the chin. "Did I not—Did I not say, Miss Aldershot, you—" He stumbled into speech, vocal cords finally working, and with a quick correction of his slip of the tongue, said, "*It*—is a beautiful drawing."

"Yes. Yes, you did," Kitty replied a little breathlessly, the look of expectation back in her eyes.

But Tom Allenby did not look at her again. He turned away, lifting Ned to his shoulders, and addressed the room. "Time we were off, or we'll miss the Yule log being carried into the Gallery. It looks to be much larger than last year's mighty specimen. Only lifting it will tell. My guess is it will take four burly lads to get it into the hearth. What do you think of that, Ned?" He looked up at his nephew. "A log bigger than last year's monster!"

"Hurry, Uncle Tom! Hurry! Ned doesn't want to miss the log!" Ned demanded, then went on because everyone in the room was looking at him, "Merry, too. And Kitty! And *him*." He pointed a finger at Prince Mordvinov. "Hurry! We must *all* hurry!"

"Coming, Merry?" Mr. Allenby said, putting out a hand to the Earl's thirteen-year-old goddaughter. "I believe your Highness is to have the privilege of lighting the log this year," he said to the Prince. "I am certain Miss Aldershot can explain what an honor that is. We shall see you anon." Then, to the excited children, he announced, "Away we go, then!" And he galloped out of the room with Ned laughing from his shoulders and Merry skipping beside him.

The children's excited chatter and Mr. Allenby's friendly voice were heard trailing off down the passageway, with the young man breaking into Christmas song for their entertainment,

> *O you merry, merry souls,*
> *Christmas is a-coming,*
> *We shall have flowing bowls,*
> *Dancing, piping, drumming!*

The Prince offered Kitty the crook of his velvet sleeve in anticipation of following the merry band to the Gallery.

But Kitty was preoccupied. She was staring at Ned's drawing. Not because she was admiring the little boy's portrait, but because, in carefully rolling it into a cylinder to put in her pocket for safekeeping, she noticed the reverse covered in writing—and recognized the handwriting. It belonged to her regular correspondent, the sister of the Earl of Salt Hendon, the Lady Caroline Temple. It looked to be a page from a letter. How Ned came to have private correspondence in his possession, she could only wonder at. She did not have to wonder at its content.

The first three sentences leapt out at her before she could stop herself from reading them. They were about her and Mr. Tom Allenby.

Four

The first word of the first sentence was illegible because the ink was smudged, but the last letter was clear, as was the rest of what Kitty read.

—y must be prevailed upon. She must be made to realize the insurmountable difficulties of such a marriage. His family will not welcome it, nor will his friends abide such an unequal match. It will be the ruin of TA's career

Curiosity compelled Kitty to read beyond this handful of sentences. But how could she when it was most improper and wicked to read another's private correspondence? Yet how could she *not* when the content was most personal? The first word might be unreadable because the ink was smudged, but the last letter was clearly a Y. Her Christian name ended in a Y. And the initials TA were self-evident.

They belonged to Tom Allenby. To be otherwise would be too much of a coincidence. The unequal match the Lady Caroline wrote of was the very one Kitty anticipated between Mr. Allenby and herself.

Lady Caroline was right; it would be an unequal match, but if Kitty—if *they*—were in love, what did their circumstances matter?

Such had been her abiding belief, until now. That an unequal match would be the ruin of Mr. Allenby had never entered her mind until seeing it written in Lady Caroline's hand. She did not want to be the ruin of the man she loved. But what hurt, what brought the tears welling in her eyes, was that Lady Caroline, whom she considered her one true friend, was not in favor of such a match.

What was the use now of orchestrating a private moment with Mr. Allenby? How could she tell him her feelings if she could not, in good conscience, accept an offer from him? Not if a marriage with her would not only ostracize his family, but also ruin his future prospects as a parliamentarian.

Suddenly all the joy, the merriment, the meaning, and the hope of the Christmas season drained away. She was left with a headache and an aching heart. Still, it said a great deal about her kind and caring nature that when Prince Mordvinov's voice pricked at her subconscious, she willed the tears behind her lids and swallowed her distress.

"Miss Aldershot? Shall we to proceed downstairs?" asked the Prince.

Brought out of her abstraction, and to the embarrassing realization she was being neglectful and rude, she quickly thrust the rolled drawing under her gossamer apron and through the slit in her quilted petticoats into the concealed pocket tied about her waist. For the first time since having the Prince as her shadow, she was grateful for his incessant questions. If anyone could distract her from depressing ruminations, it was he.

A Fairy Christmas

Suppressing the urge to flee to her room to read the rest of the letter fragment, then fall upon her bed in a flood of tears of despair, she placed her hand in the crook of the Prince's arm and went to join family and friends gathered in the Gallery, the largest public room in the Earl's Jacobean mansion, and the only one with a fireplace wide and deep enough to accommodate the Yule log.

"This—Yule log? Yes! *Yule* log!" the Prince said conversationally. "I am very interested for you to tell me all about it, Miss Aldershot." He was not blind to Kitty's distress and knew it had everything to do with the drawing in her pocket. He had seen the writing on its reverse and had watched the change come over his lovely young companion as her eyes scanned the words. Still, he pretended ignorance and did his best to keep her mind occupied. "It is a great trunk from a great tree, yes?"

"Yes, Your Highness. The biggest trunk that will fit the hearth, for it must stay alight until Twelfth Night, which is Epiphany," Kitty explained. She rattled on so the tears again filling the rims of her eyes did not spill onto her cheeks. "Choosing the right log is very important, not only because it must be of a size and seasoned well so the wood will burn for twelve days, but also because the right log is said to contain magical properties. It brings good luck for the coming year to all who give of their strength to haul it to their master's hearth. Its ash must be left to cool in the hearth until after Epiphany, and then it is collected and strewn on the vegetable gardens to bring a better harvest."

"Then I imagine great care is taken when selecting the tree to provide this log? And that every one of Lord Salt's laborers volunteer to be of service in this endeavor?"

"Very true, Your Highness. The men are not only rewarded with good luck for the New Year, but once the log is in place, they also receive small beer and a hot meal of soup and mince pies for their services."

"A fair exchange for the use of their brawn. No doubt all

of their hungry friends are there to provide support with shouts of encouragement, if not with physical labor. Are they, too, on the receiving end of his lordship's generosity?"

"Oh, yes. But the Yule log feast is only one of many at this time of year," Kitty explained. "All across the counties, doors are open wide in invitation. Every man, woman, and child may partake at their master's table. So it is not only Lord Salt who plays host to all manner of men. Even vagabonds and journeymen are given a warm meal. No one goes hungry at Christmastide. Nor should they—the birth of the Son of God should be celebrated by all, from laborer to lord. Do you not agree?" She smiled at the Russian prince. "Which is why Christmastide is my favorite holyday."

"I can see why that is so, Miss Aldershot. What you tell me offers an explanation for an incident that occurred at dawn and is the reason I was late to the breakfast table." The Prince stopped to allow Kitty to go before him, up a short flight of stairs and then down three steps to another corridor. When her hand was back on his arm, he continued. "Yuri, my valet, thought the house was being overrun by peasants, so he rushed into my bedchamber, screaming of revolution. That we—that I—was in danger of having my throat slit! But now I understand; he mistook the men from the field and the vagrants entering this house seeking food as a peasant uprising." The Prince shook his head and rolled his eyes. "Yuri is a most exceptional valet, but this is his first time away from Petersburg. So he is as stupid as the bird who sees its cage door open but does not see an opportunity for escape!"

When this elicited a polite laugh from Kitty, the Prince shrugged, then was suddenly conspiratorial. He stopped in an alcove under the light of a wall sconce, beckoned her closer, and lowered his voice.

"I will tell you and no other, Miss Aldershot. A moment after I was woken by my valet shrieking rebellion, I did believe him. Of course, I was only half awake. That is my excuse. Never have I scrambled from under the bed covers as I did this morning! You English may not have had a peasant uprising since your King Richard, and thus you sleep in your beds contented and without fear, but we Russians blink, and there it is!" He snapped his fingers. "Another peasant revolt! Since our beloved Empress ascended the throne a mere five years ago, it seems that a month does not go by without a group of peasants somewhere in the country causing ridiculous and fruitless upheaval. Their rebellions are for naught, but they continue regardless. So one learns to keep an eye over one's shoulder. Al—Lady Reanay scolded me for being ridiculous... She—she—*giggled*."

The Prince widened his eyes in disbelief. "Can you believe it, Miss Aldershot? She did. But I tell you in all sincerity, if not for her giggling, I might well have run out of the house, into the snow, barefoot and in my nightshirt, and *that* would have made me appear most ridiculous, indeed!"

The Prince gave a little shudder at the memory, then squared his shoulders as if shrugging off the embarrassment. He had confided the incident to divert Kitty from whatever was troubling her. He had succeeded admirably, because she was staring at him in puzzlement as if she was not entirely certain she understood what he was talking about. But after a week in her company, he knew that under her sparkling exterior was an astute young woman. So he was very sure that if he gave her a moment to think matters through, she would discover more than he had intended to reveal.

To continue to divert her thoughts, he pointed the tip of his walking stick at a dark passageway off to their left and asked in a voice he hoped expressed disinterest, "If I were to go down there, what would I find?"

Kitty looked at him with alarm. "*Find*, your Highness?"

He waggled his walking stick in the air. "I am not worried about peasants leaping out at me, revolting or otherwise, if that is your concern." He swished the stick to the right to touch the wooden frame of a painting hanging under the lighted wall sconce. "It's just that I have seen this painting before..."

Kitty was still trying to make sense of the Prince's confidence regarding his valet mistaking farm laborers for Russian revolutionaries, as well as Lady Reanay's part in the little melodrama. But she was most startled to think of Lord Salt's elderly aunt giggling. Only children and young girls giggled, or so she had supposed. Thus, it took a moment to realize that she had not answered his question.

Her gaze followed the length of his walking stick, which still pointed at a painting of a flock of sheep and a solitary cow in a pasture. "Lady Reanay's rooms are at the end of that corridor, your Highness."

"Are they? Are they indeed?" the Prince muttered.

He could have kicked his own stockinged shin for his stupidity. Instead of diverting his fair companion, he had instead heavily underscored her ruminations regarding Lady Reanay. The Earl's aunt Alice would not be pleased with him for his lack of discretion and would tell him so in her own blunt way. *Good.* Let them argue about it. Perhaps then what was whispered in private would finally be stated openly. Besides, he wanted an end to their game of subterfuge, and he could think of no better time to do so than on Christmas Eve, with the lighting of the Yule log when all her family would be present.

The Prince removed his stick from the wall, shifted out of the candlelight, and, with Kitty at his side, walked to the end of the passageway, where a liveried footman opened wide the double doors that gave on to the Long Gallery, allowing them to step into a room filled with light and chatter.

The Earl and Countess, their family, farmers and their kin, neighbors, and honored guests—all were gathered around an enormous hearth, sharing drink and conversation, with an indulgent eye on the children, both low- and highborn, running about the room, playing at Hoop and Hide.

The village vicar was there too, to bless the Yule log with words and wine. Then the Yule log would be set alight by the guest of honor using a preserved scrap from the previous year's log, and the twelve days of Christmas would officially commence.

All of this Kitty was explaining to the Prince when the inimitable Lady Reanay swept up to them.

She was dressed for the occasion *a la Turque*—atop her upswept silver coiffure sat a small green and red silk turban, which matched her loose petticoats. A silk burdash wrapped about her waist, which accentuated her décolletage. Silk slippers with upturned toes adorned her small feet, and she wore half a dozen gold and silver bracelets about her wrists. With the closed sticks of her fan, she tapped Prince Mordvinov on the sleeve.

Kitty instantly stopped talking, and the Prince turned to greet her ladyship with a bow. By the flush to Lady Reanay's cheeks and the twinkle in her eye, he suspected she had enjoyed more than one cup of punch while the crowd awaited his presence. Her pronouncement confirmed his suspicion.

"I want to assure you, Your Highness, that you are quite safe. None of the men in this room are peasants, Russian or otherwise. Nor are they revolting!"

Five

"How droll, my lady," the Prince replied dully. "I'll wager you've been waiting all day to say that."

Lady Reanay unfurled her fan to hide a spreading smile, while the Prince unfobbed the enameled lid of his gold snuffbox, gaze never wavering from her ladyship as he took a pinch of powder between thumb and forefinger.

Kitty looked from one to the other, puzzled. There was a look of mischief in Lady Reanay's eyes she had never seen before. Ned had that same playful expression whenever he was naughty, or about to be. But she never expected to see the Earl's elderly aunt being mischievous. Prince Mordvinov's response was as much a surprise, for while his reply had all the hallmarks of sarcasm, his eyes were bright and playful. When the silence between the elderly couple stretched, Kitty felt that she should say something, if only to alert them to her continuing presence, which they seemed to have forgotten. But an interruption at the far end of the Gallery had all heads turning that way.

On the butler's announcement, the crowd respectfully parted to allow the Earl and Countess to welcome the newest arrivals, Lord Temple and his wife, Lady Caroline. Their hosts embraced the tall gentleman in his early thirties, resplendent in powdered wig and blue frockcoat, and a petite, titian-haired beauty, not much older than Kitty, at his side. Children appeared within the cluster of adults and, seeing the Temples, excitedly waited to be noticed, then threw their arms about the couple. Animated conversation and laughter followed.

"Oh look!" Lady Reanay announced. "It's Antony and Caroline arrived at last! Thank heavens their carriage made it through the snow, and in time for the lighting of the Yule log." She turned back to Kitty with a smile. "Now you'll have company your own age, Kitty dearest, which is as it should be. You will no longer be burdened with His Highness—"

"His Highness is no burden, my lady," Kitty quickly assured her.

"Of course he is! You are a young girl, and he is a tottering old man," Lady Reanay countered. "Is that not so, Your Highness?"

Kitty's mouth involuntarily dropped open at the lack of respect for the Earl's esteemed guest. Either the Prince did not seem to mind, or he was too polite to show offense. He merely threw a lace-ruffled hand in acceptance of Lady Reanay's blunt assessment.

With a sniff of annoyance that was at odds with the look in his eye, he said, "If Lady Reanay says I am a burden, then I am a burden . . ."

"Oh, no, Your Highness," Kitty contradicted earnestly. "I have very much enjoyed your company and your stories—"

"Stories?" interrupted Lady Reanay with alarm and peered at the Prince. "Timur?! What stories have you been telling dearest Kitty? I hope you have been behaving yourself."

"When do I not behave myself, my lady?" the Prince replied blandly, not a glance at Kitty. "No! Do not answer me that, or you will get us both in trouble." He bowed to Kitty. "Please, Miss Aldershot, forgive us our ridiculous behavior. But I am certain you fully appreciate it is all the fault of her ladyship—"

Lady Reanay gasped and then laughed. "You will not force my hand in this way, Your Highness!" she said and quickly turned back to Kitty before the Prince could offer a rejoinder. "You have taken very good care of His Highness and justified the faith and trust I placed in you to be his guide. Lord Salt is most impressed and even more than a little surprised. You have shown a level of maturity and responsibility beyond your years, which has helped to persuade him to your cause—"

"M—my *cause*?" Kitty involuntarily interrupted, wondering what cause the Earl of Salt Hendon was being persuaded to support on her behalf.

"But it is Christmas Eve," Lady Reanay went on, deftly changing the subject before Kitty could ask anything further. "The Yule log must be lit before the Christmas festivities can truly begin." She placed her bejeweled hand on the crook of the Prince's velvet sleeve. "Come, Your Highness, it is time for you to put a flame to that log, before my nephew loses all patience and does the deed himself. You know how Salt is not one for small talk—Oh! And speaking of enjoying the company of people your own age, Kitty dearest, here is Tom, and with two cups of punch. One must surely be for you. Such a dear boy..."

Before Kitty could respond, the Prince and Lady Reanay abandoned her, and a cheer went up from the crowd about the hearth when the couple stepped into the light at the Earl's elbow.

Tom Allenby passed them with a nod, but he did not

turn at the sudden noise. When he joined Kitty, he held out a cup of punch and took a sip from his own to moisten his throat and loosen his tongue. He had tidied his hair, was divested of his greatcoat, and his jockey boots below his velvet breeches, which matched his dark velvet frockcoat, had been given new polish.

"I wonder—I wonder, Miss Aldershot, if I might have that word?"

Kitty took the cup of punch, his question music to her ears. She smiled up at him as if she had been blessed with ten years' worth of Christmas Cheer at once.

"Yes! Oh, yes, Mr. Allenby. I should like that very much."

He nodded, pleased and visibly relieved.

"Good. Excellent. After dinner then . . .?"

Kitty's smile vanished. "After dinner . . .?" That was too far away. She looked about. Everyone else, from family to servants, was gathered in the middle of the Gallery. A window seat was only an arm's length away—and vacant. They would still be in others' line of sight, and thus within the bounds of propriety, if they sat there for a moment. With so much competing conversation and laughter, there was no possibility of them being overheard. To her mind, there was no better time than now for Tom Allenby to have his word with her. She took a sip of warm punch and tried to keep the eagerness from her voice.

"Surely we would not be missed if we were to sit for a few minutes in that seat there, would we, Mr. Allenby . . .?"

Tom Allenby followed her gaze to an undraped window, where a bough of holly and mistletoe hung in the velvet drapes and the view was of a winter sun setting fast over snow-covered fields. He swallowed, hard. He had not figured on saying his piece here and now. To settle his nerves, he took another sip from his cup. In response to Prince Mordvinov's short speech, a roar of laughter went up from the farmers. Tom looked over his shoulder in time to witness the vicar stepping forward with the blessing cup and the Earl holding the piece of kindling kept from the Yule log of Christmas past, ready to light it.

"You do not wish to see the Yule log set alight by His Highness, Miss Aldershot?"

"I do, Mr. Allenby. But perhaps what you have to say to me at this moment is more important?" Kitty asked a little breathlessly.

His eyes went wide, and he swallowed and nodded. "Yes, yes, you are quite right. It is more important . . ."

Kitty smiled encouragingly. "Well then. Let us sit upon the window seat, and you may tell me there."

She waited for him to join her. He threw back the last drop of punch, squared his shoulders, and followed. Seated on the tapestry cushion, and with her hands in her lap, Kitty looked up at Tom Allenby with what she hoped was a friendly and not too eager expression, heartbeat thudding in her ears.

That's when it happened.

Later, Kitty would wonder which occurred first, because two incidents happened almost simultaneously. But that was no consequence. What was important was that they happened at all.

When Kitty put her hands in her lap, she felt something unfamiliar under her gossamer apron. It was the paper cylinder—Ned's drawing of her as a Christmas Fairy—in her concealed pocket. Instantly, she remembered the writing on the back of the page—those first few hurtful lines from Lady Caroline's letter—*She must be made to realize the insurmountable difficulties of such a marriage. His family will not welcome it, nor his friends abide such an unequal match*—and her head began to pound with a thud as strong as that within her chest. She suddenly felt ill and wretched. She no longer wished to hear what Tom Allenby had to say to her.

Her sigh of relief was audible when Tom Allenby was

forestalled by Ned, who called out to his uncle Tom, then ran up to them.

The little boy had hold of his mother's hand and was seemingly dragging her up the Gallery, away from the family gathering. He soon broke from her and, calling out to his uncle Tom, raced on ahead, leaving his mother, the Countess of Salt Hendon, to follow.

"Hurry, Mamma! Hurry!" Ned insisted as he reached his uncle Tom. "Papa said we have *two* minutes, that's *all*! Two!"

The Earl and everyone else gathered about the fireplace were waiting for Tom and Kitty to join them in the festivities, and the Countess agreed that lighting the Yule log would not be the same without all the family present.

But no sooner had their son and heir reached the silent couple than he forgot his reason for being there and demanded, "Kitty, show Mamma Fairy Christmas, p-l-*ease*. Uncle Tom says it is the *bestest* fairy ever!" He looked up at his mother, who now stood behind him.

"Oh, if you drew it, I am sure it must be the *bestest* fairy, my darling." Jane, Countess of Salt Hendon, smiled lovingly at her son before noticing the couple seated on the window seat. A glance at her brother and then at Kitty, and she knew that she and Ned had intruded upon a private moment. Her brother's features were always easy to read, and Kitty could not raise her gaze from her lap.

"Salt won't allow the vicar to bless the log or the Prince to carry out the ceremonial lighting until *all* the family are gathered round the hearth," the Countess told them matter-of-factly, ignoring the awkward moment. "Kitty, did you see that Caroline and Antony have arrived? You must come and greet them, particularly as they have some *exceedingly interesting* news they are eager to share with you. Tom, did you tell Kitty?"

"I haven't had the opportunity to say much at all to Miss

Aldershot," Tom said, enunciating with a hard stare at his sister and not a look at Kitty.

"The fairy!" Ned interrupted. "Kitty? Kitty, where is Fairy Christmas?"

"I don't . . . I wish . . ." Kitty began but faltered.

"Have you lost Fairy Christmas?" the little boy asked on a swift intake of breath.

Kitty shook her head and suddenly leapt to her high-heeled mules and brushed down her apron, keeping her chin lowered because there were still tears in her eyes and she was very sure she would be unable to stop them from falling this time. She hated lying to Ned. In fact, she had never lied to him and did not want to do so now. The throbbing at her temple increased, as did the sickness in her stomach.

"We can have the drawing fetched after dinner, Ned," the Countess said softly, taking her son by the hand. "Papa is waiting. Two minutes, remember?"

"Ned, shall I take you to Papa on my shoulders?" Tom Allenby suggested eagerly.

Ned pulled away from his mother. But he did not go to his uncle. He went to Kitty. He put his little hands on his silken knees, stooped and turned his head, golden curls falling back from his face, to look up into her face. His little brow contracted into a frown.

"Fairy Christmases are happy fairies, Kitty. Why are you sad?" He looked up at his mother. "Mamma, Kitty is sad."

Kitty had sniffed back tears and tried to smile at the little boy, but it was impossible. She was miserable. How could she join the family festivities when she felt anything but festive or one of the family? Being reunited with Caroline, newly returned from a five-month sojourn in Ireland and with news of a baby on the way—for what else could her *exceedingly interesting* news be?—would only underscore her own bleak prospects. Having such selfish, self-absorbed thoughts when she should have been so happy for her best friend only added to her wretchedness. She was not fit company for anyone. Was it any wonder that Caroline had written she was unsuitable to marry into this illustrious family?

"I am unwell," she whispered. "Excuse me. Excuse me, my lady. Please—*please* excuse me."

With that rush of words and a hurried curtsy, Kitty fled from the Gallery to the sanctuary of her room, where she threw herself onto the bed and gave in to her misery.

Six

When she was dry of tears, Kitty rolled over and lay on her back, staring up at the bed's pleated silk canopy. In the candlelit stillness and quiet, she fell asleep. For how long, she was unsure, but looking at the candle's flame on the bedside table, she knew it was for at least an hour, possibly two. Upon waking, she was no longer upset, just listless, which enabled her to reflect. With reflection came forbearance.

She went to the washstand, poured water from the flowered porcelain pitcher into its matching bowl, and splashed her face. Seated at her dressing table, she repinned her hair, retied the red silk ribbon into a better bow, and straightened the gossamer apron over her quilted silk petticoats. From her concealed pocket she removed the now-crushed drawing, unrolled it on the surface of her dressing table, and smoothed out the creases as best she could.

A Fairy Christmas

She stared at Ned's drawing of her as a Christmas Fairy—its big offset eyes, large mouth and bird's nest scribble of blonde hair—smiled and sighed. The drawing was so precious, and no truer words had the little boy spoken: Fairy Christmases were happy fairies. Christmas was a joyous time, a celebration of the birth of Jesus, which had brought great happiness to the world.

But lost in her own selfishness, she had forgotten the message of Christmas. She had also forgotten how fortunate she was to have the Salt Hendon family as *her* family. There were many orphans in the world, and she was no longer one of them. She had told the Prince how, at this time of year, the Earl and many noblemen like him opened their doors to offer warmth, and their larders to offer food, to those much less fortunate than themselves. Kitty would never go hungry, and she would never be cold.

That her best friend, Caroline, was expecting her first child was the most wonderful news imaginable. And what had she, Kitty, done in response to such news? She had thought of only herself, and those disheartening words written on the back of Ned's drawing, and had immediately become miserable. She should not have let such words blacken her heart, for in doing so, it had blackened everything else.

Caroline was entitled to her opinion, and was not Kitty living up to such an opinion with her selfish behavior?

As for her hopes and dreams of marrying Mr. Tom Allenby, well, she would not blame him if he did not wish to marry such a self-absorbed creature. Her childish conduct in running from the Yule log ceremony was surely evidence enough of that. Tom Allenby was a good man with a good heart, and he deserved nothing less in return. She was very sure she was in love with him, but if he did not return her regard, then so be it. She could not make him love her, nor would she. She must be resolute and let the future take care of itself. She had so much for which to be thankful—the family who had embraced her and the love they had shown her—and that was more than enough for a young girl eighteen years of age.

Decided, and feeling very much better, Kitty left her bedchamber with Ned's Fairy Christmas to rejoin the family and guests in the Gallery. She did not read the rest of what was written on the back of the drawing. It was not hers to do so. What was important was the loving message reflected in Ned's drawing.

Arriving in the Gallery, she was surprised to find it deserted but for Prince Mordvinov and a footman attending to the fire. The servant held a pair of bellows should the fire show signs of faltering; servants would now be on rotation to keep the Yule log burning until Twelfth Night.

The Prince sat cross-legged in a wingchair nearest the warmth, swirling brandy in a crystal tumbler and gazing into the hearth, his thoughts miles away. So much so, that Kitty was admiring the magnificent Yule log, her hands spread to the warmth, before she was noticed. When she curtsied, he offered the adjacent settee for her to sit on.

"You missed dinner, my dear. There were many dishes, but the one I most remember and enjoyed was a splendid venison pie. You English are very good at surprising the palate by encasing succulent morsels in mouth-watering pastry. One bite, and—ah!—it melts in the mouth. And then there are the little mincemeat pies Lady Reanay favors, and at any hour, for they are only made at this time of year, yes? But forgive me. How are you? I hope you are feeling much better? You look well."

"Yes, thank you, I am, Your Highness." When the Prince's gaze drifted back to the Yule log, she added, to fill the silence, "I like mincemeat pies too. And Yorkshire Christmas pies, because they are very large and decorative and feed so many. You will soon see. Those will be served at the feast of St. Stephen, in two days' time—Your Highness, I am very sorry I missed the blessing of the Yule log. But most particularly I am sorry I did not see you have the honor of lighting the log this year."

"Please, Miss Aldershot, an apology is unnecessary. The important thing is that I did not embarrass myself, and this massive trunk, it is now lit and shall stay that way for the—twelve?—yes, twelve days of Christmas. You see me sitting here alone, enjoying a few moments of solitude—"

"Oh! And I have interrupted you. I am sorry."

"Not at all. There is only one other in this house, indeed in this country, who I am more than happy to have interrupt my solitude. I give you such a compliment as one old enough to be your grandfather, so you are not to feel awkward or think me a senile old lecher. Ha! Now you are truly blushing! Forgive me, Miss Aldershot."

He sipped at his brandy, adding in a more conversational tone, "Everyone has gone off to do various tasks, but they have all promised to return here. Lady Reanay says we are to drink a Christmas concoction of apples and spices from a wassail bowl and then to play at a silly game called Hunt the Slipper, or was it Questions and Commands? I have not played either, but the vicar, he was not amused and said such games are for Twelfth Night only. Quite a heated exchange occurred . . ." He chuckled. "Her ladyship would not concede, and when the vicar said he must retire early to prepare for his most important sermon in the morning, my very good friend Lord Temple proposed a solution. He said that perhaps one game would not do us any harm, particularly as it was important to instruct the guest—me—in how to play before Twelfth Night is upon us. Lord Temple is ever the diplomat!"

"Yes," Kitty agreed. Adding seriously, not seeing the twinkle in the Prince's eye, "Lady Caroline says her husband will be an Ambassador one day . . . I suspect the children wished to join in the Christmas games?"

"They did. But the prospect of gifts awaiting them tomorrow morning after church was enough of an inducement to see them scamper off to bed so they could fall asleep, so tomorrow would arrive much sooner." The Prince shook his head with a smile. "Ned is a most precocious child, and his little sister the image of her beautiful Mamma. I suspect Lord and Lady Salt, with Ned's uncle Tom, are still in the Nursery saying their good nights. Such attentive and loving parents, and Mr. Allenby is a most excellent uncle. I predict he will also be an attentive father.

"When my children were small," he added smoothly, hardly stopping for breath and keeping a close eye on Kitty, whose gaze had darted to the floor at mention of Tom Allenby, "I do not think I was in their company more than once in a week. And then only when they were brought to my study for my inspection. No doubt so I could count them and see they were all alive and well. When they went off to the summer house, they did not see their Papa for months at a time . . ." He rallied and smiled. "I am much better at being a grandpapa. I have ten."

"Ten grandchildren, Your Highness?" Kitty repeated, impressed.

"I beg your pardon. I have ten children. If memory serves me, at last count I had thirty grandchildren. I was married twice. Both marriages were arranged, as is our custom. I believe that is not uncommon here, too . . ."

He shrugged, and Kitty remained silent, realizing the Prince was in a reflective mood and merely wanted her to listen.

"I never thought of the alternative—marrying for love. It was not a choice for one of my birth. But I have no complaints. Both of my wives were lovely and sweet and good mothers. The first, Anna, died in childbed. The second, Natalya, of influenza . . . To be in love is not quite what I expected . . ."

He drank his brandy, chuckling at some private thought before turning to Kitty with bright eyes. "I will tell you a little secret, Miss Aldershot. What is most unexpected is that I

A Fairy Christmas

never thought it would happen to me, this falling in love. I was not looking for it. To find myself in love for the first time at my age . . . It is quite a shock, and no doubt shocking to others. Be warned! It can hit you at any time, at any place, and at any age!"

Lady Reanay bustled up to the hearth. "I hope you are not turning Kitty's ears red with one of your stories, Timur?" she asked. "She is too young to be bothered with your age and what can hit you. Please forgive him, Kitty. I blame his English translation. I suspect, however, that even if he were to converse with you in French or Russian—or Greek, for that matter—his conversation would still be most unsuitable for the ears of young girls."

The Prince raised his long nose in the air. "I have been on my best behavior this past week; I assure you," he drawled. "Miss Aldershot will vouch for me."

"Oh, yes! Yes, he has, my lady," Kitty said earnestly before she realized the Prince was play-acting for Lady Reanay's benefit; the elderly couple exchanging a teasing look.

"How are you now, my dear?" Lady Reanay asked Kitty, spreading out her silk petticoats *a la Turque* to sit beside her on the settee. "Jane sent your maid to look in on you, but you were sound asleep. So we thought it best to leave you that way. Playing Christmas guide to His Highness has worn you thin and left you a little exhausted. No! Don't argue with me. I know it is so. And His Highness agrees with me. A dinner tray has been prepared. Do you think you might be able to eat something now?" When Kitty shook her head with a smile, she patted her hand. "Very well. Perhaps when the others return . . . Oh! Is that Ned's Christmas Fairy you have there?" she asked, spying the drawing in Kitty's lap and trying to sound uninterested. "May I see it?"

"Of course, my lady." Kitty handed her the drawing.

Lady Reanay squinted over the piece of paper, turning it this way and that, until the Prince made a clucking sound and waved a hand at her, saying what was also on Kitty's mind.

"Your spectacles, Alice. Wear them. And do not tell me they make you look old! We *are* old," the Prince said cheerfully, then grinned when Lady Reanay huffed her annoyance and pulled a face at him.

But she put on her spectacles as he commanded and saw the drawing anew, this time right way up. Without warning, she flipped it over and asked Kitty gently, her gaze on the writing, "His Highness said these words upset you . . ." When there was no reply, she looked over her gold rims. "Oh, we won't say a word about it, dearest. Will we, Timur? But we do not like to see our favorite Christmas Fairy in distress for any reason. Is that not so, Your Highness?"

"That is very true," agreed the Prince.

"I should not have read any of it, my lady. It was wrong of me," Kitty replied with a guilty blush and a glance at the Prince. "And I do not want Ned to be in trouble if, as I suspect, he took the page from amongst the letters on his mamma's escritoire, particularly as he then drew upon it."

Lady Reanay nodded, only half-listening, as she had dropped her gaze and was reading. And as she read, a change came over her. Her mouth puckered. She sat up tall. She squared her shoulders. She stopped fanning herself and looked indignant. More than once she glanced over the sheet to look, not at Kitty, but at the Prince. Finally Lady Reanay dropped the hand holding the letter into her silken lap.

"You did not read very much of this at all, did you, Kitty dear?"

Kitty shook her head. "No, my lady. I did not. It is not mine to read, and truly, I should not have read what little I did."

"You read three lines at most. Possibly to the word *career*." Lady Reanay peered down at the letter again. "Yes, to 'the ruin of TA's career . . .' Would that be so?"

A Fairy Christmas

Kitty nodded and was startled when Lady Reanay stated bluntly, "I agree. You should not have read any of it!"

"I—I am truly sorry," Kitty stammered, unaccustomed to hearing anger in her ladyship's normally placid and loving voice. "But Lady Caroline is in the right."

"Do not upset the child, Alice," the Prince advised Lady Reanay in a low voice, sitting forward in the wingchair. "Miss Aldershot says she is sorry, and that will be an end—"

"If you knew what was written here, you would agree with me!" Lady Reanay interrupted rudely.

The Prince, far from being offended to be so bluntly addressed, calmly put out a hand. "Then allow me to read it and agree with you."

"If you do, you most definitely will *not* agree with me!" Lady Reanay stated in an abrupt about-face, Ned's drawing remaining in her lap. "In fact, Caroline's argument is precisely what I have been trying to tell you all along. But you stubbornly refuse to listen!"

"I am listening now."

"I know you, Your Highness. You won't change your mind. You are an infuriatingly stubborn man."

The Prince held her gaze and then inclined his head in agreement, a smile curving his mouth as he raised his brandy glass to her. Lady Reanay sighed, threw up her hands in annoyance, and returned to fluttering her fan with an agitated movement.

"Lady Caroline is in the right," Kitty repeated, her eagerness to show her contrition blinding her to the scene being played out between the elderly couple. "I realize now that Mr. Allenby's career would be ruined were he to marry me. It was such a—a shock to see it written that way. But now that I have reflected upon Caroline's words, I realize she was not saying it spitefully, but merely as fact. I assure you both that if Mr. Allenby were to ask me to marry him—not that I am in expectation of receiving such an offer, but if he did ask me—I would refuse the honor. I do see that there are 'insurmountable difficulties' and that his friends, though I have not met them, are unlikely to approve of me. And Lord Salt cannot want me for a sister-in-law; I am an orphan without a dowry and a mere baron's daughter, while Mr. Allenby is not only the MP for Hendon, he is, to be quite vulgar, exceedingly rich, *and* he is the brother of a Countess. So I do understand how *unequal* such a union would be."

When this confessional speech was met with silence, Kitty blinked, realizing only then that judging by their expressions, the couple was engaged in a silent quarrel, and her presence was the only reason they were not vocalizing their argument. But she was wrong to think her words had gone unheard. It was just that such was the battle of wills, with neither the Prince nor Lady Reanay wishing to capitulate. Kitty looked from one to the other; they had eyes only for each other, and she was about to suggest that she was hungry after all and quietly excuse herself to call for her dinner tray when Lady Reanay came to life.

The old lady shot up off the settee and thrust the drawing at the Prince, who took it and settled back to read, first searching a deep frockcoat pocket for his spectacles. Lady Reanay then turned on Kitty, and the look of anguish in her hazel eyes was so at odds with her forthright speech that Kitty fell back against the settee, speechless.

"Rot!" Lady Reanay burst out. "What you said just now, Kitty, all of it, is utter rot and drivel! Regardless if you are an orphan with only two pennies to your name, you are a baron's daughter. As such you outrank Tom Allenby, a mere merchant's son. He is a dear boy, and Jane's stepbrother, and he will succeed as a parliamentarian. Yes, he owns vast manufacturing concerns in Bristol, which, as you say, have made him exceedingly wealthy. But for all that, he should consider himself extremely fortunate indeed to marry the daughter of a baron. If anyone is to make an unequal match of such a union, it is you, dearest Kitty! Besides which, you are the sweetest, kindest, most loyal girl imaginable, and he

A Fairy Christmas

should count his good fortune if you were to agree to marry him. Is that not so, Timur?"

"Yes. That is so," the Prince murmured, not taking his eyes from the letter fragment.

"If Tom loves you and you love him, I do not see what my nephew the Earl can object to in the match," Lady Reanay continued. "Caroline or Antony cannot object, either. And Jane only wants her brother—and you, Kitty dear—to be happy."

Kitty blushed with delight to have Lady Reanay's support, but she did not understand what had caused her ladyship's distress, for there were tears in her eyes. And the Lady Caroline's words still niggled.

"Thank you, my lady. But . . . the letter—Caroline's words . . ."

"My dear girl," Lady Reanay said with a sigh of exasperation, "what is written on the back of Ned's drawing is not about you and Tom."

"That is very true," the Prince agreed, sitting up and smiling at Kitty. He held out a clean white linen handkerchief to Lady Reanay. When she stared at him and then at the square of linen as if it were an object foreign to her, he added gently, "Dry your eyes, my dear, before the others return."

"Those words are not about me and—and Mr. Allenby?" Kitty was skeptical. "Pardon, my lady, but even though the first word is smudged and thus unreadable, the last letter, a Y is clear, and my name ends in a Y. And the initials TA—who else could they belong to but Mr. Thomas Allenby? And while you and His Highness may champion my cause—a circumstance for which I am exceedingly grateful—it does not mean that Caroline must. It is her opinion that a union between me and Mr. Allenby would be the ruin of his career."

"Miss Aldershot, let me reassure you," the Prince said with a note of apology, "that you have upset yourself unnecessarily." He glanced fleetingly at Lady Reanay. "It is not Mr. Allenby's career that is to be ruined, it is mine. And it is Lady Reanay who will be its ruin." He held up Ned's Christmas Fairy. "This is not about you; it is about *us*."

Seven

"About *you* and—and Lady Reanay? But how can it be?"

In her utter astonishment at Prince Mordvinov's pronouncement, Kitty forgot her manners. She stared at him and then at Lady Reanay. Both regarded her with sympathy. She did not know what else to say, so she patiently waited further explanation.

The Prince set aside his brandy glass, pocketed his spectacles, and picked up his walking stick. He rose slowly from the wingchair, and being slightly unsteady on his feet, Lady Reanay was quick to take his arm, an attentive, sharp-eyed footman one step behind. The servant took the brandy glass and, with a bow, returned to his position by the fireplace, one of his fellows coming up to take his place and attend to the fire.

"Forgive me. I have been sitting too long," the Prince said, leaning on his walking stick. "You know what that does to my weak knees," he added as an aside to Lady Reanay, who had him by the elbow. He held up Ned's drawing and addressed Kitty. "Under the circumstances, it would be for the best if Miss Aldershot were permitted to read the fragment in its entirety."

Lady Reanay agreed. "Yes. Under the circumstances..."

The Prince nodded. "Good. While Miss Aldershot does so, let us take a stroll about the Gallery. It will better prepare me for playing at Hunt the—er—Slipper—?"

"Don't be ridiculous, Timur! When I suggested the family play Christmas games, I did not include us in their number. We will do what the elderly always do: watch on in silence with indulgent smiles."

"But . . . I would like to play Hunt the Slipper—with you," he teased, and turned to give Kitty a quaint little bow before Lady Reanay could respond. He handed Kitty the drawing. "Forgive us our silliness. Here. Read. If nothing else becomes clear, it will at least convince you that this has nothing to do with you and Mr. Allenby." He smiled crookedly. "I believe the Y is the last letter in the name *Reanay*, her ladyship's name. The T and A are the initials of my first names, *Timur-Alexi*. No doubt Lady Caroline was doing her best to conceal whom she was discussing. Unfortunately, her efforts were for naught, as she went on to mention the Empress and the Imperial Court. But please, read first, and then we will talk. Come, Alice, let's leave her in peace to do so."

Kitty silently watched the couple slowly walk off arm in arm up the Gallery, both falling easily into the French tongue, which was their custom when alone together. When they were halfway up the length of the long room, Kitty shifted to the wingchair by the enormous hearth to be closer to the warmth and light. With the soft crackle of the burning Yule Log in the background, she dropped her gaze to the letter fragment.

A Fairy Christmas

—y must be prevailed upon. She must be made to realize the insurmountable difficulties of such a marriage. His family will not welcome it, nor will his friends abide such an unequal match. It will be the ruin of TA's career, so says Antony, and all he has achieved will be for naught. As for her, I am saddened to admit that though I love her dearly, family history is against her. The title of "princess" will not eradicate her past. With one divorce and an elopement to her discredit, she will never be received by the Empress or at the Imperial Court. She will be consigned to wait in her drawing room for visitors who will never come. I do not want to see her suffer so.

You say she is sensible and can be persuaded to do what is right by him. But I am not convinced. She is of an age when reason is thrown to the winds. What has she to lose? What has he? No doubt they have convinced themselves they are in love, so there is little hope of reasoning with either side. Thus I beseech you to advise Salt to caution her gently. I do not envy him the task, but as head of the family, he is the right and proper person to do so.

I hope you, dearest Jane, have counseled it be done before Christmastide, before the family gather for an occasion that should be joyous in every sense, though I fear our pudding, our prayers, and our Twelfth Night gambols will be heavy with her sad disappointment.

If Kitty was left wide-eyed with new knowledge after having read the fragment, she was dizzy with relief that she and Mr. Tom Allenby were not the object of Lady Caroline's letter. With relief came the realization that she had been needlessly foolish, filling her head with all sorts of unnecessary worry and conjecture. Yet it said a great deal about her caring nature that relief was soon replaced with concern for the future happiness of the couple now strolling the Gallery.

She knew a little about Lady Reanay's checkered past. Three decades ago, the Earl's aunt ran off to the Continent with a knighted jeweler while still married to her husband, leaving a small son behind. Her family had consequently disowned her, and Society had turned its back on the notorious Alice Sinclair St. John, as she was known before her eventual marriage to her lover, Sir Tobias Reanay. It had only been a handful of years since her return from abroad, and at the kind invitation of the Countess of Salt Hendon, her notorious past had been forgiven, if not forgotten.

It seemed she was once again inviting the ire of her family, this time because of her love for a Russian Prince.

It never occurred to Kitty that the elderly was capable of falling in love, least of all given to courting. She had wrongly assumed love and courtship were the exclusive realm of the young. But watching them paused in their stroll, the Prince adjusting the red woolen shawl about Lady Reanay's shoulders as she issued instructions to a liveried footman, Kitty saw them with new eyes, and it was a revelation.

It occurred to her that since arriving at Salt Hendon, the Prince had been courting Lady Reanay, and under Kitty's very nose! She recalled the times the couple had sat together in a corner of the Nursery, taking tea while she helped with the children, or when they retired after dinner to the farthest settee in the drawing room to talk while the rest of the family played at cards or enjoyed an evening musical recital or read aloud. The couple had always managed to slip away to an unoccupied window seat or settee to be alone. Preoccupied with other family members, caught up in the endless preparations for Christmastide, or daydreaming of what she would say to Mr. Tom Allenby when he joined the festive celebrations, Kitty had been oblivious to it all. Was the rest of the family equally blind? Based on Lady Caroline's fragment, not all of them could be.

A Fairy Christmas

Being no longer blind, and of a romantic disposition, Kitty wondered what the Earl of Salt Hendon and his family could have to object to in a marriage between a couple in their twilight years. The Prince must have read her mind, for when he and Lady Reanay returned to the Yule log, he offered Kitty his arm to take a stroll with him, while her ladyship said she would keep Ned's Christmas Fairy safe until their return.

Two minutes up the long room, and Prince Mordvinov startled Kitty by confiding, "Miss Aldershot, allow me to tell you that I come from a strict noble family who have never married outside their social strata. I have always done what was expected of me, so now, at my advanced stage of life, I have earned the right to do what pleases me, do you not think so?"

"Yes, Your Highness, I do."

He smiled and patted her hand, then again became serious. "I have waited a long time to marry Lady Reanay. I fell in love with her while she was still married to Sir Tobias; I did not tell her then. We corresponded for many years. Believe me, Miss Aldershot, there is no better way to truly understand a person than through the exchange of the written word. Were you aware that she has roamed the Continent from Oslo to Constantinople, has crossed the Syrian desert by camel, and swum the Nile when her felucca capsized? Ah, the stories she can tell! She makes me laugh, and I make her giggle. That is important. If there is no laughter, how, then, can you truly be comfortable with each other? Miss Aldershot, you are young and have the whole of your life ahead of you. May I offer you some advice?"

"Of course, Your Highness. I would be glad of it."

"Spend some months exchanging letters with Mr. Tom Allenby. In that way, you will become friends. And then, when the time is right, and you both feel you know each other well, the next logical step will present itself."

"Your Highness, Mr. Allenby has not asked to correspond with me. How—"

"But you would like to exchange letters with that estimable young man, would you not?"

Kitty paused, then nodded, blushing, unable to hold the Prince's gaze when he grinned, a knowing light in his blue eyes. "Good. That is what I told him," he said matter-of-factly.

Ignoring Kitty's wide-eyed stare that he'd dared do such a thing, the Prince returned her to the hearth, where Lady Reanay held up the drawing. She turned it over to show them the reverse. The writing was now covered with a thin sheet of silver paper.

"Only lightly glued, but it will suffice to stop any questions. You, dearest Kitty, may now show the proud mother her son's exceptional drawing skills. And here they come now," Lady Reanay announced, returning the drawing to Kitty.

The Earl and Countess of Salt Hendon, with Lord Temple and Lady Caroline a step behind, entered the Gallery, all four full of good cheer and conversation. Mr. Tom Allenby was soon to follow.

"Thank you, my lady," Kitty replied sincerely, turning to Lady Reanay and kissing the old lady's cheek. She smiled at the Prince but said to her ladyship in a whisper, "Christmas Eve would be the perfect occasion to tell the family of your wonderful news. I am sure His Highness wishes to make an announcement. May I be the first to wish you both very happy?"

"Oh, my dear girl, of course! I am delighted to hear you say so!" Lady Reanay looked across at the Prince. "Did I not always say that dearest Kitty was an angel, Your Highness?"

"An angel?" the Earl cut in, taking out his snuffbox and looking about at his family. "I thought Kitty had been crowned our resident Christmas Fairy."

A Fairy Christmas

"She has, my lord," Jane, Lady Salt, said with a smile. "Observe your son and heir's extraordinary drawing talent." She took Ned's drawing from Kitty and held it up for the Earl's inspection. "This is Kitty as Fairy Christmas."

When the Earl raised an eyebrow, but diplomatically refrained from commenting, the Countess laughed and squeezed his silken arm.

"Oh, Kitty, are you feeling better?" Lady Caroline asked, embracing her best friend. "Did Jane tell you . . . that Antony and I are expecting?"

"It is the most wonderful news, Caro, and I wish you both very happy," Kitty said, embracing Caroline, then kissing her cheek. She looked over her shoulder at the Prince and said, "As it seems the hour for news, perhaps there are others who wish to share on this Christmas Eve?"

Prince Mordvinov looked at Lady Reanay, and she at him. Both had such a conspiratorial gleam in their eyes, they could not help laughing at the absurdity of their situation, Lady Reanay behind her fluttering fan, the Prince into his fist. Both hesitated, wondering what the response would be to their announcement. The Prince's family had reacted badly and threatened consequences, which the Prince had disdained. At his age, he would do as he pleased; so would Lady Reanay.

Antony, Lord Temple, rudely waggled a finger at his Russian friend, turning to the Earl and saying bluntly, "I told you! You owe me twenty pounds. His Highness has asked Aunt Alice, and she's accepted!" He stuck out his hand to the Prince, then kissed his aunt's cheek. "I—*we are all*—exceedingly happy for you both."

Lady Reanay blinked up into her nephew's handsome face. "Are you sure, my boy?" She looked around at the rest of her family, who were all smiles. "Are you all *very* sure?"

"Of course," the Earl said. "Even Caroline—"

"Salt!" Lady Caroline gasped.

"—was persuaded, once she'd met the Prince. No

offence, Your Highness, but we couldn't have Aunt Alice marrying just anybody."

The Prince threw up a hand good-naturedly. "None taken, I assure you," he murmured politely, a little shaken that their news, which he'd hoped to announce, had been usurped by others'. Still, he was relieved that the engagement was now public and well-received. He caught Lady Reanay's hand, kissed it, and held it while he addressed the assembled company, looking from the Earl and Countess to Kitty, whom he smiled upon.

"Thank you, all. Your support means the world to us. We will marry at New Year. You must all be there. Particularly you, Miss Aldershot. Lady Reanay, as my wife, will then henceforth be known as Her Highness the Princess—"

"Rot, Timur! My family will continue to call me Aunt Alice. And when we are in England, you will be known as Uncle Timur. I insist."

The Prince's look of mock horror sent everyone into whoops of laughter, and with a round of congratulations, the wassail bowl was brought out and toasts made: To the happily engaged couple, to Antony and Caroline's news of a baby on the way, and to the goodwill that Christmas brings. Kitty was so caught up in the merriment, she was unaware that Mr. Allenby had been standing beside her for quite some time, until he offered to have her wassail cup refilled.

"I wonder—I wonder, Miss Aldershot, if I might have that word . . . ?"

Kitty smiled up at him. It was a smile full of such optimism that to Tom Allenby it was as if the sun had come out at night. It made him lose all hesitancy. The couple moved a little away from the animated conversation about weddings and babies.

"Miss Aldershot," he said firmly, "may I have permission to write to you? After Twelfth Night, I return to London for the resumption of Parliament. The days will be long . . . Knowing a letter from you awaits me upon my return home of an evening would make the hours go by so much the quicker. May I write to you, Miss Aldershot?"

Kitty did not hesitate in her reply. "Yes, Mr. Allenby. Nothing would give me greater pleasure than to be your correspondent." She raised her wassail cup. "Merry Christmas, Mr. Allenby."

Ned's Fairy Christmas you may be, dearest Kitty, he thought. *But to me you will always be my Christmas Angel.*

Naturally, Tom Allenby did not voice his thoughts. Yet he was confident that by next Christmas, he would have the right to do so. This Christmas Eve, he was content to raise his cup.

"And a very merry Christmas to you, Miss Aldershot."

Read more about the Salt Hendon family in Salt Bride: A Georgian Historical Romance and Salt Redux: Sequel to Salt Bride

ABOUT LUCINDA BRANT

Lucinda Brant is a *New York Times* and *USA Today* bestselling author of Georgian historical romances and mysteries. Her award-winning novels have variously been described as from "the Golden Age of romance with a modern voice" and "heart-wrenching drama with a happily ever after."

A graduate of the Australian National University and post-graduate of Bond University, Lucinda has degrees in History, Political Science, and Education. When not writing and researching, Lucinda loves watching BBC period dramas, Sci-Fi, and classic murder mysteries.

Visit her 18th Century world on Pinterest: http://pinterest.com/lucindabrant/

"Quizzing glass & quill, into my sedan chair & away! The 1700s rock!"

Visit Lucinda's website: LucindaBrant.com
Follow her on Twitter: @LucindaBrant

A Christmas Promise

by Sarah M. Eden

My mother named me Thomas, but everyone calls me Old Tom.

"Make us laugh, Old Tom," the other children often said as we'd lean against the gasworks wall, resting our legs from our childhood sport.

"What of the lad who chased after the banshee?" I've often been asked.

Or, "Tell us a tale of the wee folk."

The requests never changed, never stopped, even as I grew into the name they'd fashioned for me.

"His eyes are old," 'twas always said of me. "Old eyes speak of an old soul." Then they would ask me to tell them a story. And I did. Every time. Tellers of tales are not *born* in Ireland; we are *made*.

"I've a mind to hear something sad," said the man dispensing pints in the pub, dangling before me the promise of something for wetting my thirst if only I'd weave a tale.

And I obliged him, as is the custom in these parts. Kilkenny is an aged city, its people more ancient still. We tuck our souls into the spaces between the words of the stories we tell, feeling them safely hidden away there. We care not that a story be true, only that it be well told.

This one, though, is true *and* real. 'Twas not in my time, nor in yours, but it was in someone's time just the same . . .

One

Late 1820s

Not all roots take hold in County Mayo. For that reason, a certain Sean Kirkpatrick, his feet unsuited for firmly planting in the western lands, set those feet eastward on the promise of a position as a stable hand at Kilkenny Castle. He'd been challenged to prove his worth by driving a team of high-spirited nags from Dublin to Kilkenny in a given amount of time with not a scratch nor hair missing on either of the beasts. Arriving in one piece himself was not a requirement.

Sean had in his possession a map of questionable authenticity but no other thing to aid him in finding his destination. He might as well have tossed a length of yarn on the seat beside him and obeyed its twists and turns for all the good the map was doing. He felt certain he'd passed the same outcropping of rocks a half-dozen times, and the trees seemed to be mocking him at every turn.

"A fine lot you are," he muttered at them. "Couldn't give me so much as a hint, could you, say a branch pointing me in the right direction?"

Winter had arrived weeks earlier, though the branches were not yet bare. Somehow their refusal to act as divining rods made their half-emptied state all the more dispiriting. If he had to be lost in the vast circular mess that was the road to Kilkenny, he felt Mother Ireland ought to at least have given him a bit of color to enjoy.

Those were days of poverty, they were. Want and desperation had led many a man to do far worse than speak harshly to trees. And, though it would seem otherwise at first glance, Sean was not, in fact, mad. Lost, yes. Frustrated, decidedly. But he'd not entirely lost his mind.

Rain had fallen cold and steady all that morning, and, it now being quite firmly the afternoon, the effects of a wet morning were felt everywhere: the dripping trees, the muddy road, the wet state of Sean's backside. He was none too happy to have not yet reached Kilkenny as he ought to have. How easily he'd pictured himself arriving at the stables a day ahead, horses in fine feathers, himself not looking the least shabby. But rain and roads had conspired against him.

Don't you go about thinking that the Irish are a superstitious people. We *are*, of course, but I'd rather you didn't think it. Still, honesty compels me to admit that Sean Kirkpatrick, upon passing the same collection of very large rocks for the seventh time in a single day, felt he'd best turn off the road and follow the rocks, seven being a lucky number and he being Irish and, therefore, not one to take chances with luck. Call that superstitious if you will. We prefer *cautious*.

The path he guided his cart along led past one field after another, each divided from the next by low walls made of stone. Buildings dotted the landscape now and then, rough stone structures no doubt housing hay or animals. He thought he even saw, a great distance off, a thatched-roof cottage with a river-rock chimney and yet another rock-made wall. Ireland rather specializes in rocks.

Sean continued on for a full Irish mile, a distance far shorter than an actual mile but long enough for calling it a mile when sharing the story later and wishing to make things sound more desperate than they truly were. He saw no people, no animals even. He'd stumbled upon a great deal of nothing—another Irish specialty—but he'd not yet found the road to Kilkenny.

He came upon a hay barn filled nearly to the rafters, a rare enough sight during a time when the only thing most families had up to the rafters were children. Sean slowed his horses as he passed, watching for signs of life inside. There were none.

'Twas little point continuing down a path that could only end in muddy disappointment. He turned off and drove a bit past the hay barn, meaning to turn his cart around when he could find a bit of space to do it.

He urged the horses to the left and leaned himself a bit as well in anticipation of the turn of his vehicle. Anticipation, however, does not always prove reality. The horses moved, but the cart did not.

The horses made valiant efforts to move along, tugging and pulling and glancing back at him as if in blame. The cart was utterly stuck.

Now, most men, no matter how stubborn and hardheaded, recognize the futility of continuing when a pursuit has proven impossible. But the promise of wages when one has none can override sense with the greatest of ease. Sean, operating under this particular flavor of desperation, hopped from his perch and strode, as much as one can stride through thick mud, to the horses' heads.

He eyed the pair of them with as fearsome a look as ever his mother had produced when he'd caused mischief as a lad. He knew the look well. "Are you not eager to reach your new home, then? You'd rather play about in the mud than keep on?"

Sean swore that the beasts rolled their eyes at his scolding as if to point out that he, and not they, had been the one harebrained enough to drive into a muddy field in the first place.

"Well, you might've warned me, you might." He pulled off his sodden hat and slapped it against his thigh, sending droplets of water in all directions, punctuated by the very Irish disposition for colorful and detailed cursing.

He pointed a warning finger at the horses in turn. "Don't you go letting anyone steal you away, now. I've a job waiting, and it depends on you two bein' here when I return. Do a lad a favor and don't go wandering about with any strangers."

A nicker was all he received in response. That'd have to do, he supposed.

He trudged back along the short path he'd taken past the tall hay barn, knowing that doing so would put him back on the road he'd been on before, the one that led through the fields and past the distant buildings. If he could make his way to the cottage, someone there might lend him a hand, and, in doing so, save his neck.

Admitting he'd clearly taken a wrong turn in his attempt to find Kilkenny, that he'd been unable to find it at all, would be embarrassing, to say the least. Adding to that the confession that he'd managed to get his cart stuck in the mud, and it was enough to make him consider simply turning around and walking back to Mayo.

As he walked around the barn, a bark so loud and deep that it echoed through him in stomach-turning vibrations destroyed what little peace he still felt. He knew of only one dog with such an enormous voice: the Irish wolfhound, a breed so large, not another dog in all of creation stood as tall or as menacing. And he, apparently, was about to encounter one.

Sean searched his brains, trying to remember who was the patron saint of "not being devoured by a man-eating dog." A second bark rumbled through the air, overlapped by another and then another.

Three dogs. They bounded around the corner and directly at him, a hungry gleam in their ferocious eyes.

And that is what comes of traveling in Ireland without a reliable map.

Two

Here in the Emerald Isle, we've a great many terms for a woman so beautiful that the entire island sits up and takes notice every time she leaves her house: Irish Rose. The Gem of Ireland's Crown. If a man is wise: my wife. But we lag far behind in universal terms for women who are quite pretty but who don't stop the earth's rotation simply by arriving somewhere. Were there such a term, Maeve Butler could have adopted it as another given name.

She was lovely; all who saw her could confirm as much. Her eyes were fine, her hair dark and thick, and her smile filled with laughter. But those who took time to meet her learned quickly that her best feature was her quick wit. The woman was, in a word, clever.

Thus, she needed only an instant to realize that her dogs had caught a scent. The beasts had bolted, raising such a racket their barks must've bothered the Marquess and his family clear up at the castle. She further sorted out, by virtue of the beast's overwhelming enthusiasm, that whatever they'd taken to chasing was a bigger prize than a rabbit or bird. That left two possibilities: an unfamiliar dog or an unfamiliar person.

She'd not seen anyone pass the hay barn, where she'd been inspecting the stacks after the day's rain. But then, she'd been clear in the back.

Maeve pulled her scarf more snuggly around her neck and slipped out of the barn, whistling a jaunty tune. She'd always enjoyed the first cold days of the year, when harvest was over but the bone-chilling air of winter wasn't biting her yet.

She spotted her dogs quickly; they were roughly the size of small horses, after all. And standing on a tall rock in the midst of the barking beasts was a man. Even from that distance, she could tell he wasn't someone known to her. Not many people wandered up to the farm. Those who did were familiar, so much so that the family could generally identify them by their coats alone.

One time, Finley Donaghue had come visiting in a new coat of which he was quite proud, and Maeve's brother Kieran had nearly shot him, thinking he'd come upon a stranger bent on robbing them rather than their nearest neighbor.

The man on the rock wore an entirely unfamiliar coat.

"*Fág é!*" She called. The dogs backed off at once, still eying the stranger but no longer "hunting" him. "*Anseo.*" All three dogs returned to her at once. They were large and intimidating—the very reason her brothers insisted she keep them nearby—but they were also intelligent and well trained. And they only responded to commands issued in Irish, which marked them as far superior to dogs who preferred English.

Maeve moved near enough to be heard by the stranger, who still stood on his rock but remained at enough of a distance to let him know she didn't entirely trust him. Too many years of want and hunger had left Ireland's people wary of strangers.

"Are you so fond of rocks, then, that you go about standing on them whenever possible?" she asked.

"I'm trying to avoid being your dogs' next meal."

She scratched behind one of the dogs' ears. "These little lambs? They'd not hurt a fly."

"Perhaps, but I'm not a fly, now, am I?"

Like any true Irishwoman, Maeve Butler held decided opinions about every topic, even those she'd not yet heard of.

She was, for example, a firm believer in not cursing in church or walking heavy-footed through a graveyard. She also believed that a man ought to be quick-witted if he could at all help it. And this man seemed to be just that.

"Have you a name, stranger, or do we simply call you 'He Who Stands on Rocks'?"

He stepped onto the ground but without letting his wary gaze move the slightest from Maeve's protectors. Her loyal companions flanked her, not looking away from the trespasser. They wouldn't attack, however, unless she told them to or unless He Who Stands on Rocks did something foolish like rush at them.

"I'm Sean Kirkpatrick," he said. "And I'm a bit turned about. I'm trying to reach Kilkenny."

"You're close," she said, "but you've turned off the main road. This here's a farm, not a thoroughfare."

He looked about as if surprised. "I thought it seemed a touch too quiet."

Miss Maeve Butler had a soft spot for smart men, 'tis true enough, but if a man also had a fine sense of humor and a bit of a handsome face, she was lost. Fortunately, she had a knack for keeping a disinterested expression on her face when her heart was leaping about. Being the only sister in a house with two brothers made it a necessary skill.

"I'll not say you're as sparkly clean as a king lazing

about on his throne, but you're not dirty enough to have been walking the roads on such a wet day." He must've had a horse or cart or something somewhere nearby, but she didn't spy one.

"My team and cart are stuck in the muddy road on the other side of your barn."

She glanced in the direction he indicated. "Muddy *road*? That, my friend, is a field."

"Yes, well, my map wasn't terribly helpful."

"I'd say not." She gave him a quick nod. "Best of luck to you." To the dogs, she called, "*Tar liom!*" They followed obediently at her side as she walked in the direction of the curing shed.

"Hold up there a moment, lass. You'll not be leaving me stuck, will you?" He caught up to her quickly.

Rufus, the largest of her hounds, objected—loudly. Sean jumped backward.

"*Buachaill maith*," she told Rufus, pointing for him to back down. She eyed the newcomer a moment. "I suppose it'll not do to let your horses suffer." Maeve pretended to deeply ponder the horses' well-being. "That does it then. I'll send my brothers back with a few draft horses and a strong length of rope. They'll have your cart out, but they'll rib you something fierce. If you've any bits of your ego left intact, best tuck them firmly away. Your pride's about to take a beating."

He pulled his coat more firmly around himself. "If they'll help me get my team to the castle stables in one piece, I'll gladly serve as the fodder for whatever jokes they choose to make at my expense."

Maeve was an expert at letting a smile form slowly enough that anyone seeing it couldn't mistake its significance. An odd talent, perhaps, but a useful one. "Once they've pulled you free of the mud and you've endured their humor, let me know if you're as 'glad' about it as you expect to be."

"They're that bad, are they?"

Telling silences are also a talent of some rarity. Maeve, in addition to being clever, was rare.

She left Sean to ponder the mess in which he'd landed himself. She was doing a fine bit of pondering as well. Pondering a witty conversation. Pondering a man with terrible taste in coats but an impressive lack of arrogance. Pondering what it would take to convince her brothers to let her make a trip to Kilkenny if Sean Kirkpatrick meant to be there long, though she'd not mention that last part to them.

Lest it seem Maeve Butler was a woman of weakness, too timid to stand up to the dictatorship of her brothers, hers was not a concern about obtaining their permission so much as not wishing them to tag along, scaring Sean off with their relentless, if playful, tormenting. She loved her brothers, but like any sister worth her salt, Maeve found them tiresome.

She came across Liam not far down the road and waved him over. "We've a stranger on the land. He's managed to get a cart stuck in the mud of the fallow field just beyond the hay barn."

"What's your man doing driving a cart through a field in the first place?"

The Irish have a few quirks in the language, quirks of which we're rightly proud. One of these is the tendency to refer to a person as "your man" when we've no intention of making any real claim on a fellow. Maeve knew this. Liam knew this, and he hadn't meant to inspire in his sister any kind of connection to this stranger who had such a poor sense of direction.

Yet his words did just that.

Fortunately, for Maeve more than anyone, she truly was as smart as the neighborhood gave her credit for being. Smart enough not to fancy herself in love with a man she didn't even know.

And smart enough not to dismiss him entirely.

Three

Liam and Kieran Butler hadn't stopped laughing since introducing themselves. Sean attempted to take their teasing in stride. Attempting doesn't always mean succeeding.

"Do all lads from Mayo not know the difference between a field and a road?" Liam, the ginger one with at least a stone's worth of muscle on his brother, had latched on first thing to Sean's home county.

"And what was it, Sean from Mayo, that convinced you to lead these beasts into the mud?" Kieran had also made a point of mentioning Sean's home in nearly every sentence.

"It didn't seem so terrible an idea on the map," Sean muttered, hands thrust into his coat pockets.

The men's identical grins only widened.

"And do you always let a map do your thinking for you?" Liam asked. "Or only on rainy days?"

"Around here," Kieran jumped in, "every day's a rainy day."

"Meaning," Liam added, "he's somethin' of a muttonhead every day."

Sean ought to have been rewarded with a fancy title, or at least an estate, for the forbearance he showed that afternoon. Having his intelligence called into question again and again pushed his endurance to its limit.

But these two jesters had brought with them three very large draft horses, likely about the only thing that'd get Sean's cart free of the mud and, in so doing, save his hide. So he kept his mouth shut. Never let it be said the Irish haven't a knack for strategizing.

"Seems less than proper, though, leavin' these fine animals stranded this way," Kieran said. "Seems we ought to do something about them."

"Seems." Liam nodded, as if pondering deeply.

"I assumed that was the reason you brought the horses along." Sean indicated them with a jerk of his thumb.

"Oh, not at all," Liam insisted. "They're fine company, they are, tell the best jokes. There's this one about a muttonhead who gets his cart stuck in the mud. It's hilarious, I tell you."

"Now, I've a difficult time believing that, brother," Kieran said. "Not the bit about the talkin' horses. *That* I could imagine happening. But a fella driving a cart into a muddy field? That seems unlikely."

Sean shook his head at their nonsense. "Your sister told me that the pair of you would rib me over this. I think she made rather light of it."

"Well, but she didn't let her dogs eat you," Liam pointed out. "That tells us there's more to you than a stick in the mud." He turned to his brother, grin growing. "*Stick in the mud. The mud.* That wasn't half bad, now, was it?"

"I'll tell you what *is* half bad: this cart." Kieran gave it a firm tap with the toe of his boot. "He's managed to sink this thing deep. We'll not be pulling it out on our own."

"Again, I figured that was why you brought the horses," Sean said.

The brothers laughed, and, though Sean still wasn't enjoying being the recipient of their teasing, he found that he could smile along with them.

"We could try pulling the cart out with these beasties." Liam patted one of the very large horses they'd brought. "But I fear it's too stuck for that and would only splinter."

Sean shook his head. "Can't let that happen, lads. The cart's not mine. It belongs to the castle, as the horses do."

"Fortunately, *they're* not stuck," Liam said. "We can take them to the barn to warm up and get a bit to eat. Then I suppose we had better send for Donaghue and the up road Butlers and dig out the Marquess's cart." He looked at Sean. "Did you know that the owner of the castle was recently made a fine Marquess? I'd wager he'd be none too happy to hear that his new stable hand went and broke a cart."

Sean's day hadn't been a great one; that declaration didn't help. "The cart and animals have to be to Kilkenny stables by tomorrow at nightfall. I'd hoped to arrive early to impress a few important people. You see, I need this job the way crops need the sun—desperately."

Much of the humor in the brothers' faces eased into an optimism tempered with concern, an expression one often sees on faces in Ireland. Even when we know there's little reason to expect a happy ending, we expect it anyway. Some might blame that on the Guinness. But truth be known, 'tis nothing more nor less than being raised to believe in better things to come. We've had to make that way of seeing the word a choice, as there's been precious little these past centuries to be hopeful about.

Yet hope arrived for Sean Kirkpatrick in the form of a burly farmer by the name of Finley Donaghue and another pair of brothers with the surname of Butler, though with the added distinction of being "up road" Butlers. It was the custom in days gone by for people to adopt the same surname as the nearest family of distinction. That, in Kilkenny, was the Butler family of Kilkenny Castle. And, thus, the countryside for many miles in all directions was littered with Butlers who had no more claim on the imposing structure than they did on Dublin Castle. But Butlers they were just the same.

The six of them were digging out Sean's cart until past nightfall, a time that comes early in winter, long before anyone is truly ready to retire to his bed. Sean's cart emerged a bit worse for the experience, but in the course of that muddy undertaking, he made his first friends in this new county. Liam and Kieran invited the lot of them to take supper up at the cottage.

"Won't your sister have something to say about that?" Sean had learned from his own sainted mother that a man who valued his continued existence didn't spring guests upon a woman without warning.

"Oh, Maeve'll be expecting us," Kieran insisted.

"Give the lass our regrets," one of the up road Butlers said. "We've a few chores yet to see to, and we mean to do them before the night grows too cold."

Sean shook their hands firmly, hoping to communicate that he wasn't an utter idiot despite the predicament they'd found him in upon first meeting. "I thank you again for your help."

"You're in Kilkenny now," up road Butler the second said. "We look after one another."

"I'm appreciative."

A few more firm nods split the group. Sean, Liam, Kieran, and Finley Donaghue made their way to the cottage.

"You're certain Miss Maeve'll not mind us dropping in for supper?" Sean asked.

"She'll not mind," Liam said.

"And how is it you're so confident of that? Have you the second sight?"

"If I had, I'd've locked the gate this morning to keep troublesome lads from Mayo off our land, now wouldn't I?"

They'd only just reached the door of the cottage—precisely like every other cottage one generally sees in the countryside, from its thatched roof and white walls to its red door and small windows. It isn't that we aren't a creative people; we're simply limited by the materials on hand and by the somewhat crushing weight of not ever having any money.

Irish cuisine is about as varied as Irish country architecture. Had Sean been asked to hazard a guess as to the menu Miss Maeve Butler had concocted, he'd likely've hit quite close to the mark. He knew in an instant, as does every Irishman, the aroma of colcannon and soda bread, and that was precisely what he smelled the moment they stepped inside.

"You're late, lads," came the greeting from just out of sight around a corner. "I've kept your meal warm, but if I hear a word of complaint about it bein' over cooked, I'll skin the lot of you and serve you to my hounds for breakfast." Maeve stepped into sight, offered them all a brilliant smile and added, "Dinner's on, then."

There's hardly a soul who's not heard of love at first sight. Yet, more often than not, 'tis a good dozen or so sights before a heart begins to realize it's in danger of never being quite whole again. Sean needed neither one nor twelve sightings of Maeve Butler to begin falling rather irreparably into the first stages of love with her, the first being something along the lines of, "that fine lass has caught my attention, and I'm wishing to know her better." Sean needed only two sightings to reach that starting place.

The first sighting had mostly been about her dogs and his horses. But the second one, *this* moment, with Maeve standing there, her apron dirtied with dinner, her hair hanging every which way, her large wooden spoon aimed at them all like a queen making a royal accusation—that moment did it for him.

He was well and truly gone, or at least pointed in that general direction.

Four

Different lands have their own unique ideas about those things that make a man attractive to a woman. In Scotland, they put a great deal of importance on kilts and tossing tree-sized logs about. In England 'tis of great importance for a man to sport particularly clean clothes and fine manners. No one quite knows what to make of the Americans' approach to almost anything.

But in Ireland, a man coming in from the fields, smelling of earth and fresh air, invigorated with the satisfaction of a job well done, and glowing with pride of ownership is . . . not terribly realistic. Most men newly returned from the fields smell of things far less pleasant and shine with nothing so much as a heavy sheen of sweat. I'd not say *that* is the key to an Irishwoman's heart. But a man who won't work hard or is too dainty to dirty his hands won't get far in the countryside.

Sean arrived in Maeve's home, smelling and looking like he'd been rolling about in a mixture of mud and wet dog fur. She ought to have been entirely put off on the man, yet something about the filthy smelliness of him had quite the opposite effect. Seeing proof of his hard work, and a smile on his face despite the struggle he'd had that afternoon, couldn't help but inspire admiration. And if a man can earn a woman's admiration, the task of earning her affection becomes far more feasible.

"You were planning to wash before sitting at my table, weren't you?" she asked him.

He took up her dry tone of teasing. "Indeed. But I couldn't imagine your brothers' having any idea where I might accomplish that, so I thought I'd best ask you."

"Sorted them out straight off, did you?" She laughed at her brothers' looks of feigned offense. "There's a well a few yards back of the house. You can wash up there. And the rest of you, as well. I'll not have you turning my kitchen into a muddy field."

"We had best avoid that," Liam agreed, "else Sean'll likely get himself stuck in here as well."

Sean took the ribbing in stride. "And do the two of you intend to let me fall in this well of yours, stumbling about as I will be in the dark?"

"You'll have to take your chances." Kieran slapped a hand on Sean's back.

The lads were outside in a moment. Though she ought to have set herself to the task of placing bowls and cups and such on the table, Maeve's mind had followed the men out the door.

That Sean Kirkpatrick is a handsome man, mud and all. And quick-witted. And not easily offended. Now to discover if he turned his nose up at simple country fare. For if a man can't stomach a woman's cooking, 'tis best for all concerned that he not come around at mealtimes. And if he'll not be around at mealtimes, there's little point in him being around the rest of the day, either.

But Sean quite heartily approved of her cooking, both in words and in his very enthusiastic devouring of the meal. Indeed, he referenced a good number of saints as well as the heavens themselves between bites.

"You'd best not praise her too highly, Kirkpatrick," Liam said, wiping the last of his colcannon from his bowl with a slice of soda bread. "She'll get it into her head to go work at the kitchens up at the castle, and we'll lose our cook and our sister all in one go."

'Twas Finley who responded, the first word he'd said since arriving for supper. "You'd not up and leave us, would you, Maeve?"

Where the Butler boys were rather expert at teasing, Finley Donaghue was of a more sober mien. His question was asked in absolute earnest, the kind of earnest that either endears a person or makes the entire room a touch uncomfortable. In that room, with that question, 'twas something of an endearing discomfort.

Maeve took another quick bite before answering Finley's question. "Seems to me, seeking one's fortune up at the castle is becoming quite the fashionable thing." She allowed the quickest glance in Sean's direction. "And *I* actually know how to get to Kilkenny."

"Perhaps you'd accompany me there, Miss Maeve, to make certain I don't lose my way again." A slow smile tugged at Sean's lips. "T'would be a shame if I drove into another field."

Liam spoke before Maeve could manage even the quickest of answers. "You'll not be driving anywhere tonight." Liam, being oldest, tended to make declarations for other people as if he were the law. "But come morning, Maeve and one of her hounds could take you up the road."

"If *I* choose to." Maeve, being the much-put-upon

younger sister, tended to correct Liam's declarations as a reminder that he was not, in fact, the law.

"And *do* you choose to?" Sean held her gaze.

Maeve had never been one to let her heart override her head. But now and then the struggle between those two parts of herself proved a close-run thing. Sean's question set her insides flipping about. Did he *want* her to go with him? A bubble of wonderment formed deep inside, growing as his gaze remained steady on her.

"I suppose Rufus and I could spare some time in the morning to see to it that you don't get yourself lost again." She took a bite and half-shrugged. "If you're needing me to, that is."

"I do believe I most decidedly need you to." His smile tipped a bit even as a laugh entered his eyes. "Though I could do without Rufus coming along."

"Rufus is going," Liam added with the firmness of an older brother when a near stranger proposes walking out with his younger sister without a chaperone. And Rufus was a fine chaperone. The hound wouldn't stop at simply shooing away a suitor making advances; Rufus would likely *eat* him.

"Good," Sean said, much to Maeve's surprise. "He can help pull the cart."

A sense of humor he had, to be certain. Maeve found herself very much looking forward to joining Sean Kirkpatrick on his way to Kilkenny in the morning. Indeed, it might be worth her while to get him a little bit lost and prolong the outing.

"It has occurred to me, Miss Maeve, that you may be of a mind to misdirect me so as to steal a few extra minutes with me." Sean kept driving his cart as though the remark wasn't the least bit remarkable.

Maeve knew otherwise. The man had all but read her thoughts the night before. She didn't truly intend to mislead him, but she'd most certainly given it some consideration. "If I'd wanted a few extra minutes of your time, I'd've made you help wash dishes last evening instead of allowing you to seek your bed first thing."

"I'd've helped, you know." He expertly guided his team around a bend in the road. "Your brothers, however, saw me as a wounded sparrow in need of tucking safely in a nest."

Maeve laughed long and hard, for she knew far better what her brothers had seen him as. Not a bird in the nest, but a fox in the henhouse. If not for Rufus running alongside the cart, standing nearly as tall as the horses themselves—and the admittedly short distance to Kilkenny—she'd have been the one tucked "safely" away at home.

"And have you a knack for washing dishes?" She threaded her fingers through each other.

"I'm almost as good at it as I am at reading a map." He wiggled his dark eyebrows in the way that's meant to indicate one is aware of how idiotic one is being, all while pretending to not be idiotic at all.

"Well, what does your map tell you is up in the distance?"

"Kilkenny?" He let his doubt show. "But we've only been driving a quarter of an hour."

"I did tell you you were close, now, didn't I?" Her laughter died out when she saw the tightening of his lips and jaw.

"A quarter of an hour?" he repeated, tension in his tone. "I was a mere fifteen minutes away?"

Would the mild-mannered Sean Kirkpatrick show himself to be a man with a violent temper? She could abide a great many faults in a man, but an overly hot disposition was not one of them.

"Saints, I could've walked that far."

Maeve shook her head. "Not in the dark, you couldn't have. 'Twas only a sliver of a moon last night. And we know full well the unreliable nature of your sense of direction."

His head turned slowly toward her. She watched for any signs of an explosion. Even Rufus slowed his trot a bit to come up more evenly with her.

"Are you meaning to goad me over that for the rest of m' life?" His eyes, thank the heavens, had begun to dance. Not a jig, necessarily, but not a dirge, either.

"Are you saying you mean to keep my acquaintance for the rest of your life?" She was likely being too bold, but Maeve never had been one to err on the side of bashfulness.

He only smiled and focused once more on the road. Maeve allowed her own smile to blossom. How was it that having known him only since the previous afternoon, that she was already turning about inside at the thought of seeing him again and again? Perhaps she wasn't so levelheaded as she liked to believe. But levelheadedness, in general, is rather overrated. Tis a fine thing to be a wee bit mad now and then.

"Am I needing to make any crucial turns, Miss Maeve?" Sean asked.

"This road'll lead you directly past the castle, Mr. Sean," she answered.

"*Mr. Sean?*" He clearly objected to her choice of name for him. But, then, she was finding herself objecting to *his* choice of name for *her*.

"*Miss Maeve*," she pointed out.

He shook his head quite firmly. "I'm being entirely too forward as it is, having you accompany me on only the second day of our acquaintance, and with only a dog along for propriety."

"Are we so very fine and fancy now?" She sat up quite straight and proper, adopting her best English accent, which wasn't very good at all. "Why, Mr. Kirkpatrick, how very bold you are, sir. Why, I shall swoon straight off if you do not assume a bit more indifference."

Far from indifferent, Sean laughed long and hard. His booming enjoyment even startled the horses and brought Rufus's eyes around to him, a look of suspicion in their depths.

"What'd it be like living in England, do you think?" He talked through his continued chuckles. "Having to be so stiff and proper all the miserable time?"

"The English are likely not quite the way we imagine them." 'Twas a more generous statement than most in Ireland made about their less-than-congenial neighbors to the east. History had tainted the two people's views of each other. Centuries of hatred tend to do that. "Just as we're not the mindless animals they so often claim we are," she added.

"Do you think, Miss Maeve, that Ireland will ever be a real country, free to rule herself?" Contemplation sat heavy on Sean's posture and expression. An earnest question, then, not idle conversation.

It was saying something for two people to be comfortable enough for perplexing topics when they'd only just met.

"If the Americans can manage it," she answered him, "anyone can."

That brought another round of laughter, from Sean and Maeve both. The two made quite a pair riding together, smiling and quite at ease in each other's company. The castle came into view in the next moment, something that happens quickly upon the approach to Kilkenny.

"There's a sight for your sore eyes, I'd imagine." Maeve indicated the imposing structure. "The stables are just across from the castle." She motioned in that direction.

Sean whistled appreciatively. "Those're stables? The house I grew up in could fit inside them one hundred times over."

"Indeed. It is a bit showy, for sure, but it also makes the

town seem a tad more fancy. And it's a fine-looking structure. Nothing to be ashamed of, at least." Maeve took a moment to be amazed at how many ways she'd found to compliment a stable.

"I've only realized—you have no means of returning home." 'Twas an admirable quality in a man to be concerned over a woman without being overbearing about it.

"As you said yourself only a moment ago, I live an easy distance from Kilkenny. And today's my market day, anyway. We make this walk quite often, Rufus and I."

"Quite often, you say? And do you make this 'quite often' walk past the Kilkenny stables every time?"

She smiled up at him. "If I choose to."

He pulled the cart directly in front of the stables. "This is my stop, Miss Maeve."

"Do you think you could find your way to calling me Maeve?"

"I think I could manage." He held the horses' reins as she climbed down from the low cart. He tipped his hat. "A fine good morning to you, Maeve."

"And to you, Sean." If he could use her Christian name, certainly she could use his. She'd gone but one step when he called out to her.

"Do you, then?"

She looked back over her shoulder at him. "Do I *what*?"

"Choose to walk past the stables when you come to market from now on?"

This was an invitation she knew herself incapable of resisting, but he needn't know that. Not yet. "You keep a weather eye out, Sean Kirkpatrick, and see if I do."

Five

Sean kept a weather eye out. And a sharp eye, a keen eye, and every other kind of very watchful eye but didn't see Maeve Butler even once over the following days. He hadn't the luxury of time away from his duties. The stable master allowed him only enough time away on Sundays to attend mass. He was to prove himself a tireless and uncomplaining worker during his first week on the job, he was told. Then, and only then, would he be permitted time of his own.

Though he didn't see Maeve, he thought of her often. For some, a head of golden hair or of fiery red is quite the end all of beauty. Sean had always had a particular weakness for hair of the darker variety. And he'd always been unable to resist a laughing smile. Wit went a long way in capturing his attention as well. Maeve was all those things, but she was something more as well. She was . . . He had no idea what she was, which was precisely why he wanted to see her again. But the confounded colleen never showed her lovely face.

Late in the afternoon of a mild Wednesday—"mild" by comparison, of course, meaning rain had fallen all the day long with a fierce wind that bit through even tightly knit sweaters and thick, woolen coats—a man's voice sounded through the castle stables.

"I'm needing to borrow one o' your stable hands, Desmond."

Sean leaned around the stable door, straining to catch sight of Liam Butler. Even with the comings and goings of a large staff and a great many animals, he thought he might manage to find the man. Gingers generally stand out in a crowd.

"You'll not be convincing me that you and Kieran can't manage your animals." Desmond was the stable master and never let a soul forget it. "And I know perfectly well that sister of yours can keep her hounds in line."

"'Tis the sister we're needing help with," Liam answered.

Worries for Maeve flooded over Sean as he stood in that stall, his task forgotten, dirtied straw stuck to the end of his abandoned pitchfork.

"Nonsense," Desmond grumbled. "That lass is tougher than the both of you combined."

"Don't I know it." Liam looked about the place. He didn't appear at all like a brother worried over the welfare of his sister, but rather one plotting very nearly against her. "Have you a place where we might talk without being overheard?"

Desmond gave a silent nod. Before stepping away, he looked over the stalls and the many hands working there. "Back to your chores, lads," he barked out. "You're not bein' paid to stand about."

Sean set back to his task on the instant. He knew better than to ignore a dictate from Desmond. The man ruled with an iron fist right up until the work was done for the day, when he turned into precisely the sort of fellow one liked to run into at the pub. Days were long and grueling at the castle stables, but the evenings were a regular romp. Still, Sean couldn't quite lose himself in the merriment. His thoughts were a quarter of an hour down the road.

All those things considered, when Desmond relieved Sean of his duties a full hour before usual and even went so far as to give him the evening off, he didn't utter so much as a word of complaint. "I'm much obliged to you."

"Don't be." Desmond was a tough old bird. "I'm letting you go on an assignment, not as any kind of favor to you."

"An assignment?"

"There's family just outside Kilkenny in need of a bit of help."

Ah, yes. Liam's visit. "The Butlers?"

Desmond's eyes narrowed. "And how is it you knew that?"

"I understand there are a great many Butlers hereabout. I figured 'twas a likely guess." A wee falsehood could be excused when one doesn't wish to play one's hand where a woman is concerned.

Desmond didn't seem terribly impressed with Sean's logic. But then, Desmond wasn't often impressed. "They do happen to be Butlers, in fact. Fifteen, perhaps twenty minutes along this road. You're looking for the six boulders Butlers. If you reach the up road Butlers, you've gone too far."

It's identifiers such as these, "six boulders" and "up road" and such, that contribute to Ireland's reputation for bein' a bit adorably simple. What we're not given credit for is how very ingenious such a system truly is when nearly everyone for miles around has the same surname.

"What sort of work am I to do there?" Sean had overheard enough of Desmond and Liam's conversation to be fully curious.

"It's not for you to turn it down, so there's little point in asking. On your way, lad."

He was on his way, as instructed, his way being directly back to the same pile of rocks where he'd made his fateful turn off the main road a week or so earlier. He recognized it easily and found that, though he'd been walking for a good bit of time, knowing Maeve Butler was up the way had put a spring back in his step.

He meant to ask why it was she'd never come to see him and whether he'd imagined the connection between them, perhaps even discover where he'd gone wrong. Though men don't generally like to let on that we worry over such things, we most certainly do. And Sean *had* been worrying a bit.

He reached the familiar red door and lifted his fist to knock, but a voice stopped him.

"Have you come, then, Sean?" Kieran was even then approaching the same spot. "Liam thought you might, though Maeve's despairing of it."

"She's expected me?" That seemed encouraging, though with women one couldn't always tell.

Kieran nodded. "We let her know that old Desmond wasn't likely to allow you any time of your own this first week or two, but she kept right on hoping."

Encouraging news, to be sure. "Why did she not drop by the stables and give me a wave? She said she might."

"And she might have if not for an unfortunate tumble off the ladder." Kieran scratched at his stubbly chin. "Fortunately 'twas only a rung or two. Well, it might've been six. Eight at the very most."

"Saints above." Sean grabbed the handle and pushed the door open.

He found his Maeve in an instant, sitting in a rocking chair at the hearth, her head dropped into one upturned hand. At her side sat Finley Donaghue going on about sheep and acreage. Other than seeming rather bored out of her mind, she appeared well. Relief pulled a sigh from the very depths of Sean.

Maeve looked up at the sound. On the instant, a grin split her face. "Why, Sean Kirkpatrick! Aren't you a sight?"

"A fine sight, or a horror?" he pressed with a smile of his own.

"Why've you not come sooner?"

He crossed directly to her and hunched down before her. If Finley was surprised at the interruption, he didn't say anything, and Sean was too intent on looking at Maeve to bother eying the other fellow to see his reaction.

"Desmond won't allow his stable hands any time of their own during the first few weeks in his employ. 'Tis his way of breaking us the way some would break a horse."

"I told you so," Liam called from the kitchen.

"You've not taken French leave, have you? I'll not allow you to lose your position on account of visiting me."

He slipped his hands around hers. "Desmond gave me permission. But what's this I hear, lass, about your falling near to your death?"

"'Twasn't so bad as all that. I turned my ankle a touch and haven't been able to leave this house on account of I don't walk terribly well yet."

He rubbed at her hand with his. "How long've you been cooped up in here?"

"A week." Those two words told Sean all he needed to know.

"An entire week? Why, you must be climbing the walls."

Kieran answered before she could. "Not with that ankle, she isn't."

Maeve threw her brother a look of ill-amused scolding. For the sake of family harmony, Sean thought it best to wander off with Maeve for a time. Family harmony being quite important and all.

"Have you a riding horse?" he asked Kieran. "Or a carriage or wagon of some kind?"

"We've a hay cart," Kieran said.

That'd do. Sean returned his gaze to Maeve's lovely dark eyes. "Would you care to go for a quick ride with me in a very fine and fancy hay cart?"

"I'd be in your debt for ever and ever, Sean Kirkpatrick, if you could find a way to get me out of this house for even a moment."

He raised her hand to his lips and pressed a kiss to her fingers. "Consider it done, lass."

He stood once more and turned to face the Butler brothers, who were standing a piece behind Finley Donaghue, whom he'd nearly forgotten about. The company of a good woman can do that to a man—make him forget everyone around him.

"Point me in the direction of your barn, men. I've a cart and horse to make acquaintance with."

Liam didn't agree to the very reasonable request. "You stay here and keep our sister company—*honorable* company—and the three of us'll bring the cart 'round."

"Three?" Finley looked up at the man as though he'd marched his brain clear out of his head. "Why would it take three people to do something so simple?"

Kieran slipped a hand under Finley's arm and pulled him out of his chair. "What we've undertaken, man, isn't simple in the least."

The two brothers all but marched their neighbor from the cottage.

"It seems Liam and Kieran have it in their minds to play matchmaker, Maeve." Sean looked back at her, half expecting a look of horror. What he saw was pondering—deep and uncertain pondering.

"Does that frighten you?" she asked quietly.

"It does a bit," he admitted. "But not enough to send me running back to Kilkenny."

Maeve shrugged. "You'd likely get lost if you tried."

"Troublesome woman," he muttered.

"Admit you love the ribbing."

He didn't bother hiding his grin. "I'm beginning to."

Some women blush elegantly and adorably, with perfect pink patches bringing a rosy hue to their complexion. Other women blush in a way that vaguely resembles the measles and makes a fellow worry that something's terribly the matter. Maeve, for all her prettiness, did not fall in the first category.

"Where do you keep your coat and warm blankets?" Sean asked. "'Tis a mighty cold evening out there."

"Blankets are in the chest against that wall." She pointed across the room. "My coat is hanging on a nail in my bedroom."

When Liam peeked his head inside once more, she had her coat on and the blankets were at the ready. "Your cart awaits," he announced. "And we've a lantern for you. The evening's growing dark already."

Sean turned back to Maeve. "Can you walk at all, or do you need me to carry you?"

"I can walk a bit, but not far and not for long."

"Well, then, if your brother hasn't any objections, I'll carry you out to the cart."

Liam motioned for him to go ahead, something that, frankly, surprised Sean. He had two sisters of his own, and he and his brothers had been quite protective of them, perhaps overly so.

"You seem to have decided I'm trustworthy," Sean said.

Right on cue a deep, rumbling bark sounded from just outside the door. "Rufus is going along," Liam said.

So perhaps the Butler boys weren't entirely decided on the matter of Sean's worthiness. Still, they were allowing him to ride with their sister.

"Why is it only old Rufus is sent out as chaperone?" Sean asked. "I recall with perfect clarity that you've a few other hounds equally as large lurking about the place."

Maeve's slow-forming smile spoke of amusement.

"Rufus is the meanest of the lot, but only when he's alone. If all three came along, you might manage a bit of mischief before it's noticed."

"I doubt that. I've attempted to outrun them, you'll remember."

She shrugged a single shoulder. "I did say you would manage only 'a bit' of mischief."

Sean bent down, slipping an arm under Maeve's knees and another behind her back. She slid an arm around his neck, holding fast to him. After standing and making a few adjustments, he carried her to the door and outside to the waiting cart.

Blankets were situated. The lantern was hung on the cart's hook. Rufus took up his position directly beside the cart, eyes narrowed at Sean.

"Where would you like to go?" Sean asked Maeve. "This outing is for you, after all."

She thought a moment. "Could we just drive about for a time? I'm nearly desperate to see something other than the walls of this house."

"I'll go anywhere you like, Maeve Butler."

It often happens that a man is caught quite by surprise when realizes he's grown unexpectedly attached to a woman.

Sean Kilpatrick was no exception. And mingled with that surprise was just a tiny bit of fear. For once a man begins to love a woman, his life is never quite whole again without her.

Six

"Seems to me Desmond is something of a dictator, seems to me." Maeve didn't at all like the idea of any person trying to "break" Sean. Anyone could see he was strong and independent. She liked him that way. She liked him very much, indeed.

Sean didn't seem overly concerned, though. "He'll ease off in time. 'Tis his way of weeding out those who aren't willing to work."

There wasn't much to be seen as they drove along the paths that wove through the family farm. The sun had set, and the land was dark. But she was warm in her coat under the blanket he'd provided, and she was grateful for the fresh air and the joy of Sean's company. Finley, though he was a dear family friend, hadn't Sean's knack for conversation nor his quick wit.

"Have you had a good first week at the stables?" she asked. "Or has it been terrible?"

"It's been grand, actually. Such fine animals and the stables, Maeve." He whistled appreciatively. "They're quite the finest stables I've ever seen."

"So is it the stables you like best or the horses?"

"The horses, to be sure. I've always liked animals. Except, perhaps, for Rufus there," he added with a chuckle.

Upon hearing his name, Rufus let out a quick bark.

"I think Rufus likes *you*," Maeve said.

"Oh, certainly. He'd like me for supper, is what he'd like."

Maeve moved a bit closer to Sean, and not entirely because the night was growing colder. A week she'd been watching for him, hoping he'd come. And here he was, directly beside her, laughing and talking and lifting her spirits. Little wonder her heart was spinning about inside her.

"Which of the horses is your favorite?" she asked.

He glanced at her. "You don't truly want to hear about my boring job, do you?"

"Why wouldn't I?"

"I worked at a stable in Mayo, and m' sisters never did want to hear a single word about what I did."

She shook her head at his rather thickheaded logic. "They're sisters. And sisters are quite different from"—she wasn't sure what to call herself at that point—"from not-sisters."

"Well, then, *not-sister*, I'd have to say that my favorite horse is a chestnut the Marquess has named Chestnut."

She laughed silently. "The Marquess is not particularly creative, it would seem. Now, why is it Chestnut is your favorite?"

They rode on that way for long, enjoyable minutes, the night growing darker and chillier. She learned about the animals in his care, about the family he'd left behind in Mayo. He asked after her work and her joys. He wished to know of her late parents and her childhood.

Theirs was such an easy and natural conversation that one might be excused for thinking they benefited from a long acquaintance. And, seeing how they slowly inched closer and closer together as they drove along, even they began to feel that there was more to the evening than two near-strangers getting acquainted.

Ireland, you must understand, is peopled first and foremost by dreamers. We'll fight when we must, and we're not entirely without brains. But the trait that most defines us is the heart of a poet, and it shows most in quiet moments like that one, when a hopeful sort of love is born.

The next week, Sean came by for Sunday supper, and again the week after that and the week after that. Desmond, it seemed, felt he'd earned one night a week to himself. The change might've also had something to do with the scones Maeve brought to old Desmond whilst emitting a few heartfelt sighs of regret over never being able to see her fine lad. Desmond was a tyrant—there was no denying that. But he was also a man without a wife and in firm possession of a sweet tooth, something Maeve had managed to discover by means of endless questioning of Liam, who had known the man for many years.

Whatever the reason for the hard-nosed stable master's softening toward his newest stable hand, Maeve saw a great deal of Sean Kirkpatrick as Christmas approached. He came every Sunday without fail, no matter how miserable the weather, and she found herself watching the front windows all the day long, praying he'd come a bit early.

On his sixth Sunday visiting, when the other lads moved from the small kitchen, Sean remained behind. "I can't promise to very good at it, but I'm hoping to help with the dishes."

"You're *hoping*? Were you thinking I'd say no?" Even if he proved an absolute dolt at washing dishes, she wasn't about to turn him away.

"I warn you, I've little experience with it."

"I'd wager you're a fast learner." She tossed a large, dry rag in his direction. "I'll wash. You dry."

He was a natural-born dryer, which was rather like saying one was a natural-born breather. Drying dishes didn't require much skill.

"Donaghue is here every week, I've noticed," he said as he dried a pewter plate. "Does he come around often?"

"Finley's been visiting since he was a lad, back when all of our parents were yet living."

"An old friend, then?" Sean slid the dried dish into the age-worn cabinet.

"Quite old."

Sean raised an ebony eyebrow. "He's my age, you realize. That's not so very old."

She scrubbed a bit of potato off the large serving pot in which she'd made the night's coddle. "He was always Liam's friend. I suppose that makes him seem older. Almost like another brother."

"Is that what he is to you?"

In that moment, with an intuition most women are born with, Maeve pieced something together. Despite all of the time they'd spent together, despite her tendency to snuggle close to him when he drove her about in the cart, and despite the rather obvious cow eyes she made at him across the table every Sunday evening, Sean was jealous.

Of Finley Donaghue, of all people.

The kind thing to do would have been to put his mind at ease, to swear reassurances and speak sweet words of tenderness. But the *wise* thing was to let him discover her feelings for himself. If their pattern became her having to swear up and down to her feelings anytime life gave him reason to wonder even a little bit, t'would be a long and tiresome life indeed.

She let him chew on his thoughts as they finished the last of the washing. Sean didn't grow angry or demand answers. He made no further comment, really, only stood with a furrowed brow and a downturn to his lips that clearly said, *I'm pondering where I stand with a woman, and I'm not terribly keen on the answers I'm formulating.*

So Maeve, being a font of compassion as well as a believer in the importance of a bit of humor, decided to help him along a bit. "Did you know that Finley has nearly five hundred head of sheep, a surprising number of which have black wool? Did you further know that he's at his wit's end over a particular weed growing in his back pasture? His wit's end, Sean."

His confusion only grew. She managed not to laugh, but 'twas a close-run thing.

"And can you guess how it is that I know he's at his wit's end over the weeds in his back pasture?" she pressed. "Because he told me. He has, in fact, told me several times a week for the past three years. Weeds, Sean. *Weeds.* For three years." She took the rag from him and hung it over the back of a chair. "What was the last topic you and I chose to talk about?"

"We've covered so many in just the past quarter-hour."

Maeve stepped closer to him and set her hands on both of his arms. "Precisely, you daft man. You are the one I enjoy talking with, the one who stays behind to help me rather than taking his leisure at the fire with my brothers." She slid her hands up his arms and to his shoulders. "You are the one for whom I brave cold winter nights simply to snatch a moment of my company. Finley comes around often, as he's a neighbor and a good friend of Liam's. But you, Sean Kirkpatrick"—she wrapped her arms around his neck—"are the one *I* watch for and wait for and hope will someday come by more often than once a week."

His arms slid around her waist, and he pulled her close against him. "I'd be here every day if Desmond allowed it."

"Because you like me?"

"Because Finley, apparently, needs help with his weeds."

She leaned her head on his shoulder, settling into the warmth of his embrace. A woman could grow quite used to such a thing. "Christmas is this week."

"Is it? Didn't we just have Christmas a year ago?" His hand rubbed a slow, lazy circle on her back.

"Will Desmond be allowing you the day, or are you to be slaving away on Christmas, as well?"

His head rested atop of hers. Her heart leaped about. She held more tightly to him.

"We're to have Christmas evening to ourselves," he said.

Just what she'd hoped he would say. "Will you come have Christmas supper with us?"

"I'd love to."

She pulled back the tiniest bit, looking into his face. "Do you promise?"

His lopsided smile made another appearance. "When have you ever known me to turn down a meal?"

But she wasn't teasing in that moment. "Do you promise to come for Christmas? It's all I want, the only gift I'm hoping for. If you promise you'll come, I know you will. You'd never go back on your word, not to me."

His eyes filled with sincerity. "I solemnly swear to you, I'll be here."

"I'll be watching at the window."

Sean lowered his head. Instinct told her she was about to be kissed. And kissing instincts are seldom wrong.

Their lips drew ever closer. And closer. Her pulse pounded in her ears and neck. Another inch, perhaps less, and his lips would be on hers.

A rumbling bark filled the kitchen. Maeve and Sean both froze on the spot.

"What is Rufus doing inside the house?" she asked.

"Exactly what he's supposed to do," Liam called from the other room.

Sean grinned. "I believe that means the time's come for me to go."

Disappointment swept over her, tempered only by the knowledge that he'd be back in only a few days. As she watched him disappear into the cold, dark night, she reminded herself of that. She would see him again on Christmas Day.

He'd promised.

Seven

Christmas Day is rather less than joyful when one is working for the privileged upper classes. For, no matter the promises made of half-days and minimal duties, should the family one works for decide that Christmas Day would be utterly perfect for an unplanned jaunt through the countryside, someone must remain behind to receive the return of the carriage and horses. And that someone is then forced to spend his Christmas afternoon and evening pacing the length of the stable yard, contemplating the hurt and disappointment no doubt felt by a certain Irishwoman down the road.

I promised her. I solemnly swore. And Sean, being a decent sort of fellow, didn't care to be breaking a promise to any person, least of all his Maeve. But what could he do? Leaving would have cost him his job. Losing his job would have meant leaving Kilkenny and Maeve entirely.

There was no way of telling Maeve what had happened. She would think he'd broken his word.

"If you promise you'll come, I know you will," she'd said.

"You'd never go back on your word," she'd said.

"I never want to see you again," she'd say next.

He couldn't bear the thought. But what could he do? He was every bit as stuck as he'd been the day they'd first met. He paced back to the arched entryway to the stable yard and set his eyes on the castle across the way.

How many of the Marquess's servants were required to spend their Christmas away from loved ones? Likely quite a few. They had an advantage over him, however. He was spending his Christmas with a stable full of horses, not another person in sight. They, at least, had each other.

He stuffed his hands in his coat pockets and trudged his way past a long row of horse stalls, eyes focused on the floor ahead of him. "Maeve will have my neck, assuming she agrees to see me again."

Sean wasn't an entirely unreasonable man, and the more logical part of him knew he was likely making more of his Christmas absence than need be. But he was also a man in love, which has a tendency to override one's ability to think clearly. He didn't want to disappoint Maeve, and neither did he wish to spend the holiday away from her. Indeed, he was growing ever more convinced that he never wanted to spend another day away from her.

I might even get around to telling her that, if I'm ever allowed to leave this stable, that is. Grumbling, one must understand, is quite the most productive way to pass an evening. If nothing else, it makes a soul feel the tiniest bit better. Kicking at stray bits of straw helps as well.

Beyond the stables, voices raised in laughter and song echoed from the village. People were celebrating together, happy and contented. He, alone, was . . . alone.

It being Christmas and a holy day, he limited himself to

only the mildest of curses, nothing that would make a priest call him in for confession, but he was none too happy. Stepping back out to the stable yard, he shot a wary eye heavenward. Not a flake of snow fell, something Maeve might have blamed his absence on other than himself.

She was likely sitting at the window, watching for him to come. Or had been for a time until she'd given up on him.

The bells at St. Canice's had long since rung the call to evening mass. The sun had set. He couldn't help wondering if the Marquess's family meant to return that evening. They'd set off to visit friends who had a country home near Castlecomer. 'Twas entirely possible they'd opted to remain for the night. One benefit of being fine and fancy was the ability to cause inconvenience without consequence, at least not to one's fine and fancy self.

And so Sean sat on a stool in the empty stable yard, a weight in his stomach and on his heart. "'Twas all she wanted for Christmas," he informed the unhelpful heavens. "A visit, the chance to sit at each other's side, to talk as we always do. 'Twas all she wanted, and I promised her. I *promised* her."

He leaned his elbows on his legs and rested his head in his hands. He'd planned to tell her that he loved her. A man doesn't build up the courage to do so easily, which made the night's events all the more tragic. T'would have been quite a perfect Christmas.

But sometimes all one needs for perfection is an added measure of patience.

A mere moment after Sean had chastised the heavens, the sound of approaching hooves pulled his head up out of his hands. The family, it seemed, had returned. He'd be terribly late getting to the Butlers' cottage, but he would get there just the same. He would knock at the door for hours if necessary until Maeve allowed him to explain and apologize.

He rushed to his expected position, just inside the entry arch, and stood at respectful attention. Into the stable yard came not a fine carriage pulled by a high-stepping team, but a humble and rickety old hay cart, pulled by two draft horses and driven by a ginger farmer, with a dark-haired beauty beside him, and a tall, stick of a man behind.

T'wasn't the Butlers of Kilkenny Castle nor the up road Butlers, but the six boulders family, his Butlers. And his Maeve.

Liam pulled the cart to a stop in the middle of the yard. Sean stood in shock, frozen at the unexpected sight. His Maeve.

True to the feisty colleen she'd proven herself to be, Maeve hopped from the cart without waiting for anyone's assistance, then came directly toward him.

"I am so very sorry, Maeve. I'd not meant to—" He managed nothing beyond that.

"We've brought supper, Sean. Will Desmond pitch a fit if we eat it here with you, do you think?"

"Supper?" His thoughts swam too swiftly for making complete sense of her words.

"When you didn't arrive, I assumed you'd been made to stay here rather than being given the evening to yourself."

He nodded, his worry still too great for a verbal response.

"So we brought Christmas supper to you."

He took her hand, his own trembling with uncertainty. Did this mean she'd not lost faith in him? "I have to wait for the castle family to return with their carriage and team. I'm the newest hand, so the lot fell to me." The glove she wore was cold. Her hand beneath must have been near to freezing. "You shouldn't have come so far in the cold, love. You'll catch your death."

She reached up and touched his face. "I'd've gone clear to Mayo if need be."

"You aren't angry with me for disappointing you?"

Hers was a soft and alluring smile. "You've not disappointed me."

"Kiss the lass, already," Kieran called from the hay cart. "We've a Christmas supper to eat."

"There are empty stalls at the end of the row," Sean said. "Your animals'll be warm there."

Liam smirked a bit. "Trying to shoo away your audience, are you?"

"That is precisely what I'm doing. Now off with you."

They obliged.

Sean turned every ounce of his attention back to Maeve. He pulled her fully into his arms. "I was so afraid you'd be boilin', love. I broke m' word to you. You gave me your trust, and I broke it."

"You've not broken my trust in you, Sean. I trust you enough to have never doubted all the day long that you'd've come if you could."

He lightly brushed his lips against her forehead. "I don't deserve you."

"No, you don't." She wrapped her arms around his neck. "But you come close enough, that I'll not hold it against you."

He kissed her temple, then her cheek. Heavens, but he adored this woman. "Maeve, darlin' Maeve. I've nothing to give you for Christmas. I haven't money for a fine gift, and I didn't make it out to see you today." He cupped her face in his hands. "But I give you what I have, love. I give you my devotion and my caring, and I give you my love, all of it, every beat of my heart and every breath that fills my body."

He meant to seal the promise with a fervent kiss. She, however, was quicker than he was. She rose up on her toes and kissed him, her lips to his, making a promise without words that matched his spoken vow.

A promise of days and months and Christmases yet to come. A promise of love.

A Christmas Promise

That Christmas was not in my time, nor in yours, but it was in someone's time just the same. Sean and Maeve shared many a supper, both at the castle stables and at the six boulders Butlers' cottage. One might say their courtship was undertaken along the very road that first brought Sean Kirkpatrick to that fateful muddy field.

He'd taken a wrong turn, made a mistake. And what a grand mistake it turned out to be. By their second Christmas, the two were happily married. In time they were blessed with a daughter, who had a daughter, who had a son.

She named her son Thomas, but everyone calls me Old Tom.

ABOUT SARAH M. EDEN

Sarah M. Eden is the author of multiple historical romances, including *Longing for Home*, winner of *Foreword* magazine's IndieFab Gold Award and the AML's 2013 Novel of the Year, as well as Whitney Award finalists *Seeking Persephone* and *Courting Miss Lancaster*.

Combining her obsession with history and affinity for tender love stories, Sarah loves crafting witty characters and heartfelt romances. She has twice served as the Master of Ceremonies for the LDStorymakers Writers Conference and acted as the Writer in Residence at the Northwest Writers Retreat. Sarah is represented by Pam van Hylckama Vlieg at Foreword Literary Agency.

Find Sarah online at www.sarahmeden.com
Follow Sarah on Twitter: @SarahMEden

Twelve Months

by Heather B. Moore

One

England—1907

Lucien Baxter turned over the telegram that had just arrived from Upcreek. As he read, disbelief coursed through him. It was only two weeks before Christmas, and the message was not good. Again, he read the message, his stomach knotting.

> *Lucien,*
> *This illness grows worse. Come quickly. I must speak with you before I leave this earth.*
> *W.B. Griffiths*

William Bruce Griffiths had been Lucien's best friend since boarding school. The two made an unlikely pair, but perhaps that was what had drawn them together. Will came from a family of vast wealth and privilege, while Lucien had enjoyed a modest upbringing, and when an uncle died, Lucien's parents spent a portion of the inheritance on his education.

It could be said that Will lived life to the fullest, from betting at the horse races to having a different woman on his arm each weekend, making him always at the center of the action. Lucien could have described his role as best friend as simply someone in the background who offered a few laughs and served as a partner in crime. Not real crimes, of course, but Lucien had somehow become the broker between Will and his lady friends—of whom there had never been any shortage of.

In boarding school, Lucien had delivered letters, picked up notes, purchased jewelry, packed frilly things into trunks, redirected visitors, and had even composed lyrics for Will to sing to a lady or two. Will wasn't the only one who enjoyed romance. After the university, Lucien and Will had shared a townhouse in London until Lucien could afford to rent his own. Lucien had almost been engaged once, but when Kathleen Greene caught him at Will's house with another woman, Kathleen wouldn't listen to his outlandish, though honest, explanation.

The woman had been *Will's* latest girlfriend and had spent the night with him. She'd just awakened when Kathleen arrived. Inconvenient timing, especially since Will had left for the office earlier than usual and wasn't there to attest to the visiting woman's identity. So Lucien was left trying to explain his roommate's indiscretions to Kathleen since her sudden appearance had left Lucien no time to tell the woman to keep to Will's bedroom.

But that was all in the past and now with Will being safely married, Lucien finally had the time to focus on his own future and possible love interest.

And now . . . Lucien scrubbed his hands through his hair. And now Will was dying. The earth itself would have to stop spinning first. It was unconscionable. Surely, Will had the best physicians. But what if something had been overlooked? What if Lucien could discover the real ailment? Perhaps Will just need some cheering up.

It was already three hours since Will had written him. Three hours was a long time in an ill man's life. If Lucien didn't leave now, he might be too late. Mind made up, Lucien left his study and called for Johnson, his butler, accountant, and manservant all in one.

The short and tidy man came hurrying out of the kitchen. His face was a bit flushed, most likely from flirting with the cook again.

"I'm going to Upcreek. Will Griffiths is very ill," Lucien said, handing the telegram to Johnson.

Johnson scanned the paper, his face losing color. "Do you want to drive the car down?"

"I don't want to risk getting stuck on a muddy road from the icy drizzle over the past few days. I'll just have time to catch the first train. If you could bring the car around and drop me off at the station?"

Johnson nodded and started down the corridor to exit into the stable-turned-garage behind the house.

Mrs. Lewis came out of the kitchen. Widowed, with grown children, she'd turned out to be an asset for Lucien. She oversaw the household affairs and cooked a decent meal. "Would you like me to pack you a suitcase, Mr. Baxter?" She clasped her thin hands together.

"Thank you for the offer, but I must hurry to the station if I'm to make the train." He paused. "I might be gone a few days . . . or if things don't end well, I'll stay until after the funeral." His voice felt thick as he spoke, and he quickly turned from Mrs. Lewis' concerned gaze.

Lucien grabbed his heavy wool coat and opened the front door just as Johnson brought around the Benz.

"Thank you, Johnson," Lucien said, climbing into the back seat. The journey to the station was about fifteen minutes, and the ride to Upcreek would take less than an hour, but time was precious.

As they drove through the nearly-empty streets, Lucien was grateful it had only snowed a few flurries this winter, making travel swift. Once outside of London though, the roads would be unpredictable, which was why he didn't want to risk his own car.

When Johnson pulled up to the station, Lucien thanked him and climbed out of the car. He purchased his ticket, then made his way onto the train. After he settled into his seat, he gazed out the window as the train moved forward with the rising sun to his left. As winter fields and bare trees passed by, Lucien's memories of his best friend churned in his mind . . . Meeting Will for the first time at boarding school assembly when Will didn't close his eyes during a prayer. They'd caught each other's gazes from across the row. Will had grinned, and Lucien was forced to hide a laugh.

Of the time Will sneaked a lady into their dorm room and told Lucien to take an extended bathroom break. Will acing every test with little effort, while Lucien had to study for hours, many of them in the hallway while Will invited more lady friends over. Will drinking enough at taverns to kill two horses, yet managing to charm and joke all night. A couple of drinks, and Lucien was foxed for hours.

But Lucien never resented Will's good luck or fortune. If Will was one thing, it was generous. He'd brought Lucien on as a partner in his solicitor firm, and until about a year ago, they'd seen each other every day at their offices. When Will's father died, he'd moved to the family's estate, refurbishing it, then living in the country most of the time.

Lucien had been lonely at first without Will around, but it had been quite easy to bury himself in his work, especially after the disaster with Kathleen. He shook away thoughts of the prim-faced Kathleen, refusing to let the old disappointments return. He couldn't say he had been in love with her, exactly, but they'd been compatible, and her family was respectable. But Kathleen didn't have a sense of humor.

The sun crested the horizon just as Lucien left the last bit of London behind. From the window, the air already looked cleaner, and the change in atmosphere was like a strengthening balm. He felt he could face whatever was in store for Will, good or bad. Lucien would arrive at the estate and help in any way he could. He'd consult with the physician and discuss the best treatments for his friend. He would bring Will back to his former larger-than-life self.

And Will's new wife, Cora, would thank him for it. Lucien imagined her deep blue eyes full of gratitude. Will and Cora had married at the end of September, only a few months ago. It was easy to see what Will appreciated in Cora—she was beautiful, intelligent, and seemed devoted to Will. And, as Will had said, it was high time to settle down, especially in light of his father's passing. Cora had been the perfect choice. If Lucien had been in Will's shoes, he would have fallen in love with Cora too. And for that reason, Lucien would make sure Will was healthy enough to enjoy his first Christmas with his new wife.

Two

Three Days Later

As the minister offered a final blessing over her husband's casket, Cora bowed her head. This was not supposed to be happening. *Today* was not supposed to be happening. A funeral for her new husband, who was not even thirty years of age.

The air was still, yet frigid, at the family cemetery. If there had been a wind, she couldn't have borne it; she had enough to bear already. Her stomach rolled, then tightened, as if to remind her of the presence of the child she carried. It was difficult to believe that a creature who was probably no larger than her finger could cause so much havoc on her body.

She'd hardly eaten in weeks, and Will's sudden illness had created many sleepless nights. When the physician had announced his death, she'd collapsed. Lucien Baxter had been there, having arrived only hours before Will passed. Lucien had picked her up and carried her into one of the guest bedrooms, then ordered tea and a fire to be lit. Soon the physician was attending to *her*. There was no use for him any longer in the master bedroom.

But here, on the Griffiths family hillside cemetery, she stood on her own two feet, if a bit weak. Tears burned her eyes, then trickled down her cheeks. Beneath the ground were the buried generations of Will's family, including his parents. His father's death the prior year had brought Will back to the family estate. It was then that Will had met Cora. When Cora's family had attended the county jubilee picnic, Will had charmed her, and they'd had a whirlwind of a courtship.

From the beginning, she'd suspected Will's apparent love for her was too good to be true, but that didn't stop her from marrying him. She'd gone into the marriage to Will knowing his past. Others might think her a naïve and docile woman, but she knew of Will's reputation and had even seen letters from various women, which had arrived before and after their marriage.

The truth was that Cora didn't care about her own heart. Her previous fiancé, Major Bryson Young, had been killed in Tibet while leading the British force protecting Tibet's border. After a year of mourning, she had entered the social circles again, but a part of her had remained missing. So when Will turned his attention on her, she realized that at the age of twenty-six, she would most likely not have another offer of marriage. Besides, Will made her laugh; he could charm a weed into a rose. And if Will could make her forget her sorrows, if only for a few moments a day, marriage to him would be worth it.

"Amen," the minister said.

Amen sounded so final. It was a single word to say at the end of a prayer, but somehow it meant that Will was truly gone. As if on cue, the wind started up, gusting through the crowd, stirring the women's skirts and shawls and the men's overcoats.

People approached Cora, taking her hand or embracing her, voicing condolences that Cora couldn't quite focus on. All the while, Lucien stayed at her side, essentially speaking for her as he thanked people and wished them well. Cora had never been more grateful.

As the mourners moved away, heading back to the main house, where the cooks had undoubtedly spread a fine feast—more food Cora wouldn't be able to eat—she stepped up to the casket. A couple of gravediggers waited several paces away, probably impatient in the cold wind, yet willing to give her time. Somewhere behind her, Lucien was waiting as well. Even though Cora wished she could be completely alone, she knew the time would come soon enough that all of the relatives would depart and Lucien would return to his law practice in London.

She placed her hand on the mahogany casket, wondering how a man's entire life could be encased in a wooden box. Without thinking about it, Cora's other hand moved to her stomach where it had just began to expand, though it wouldn't be noticeable to anyone else yet.

"We won't forget him," she whispered to her unborn child. "We'll never forget him."

She blinked back hot tears. There would be plenty of time to crumple later, but she had a house full of people waiting. She half turned and looked over at Lucien. In a moment, he was at her side, and she linked her arm through his. She tried not to lean against him as they made the walk back to the house, but she was certain he was holding her up anyway.

As long as he was close by, she could stay in one piece. Once he left the room—or the house—it would be like stitches coming undone. She had no idea how long he'd stay to help settle estate matters, but it would not be long enough. Somehow, she would have to let him go too.

Three

Lucien shut the door on the final guest leaving the Griffiths household. He was exhausted, though he was sure Will's new widow was even more so. He'd seen her eyes tear up more than once, yet despite his encouragement to go rest, she had been a hostess to her close family members who stayed for a few days following the funeral. She was the ultimate hostess.

Cora's mother, Mrs. Evans, had stayed with Cora while Lucien spent a day or two wrapping up the legal paperwork for the estate. Being a trained solicitor had its advantages in this situation. But even Mrs. Evans had run out of strength and taken to her bed.

As it was, the house felt empty and too quiet.

Will was gone. It didn't seem possible, but the freshly dug grave on the top of the hill confirmed it. And now Lucien was about to approach Cora with what would surely be an unwelcome topic.

As he made his way to the sitting room, where she'd been moments before, the last minutes spent with Will ran through Lucien's mind. He'd made it to the estate just in time to hear his best friend's final request.

You must marry Cora. She'll resist at first, but I promised to take care of her. I can't break my promise, not when a child is on the way. Eventually, she'll understand the necessity and agree. I wasn't the best husband, but if she can put up with me, then in her eyes, you'll walk on water.

As if Will's pleading hadn't pierced Lucien's heart enough, his next words were impossible to forget.

She knew about the women before her, and about . . . well, there were one or two I didn't exactly let go of. I'm not proud of it, but Cora never wavered in her affection. I didn't deserve her, and she doesn't deserve the life of a lonely widow raising a fatherless child.

Of course, Lucien had agreed to honor Will's request. He wanted his friend to die in peace. Yet as he anticipated the upcoming conversation with Cora, he had no idea what her reaction would be. Would she be offended by his loveless proposal? Would she see through his suggestion and know the true source? In all the conversations surrounding the funeral, she hadn't spoken of her pregnancy once, which meant she might want to hide it.

What did that mean?

Lucien took a deep breath and turned the doorknob leading into the sitting room. Cora stood in front of the fire, her hands clasped behind her back. Where she found the strength to stand, Lucien didn't know.

She turned as he entered, her dark blue eyes taking him in as if she'd only just noticed him, though he'd been at her side for days.

Her thin eyebrows arched, and a smile played upon her face, surprising him. He'd not expected to see amusement from her. Self-consciously, he brushed at his hair. Perhaps he had a bit of lint stuck there.

"I've been expecting you," Cora said. "Why don't we sit down and get it over with?" Lucien opened his mouth, unsure of what to say. Finally, he nodded and took one of the wingback chairs. She walked over to the one directly across from him, and Lucien couldn't help but assess her figure, trying to decide if her pregnancy was obvious to the casual observer. Her waist was still small, and her curves were in all the right places. She was truly a beautiful woman, and her thick chestnut hair was the perfect backdrop to her ivory skin and dark blue eyes. It wasn't difficult to believe that a man, even one as worldly as Will, had wanted to marry her.

"There's no need to delay," Cora said. "I've been waiting days for a moment alone with you."

"I . . ." Lucien's heart raced. Was he nervous? The tables had been turned quite suddenly. "I'd like to offer my condolences once again, Mrs.—"

"If I have to listen to one more word of pity, I'll be the next one lying in a casket."

Lucien stared at her, dumbfounded. Her eyes, normally tame, were full of fire. It was a side of her that Lucien hadn't witnessed before. If possible, it made her even more beautiful.

"Don't think I'm oblivious to what Will has asked of you," Cora said, her usually gentle tone firm. "He felt guilty for being such a lousy husband, and I'm sure he asked you to make amends somehow. For you to clean up after him. Just as you've been doing since your college days."

"You know about . . . I mean, what are you talking about?"

She laughed, but there was no mirth in it. "He's used you for years, Lucien, and now he's used me." Her hand settled on her stomach. "Once he discovered I was pregnant, he went back to his old ways. It's one thing to have a past and forsake it—it's another to return to it when your new wife is carrying your heir."

And yet Will had made Cora sound like she was so

accepting, so affectionate, despite knowing about his sordid habits.

"He truly cared for you, Cora," Lucien said, grasping at what to say. At least, he *thought* Will had loved his wife. He was certainly attracted to her, and her character seemed to balance Will's perfectly.

Her smile was tight. "I knew you'd defend him; I expected nothing less. You're loyal through and through. I know as well as anyone that life is far from a fairytale." She tipped her head, gazing at him. "Had I met you first . . . Well, there's no use speculating, is there?"

Her words shook him. If Will hadn't pursued her, would Cora have been interested in *him*? No, he determined. She was grieving and saying things she didn't mean. She stood and walked to the fireplace, holding out her ungloved hands toward the leaping flames as if to warm them.

Lucien thought the room overwarm and wished the fire would die down quickly. It was awkward sitting while the lady of the house was standing, so he joined her by the mantel. "I have many faults, Mrs. Griffiths, and so did Will, although I do concede that we were quite loyal to each other. You might perceive that our friendship was one-sided, but Will was a good friend to me. For all his oddities, there was no one I'd rather have as a business partner."

Cora let out a sigh, and her shoulders sagged as she stared into the fire. "He lit up a room with his smile. He could turn any depressing situation into a joke. He always knew the right thing to say, even if it wasn't true." She gave a small laugh. "He was like a little boy, really. Never tiring, taking delight in every small thing, and never wanting to be told no."

Lucien found himself smiling and nodding. "No one could tell him no."

Cora turned her head, and their gazes met. "But now he's gone, and I can't let you continue to make up for his failings, Lucien."

His breath left his chest.

"In his last days," she said, "he was desperate to talk to you, and at first I thought it had to do with business." She folded her arms. "Soon I realized it had to do with me." Her eyes stayed on him, challenging, waiting.

Lucien cleared his throat. "You're right, Mrs. Griffiths. Will's final request had everything to do with you."

Four

Where she found her courage to drill Lucien with questions, Cora didn't know. By all accounts, she should have been nestled under a pile of covers, putting the awfulness of the past weeks behind her. She should have been making decisions whether to remain in Will's family home or to return to her parents'. Loneliness in a massive house or being fretted over in her parents'? Both thoughts were equally depressing.

But as Lucien explained how Will had asked him to watch over Cora and her unborn child, she knew her deceased husband had passed on yet another project to his best friend. Cora had heard all about the other projects. She wasn't entirely sure if Will had ever told her exact truths, since he tended to reveal his secrets when he was drunk, but the general information was plenty to go on.

Twelve Months

She knew now that she'd made a mistake in marrying Will. If only she'd paid more attention to Lucien when they'd first met. He'd been at the same county picnic but had been a nondescript background gentleman. Will was always front and center of attention, so when he turned his eye on her, it was difficult for Cora to remember anyone else.

But the past few days with Lucien at her side had certainly moved her attention to him—when he'd held her up when she could no longer stand, when he'd spoken for her when all she could manage was to breathe in and out; he'd even insisted that she eat and sleep. Lucien had reminded her of Bryson—loyal with every fiber of his being.

"Mrs. Griffiths," Lucien was saying, "believe me when I say it would be an honor to enter into a marriage agreement with you."

Cora wanted to cry and laugh at the same time—cry because the words were coming from Lucien out of *duty*; laugh because he was being so formal. If Will were the one standing before her, he would have probably just kissed her. But Lucien was too proper for anything so impulsive. For some reason, his formality endeared him to her—a fact she'd have to forget all about, because she wasn't about to become charity.

With what little she knew about Will's estate settlement, she would be well provided for. She'd be the caretaker of Griffiths Estate until her child reached majority age and inherited. The life looming before her was a quiet one. Cora had been very unlucky in matters of love, and she didn't want to add Lucien to that tally. No matter how his gaze beseeched her, no matter how nice it might feel to have such a man's arms about her.

Cora reached up and patted Lucien's cheek, much like a mother would a small child's. "I *am* grateful for your offer, Mr. Baxter, but I cannot take it. I cannot believe for a moment that you are willing to wait for my year of mourning. So much could happen during that time. You could meet someone else."

Lucien started to protest, but she stopped him. "Despite the many events taking up my attention these past days," she continued, "I've thought through all of the possibilities and the consequences of each. I plan to raise Will's child in loving memory of him, and the child will grow up well-cared for. If the child is a boy, he'll inherit when he becomes of age. If it's a girl, I've an inheritance that will take care of the both of us for life, and I'll most likely move back to my parents' home, and the estate will pass to Will's first cousin." She tried to smile at him, but instead, her lips trembled. She dropped her hand quickly and clasped her hands. "And I'm sure the child would love to have a godfather such as you."

In a surprising move, Lucien grasped her hands in his and leaned close. Close enough that Cora almost regretted her rebuff. "You needn't decide today," he said, voice low. "Take your time. As you said, you've a year of mourning ahead of you."

Cora moved her gaze from their clasped hands up to Lucien's steady brown eyes. Even his eyes were different from Will's intense green ones. Lucien's eyes made her feel safe, comforted. But there was one thing Cora couldn't abide, and that was pity. She'd lost her true love three years ago, and then she'd married Will in hopes of living a life of hope and affection. That had disappeared after conceiving her child. What could Lucien offer that she hadn't already experienced? Marriage wouldn't be fair to him. Perhaps he'd meet the love of his life at his next social event.

She withdrew her hands slowly, reluctantly, from his grasp. "I am truly sorry, Lucien. I don't need more time to reconsider. I've given my final answer."

Five

The sun had yet to rise, but Lucien could have sworn someone had been looking down on him from the upper window while he waited for the car to be brought around. It could only be Cora. If he stalled a few moments, would she come out to say goodbye?

Lucien glanced up again at the movement in the window on the second floor of the Griffiths mansion. The hour was early enough that no one was awake. Last night, he'd notified the butler that he'd need a ride to the station to make the early train.

That was a ridiculous idea. They'd said their goodbyes the night before. Why prolong their farewells? She'd made her decision, and she seemed determined to stick by it. Besides, as Cora had pointed out, she'd be in mourning for a year. A lot could happen in that time. To him and to her.

The butler arrived, driving Will's car, and as Lucien climbed into the backseat, he felt as if he'd forgotten something. But his mind went through his preparations of the night before, and nothing seemed amiss. He shook off the feeling and considered all that needed to be done once he returned. With Christmas only a few days away, business would be lagging; he'd be able to catch up on paperwork by the time the New Year rolled around.

When they reached the train station, the sense that he was forgetting something persisted. But he hadn't left anything at Cora's estate; he knew it. He climbed out of the car and thanked the butler, then headed for the platform. As he waited, apparently the only passenger at the station, his thoughts were consumed by Cora. How could he leave Will's grieving widow to celebrate Christmas practically alone? When he'd asked about her holiday plans, she'd said her father wouldn't be able to return, as he was on the board for the annual Christmas Ball in her home town.

"It will be a quiet holiday with just Mother and me," Cora had said. "I'm not even putting up a tree. It's not worth the bother. Mother's not feeling well anyway, and I prefer the quiet after so many guests during the funeral."

That was how Lucien had justified leaving her.

But how could he continue onto London, knowing Cora would have a lonely Christmas? By the time he heard the train's approach, he'd already left the platform and was walking back to the estate. The sun was well on its way to bringing in a bright morning. Lucien might be a fool, but as he strode back to the Griffiths Estate his heart felt lighter somehow.

When he arrived back at the estate, he hesitated before ringing the bell. The time was still quite early. What would Cora say about his return? Would she assure him that she was fine and send him away?

He decided to walk in the gardens and wait there a bit, give the household time to rise. Although Cora was an early riser, he didn't want to request her presence before she was ready to receive visitors.

After at least half an hour of aimless walking across frozen ground, he sat on a bench. It wasn't long before he started to feel foolish. He'd proposed to Cora, and she'd turned him down, yet here he sat, unable to leave.

He leaned forward, propped his elbows on his knees, and closed his eyes. The air was properly cold, but as the morning sun warmed the bench, he relaxed into a doze.

"Lucien?"

Now he was dreaming about her? Then the voice came again, and he realized that he wasn't dreaming. Lucien opened his eyes. Cora stood before him, dressed in a riding habit.

"You missed your train?" She tilted her head, peering down at him.

He rose to his feet. She wore a riding habit, and he couldn't help but notice the pink of her cheeks from the brisk morning air and the way the winter sun glowed off the wisps of hair that had fallen from her loose bun.

"I didn't hear you coming," he said. "I . . ." He exhaled, trying to regain command of his thoughts. "I plan to stay through the holiday. No one should spend Christmas alone."

Her eyes widened, but instead of saying no as he thought she would, she remained quiet for several moments. Then her face softened into a smile. "That would be lovely. Thank you."

She'd agreed? Just like that? Lucien let out the rest of his breath. He held back a smile. "Are you going riding?"

"I am," Cora said. "Care to join me?"

"Is it safe? You know, for the child?"

She lifted a brow. "I'm feeling well enough." A smile played on her lips. "But thank you for your concern."

Was she teasing him? Berating him? Had she been this way with Will? A knot formed in his stomach as he thought of how Will had seen other women while married to Cora. "I should come along, then, if only to make sure you are safe." His excuse to accompany her was offered quite lamely, but he realized that his tone was teasing, as well.

    He stepped beside her and held out his arm. When she took it, the knot in his stomach loosened. Maybe, just maybe, he could make up for some of what Will had put her through.

Six

They rode their horses all morning and would have continued longer if they'd brought a bit of refreshment, but as it was, Cora was parched with thirst. And the truth was, she was feeling a bit queasy. Maybe she would have to give up riding sooner than later after all. It would be a sad moment; riding had always given her the escape she needed to endure her marriage. Most days, she was fine, but once in a while, the realization that she wasn't the only woman in her husband's life had seeped into her soul. To breathe again, she rode. Rain or shine, cold or hot, windy or calm. She rode. And forgot.

On their ride, Lucien had been quiet at first, as had Cora, but as their horses cantered together, she asked him about his work, and then his clients, and before she knew it, they were both talking about their families and upbringings.

"We should turn back," Cora said, glancing over at Lucien. He made a fine figure on a horse and seemed to be in complete command.

He didn't question her, instead simply slowing and turning his horse around, then waiting for Cora to do the same. They had been discussing their favorite composers, and Cora told him she played the piano. Cora knew Lucien had written some songs, but she was curious to see if he'd mention it himself.

"Do you play any instrument besides the piano?" Lucien asked.

"I tried the clarinet for a while, but I didn't care for it."

A brief smile touched Lucien's face. "I never moved beyond the piano myself."

"Oh?" This was the lead-in Cora had been hoping for. "How well do you play?"

"Well enough." His tone sounded reluctant. Then he went quiet, and Cora pulled her horse to a stop. When Lucien realized she was no longer beside him, he turned his horse around and approached. His eyes scanned her face, and possibly more, concern pulling on the corners of his mouth.

"Are you all right?" he asked.

"Will said you composed music. I'd like to hear some."

Lucien looked away for a moment, and then his brown eyes settled back on her. Cora didn't know what to make of their depths. Was his composing something he didn't want anyone to know about? "The music I've written isn't polished. It's more of a hobby, or p-part of a hobby, not even a full hobby."

He was practically stuttering, and Cora thought it was endearing. Who would have thought that sensible Lucien could get flustered?

"How about we play the piano for each other?" Cora said, urging her horse forward.

Lucien had to turn around again to match her, and in a

moment he was by her side again. "I've never played any of my compositions in public before."

"I'm not the public," she said. "And . . . you played for Will. We're practically family."

Lucien's face went still. "It's been a long time," he finally said.

"How long?" Cora asked. This was a side of Lucien that intrigued her; she hoped her persistence would pay off. Why she was so interested, she couldn't say.

"It's been a couple of years since I've played for anyone."

"I haven't played for longer than that," she said. "Tell you what, we'll both give it our best, and if we fail, we tell no one."

Lucien chuckled, and for the first time since Will first became ill, she laughed.

She guided her horse into a faster canter, Lucien keeping pace. She didn't look at him again as they rode toward the estate, but a quick glance at him told her he was still smiling. Although it was cold, and her fingers would take ages to thaw, her heart had just warmed up a few degrees.

Seven

Lucien lightly ran his fingertips over the piano keys. It had been too long since he'd played. His townhouse didn't have a music room, and every time he returned home, there was no end to the questions from his mother of when he'd marry. He'd actually composed a couple of songs without the benefit of a piano, ones he'd yet to try out.

He'd never volunteered to play at musicales at friends' homes, and only when Will insisted on something nice for one of his ladies did Lucien copy off a few lines. He had no idea what lyrics Will had added to his notes, nor did he ask.

A couple of pieces battled for remembrance in his mind, and Lucien dropped his hands in his lap. Cora was still upstairs changing her clothing, and the longer she took, the less playing his compositions for her sounded like a good idea. His parents and Will were the only ones to ever hear Lucien's compositions.

Twelve Months

He prided himself on his organization, education, and practical approach to solving matters of the law, even when they were complicated. But music was different. It moved in unpredictable directions, and it didn't end when it was supposed to; it was loud, then soft, shouting emotions that Lucien didn't always want to shout.

The door behind him opened, and Cora entered. Lucien shot to his feet and stepped away from the piano. Before she could speak and change his mind, he said, "I'm out of practice. I'd much rather hear you play."

Cora walked toward him and stopped a few paces away; he could clearly see amusement in her blue eyes.

"I see." She folded her arms, and Lucien forced his eyes to stay on her face, despite the fact that her black dress nipped at her waist. "It's only us, Lucien. Mother is in her room. We can shut the doors so not even the servants will hear."

Lucien did so, then crossed to the windows and looked over the drive leading up to the house. The trees lining it were wind-stripped, and the sky was a bleak gray. The morning sun had disappeared with the gathering afternoon clouds. "How about we make a trade?"

"Such as?" Cora took a few steps toward him.

"You allow a Christmas tree, and I'll play you one of my compositions." He watched several emotions flicker across her face one after the other.

She'd planned to skip all semblance of Christmas this year—her first as a married woman and the mistress of the estate. She'd made grand plans, yet had cancelled them all when Will died.

"You may bring in a tree, but decorating it will cost you another piece," Cora said, a slight smile on her face.

Relief warmed Lucien. "What if you don't like my compositions? Sitting through two may be torture, and you would still have to keep your end of the bargain."

"I'll have to take that risk." She crossed to the chair

closest to the piano and sat down, arranging her skirt, waiting for him to play.

"Now?" Lucien said, stalling, knowing she was waiting.

She lifted her chin, her gaze steady. "Now."

He was grateful she'd accepted the bargain, but now that the need to play for her was staring him in the face, his pulse drummed. Would she give him her honest opinion, or would it be simply a tight smile and polite applause?

She pointed to the piano bench.

He swallowed against the dryness in his throat and strode forward. If this was going to be a disaster, it would be a spectacular disaster, and he knew just which piece to start with.

His first notes felt awkward and stilted. He lifted his fingers, rubbed his hands for a couple of moments, then began again. The same awkward notes arose, but this time he pushed through them. He played a medium-tempo melody, recalling the inspiration behind the piece. It was a hunting melody, really, a thrilling fox chase. The music mimicked a half-dozen riders and their hounds streaming through the woods, in and out of meadows and trees, over a broken fence, across a shallow river.

Then one dog and rider broke off from the rest, following another scent, and soon he was alone, riding valiantly on, hoping to catch the prize. The music simplified, slowed, yet remained heavy with anticipation, until finally . . . the lone hunter was rewarded, and the others of the hunting party caught up and began to celebrate.

By the time he finished, Lucien was out of breath. He reached up to loosen his collar, and his arm bumped someone next to him. He startled. Cora had joined him on the bench sometime during the song. As caught up as he was, he hadn't noticed.

"That was amazing, Lucien," Cora said in a soft voice.

He didn't dare look at her. The next piece would take even more out of him, and he didn't want to see what her expression might be now, after his first piece. He needed to wholly concentrate on the next piece; it had been years since he'd played it, written about his mother in memory of the day he'd left for boarding school.

He placed his hands on the keys and started to play again. The opening melody started out fractured but cheerful, as he imagined his mother putting on a brave face interspersed with hiccups of emotion. As she watched the carriage drive away, the melody mimicked the rapid beat of her heart as if in time with the horse's hooves. The melody grew melancholy as she walked back into the house and into her child's empty room. He'd been gone only moments, but she missed him already. The melody sped up again as she thought of the things her son would experience, of the education he'd get. And her heart became light again, despite the tears.

After Lucien had played the final notes, the world came back into focus, and he realized that Cora had laid a hand on his arm. He blinked a few times, clearing his mind, and looked over at her.

Her eyes were wide and a darker blue than he remembered. There was moisture in them, as if she'd been touched by the same emotion he'd felt while playing. His gaze fell to her slightly open mouth. It was like something was tugging them together. He leaned down. She leaned closer, her face upturned, her eyes fluttering shut.

Without thought, Lucien tilted his head and closed his eyes. He felt her warm breath on his, and then it was gone. He opened his eyes. Cora was facing forward, her hands on the keys.

"Teach me the piece you just played," she said, her voice breathless. A blush covered her neck and cheeks.

Lucien exhaled. What had just happened—what had *almost* happened?

Eight

Cora blinked rapidly against her encroaching tears. She wouldn't let a single one drop. To prevent it, she kept her focus on Lucien's hands moving on the keys as he played a few measures at a time. Then she mimicked the notes one octave higher.

She'd almost kissed him—or was it that he had almost kissed her? She wasn't quite sure, now that she thought about it. Regardless, she was mortified. Her husband hadn't even been in the ground for a week, and she had nearly thrown herself into the arms of another man.

Granted, Will hadn't been faithful to her, but that didn't excuse *her* behavior. She was not her husband. She was a woman of integrity and practicality. She might have judged Lucien for his propriety, but the truth was, Cora depended on it as well. And they had both almost thrown all propriety out the window, which could only lead to disaster.

The tension in the room was tangible. Not an uncomfortable tension, but a heart-racing, pulse-pounding one. How could this be happening? There was only one explanation. It *wasn't* really happening—she couldn't be falling in love with Lucien. She was in full mourning, and Lucien was the one who knew her husband best. Opposite personalities, to be sure, but Lucien had known her husband even better than she.

She was clinging to him because of that. Nothing else.

Besides, carrying a child had made her more emotional, needy, and definitely irrational. Spending Christmas together with Lucien was not a good idea after all. If one or two pieces of music could make her melt in another man's arms, what would spending several days with him bring her to do?

"You're a quick student," Lucien said, pulling Cora out of her thoughts. His deep voice seemed to rumble through her, making her aware of how close they sat together at the piano bench, pecking at keys only a couple of octaves apart. Cora didn't need to be touching Lucien to feel as if her skin were in contact with his.

"Your compositions are beautiful," Cora said when she again felt that she had command of her voice. "You should have them published into a collection."

Lucien rested his hands on his thighs and chuckled. "You sound like my mother."

Cora looked up at him, willing herself not to get caught in his warm gaze. "I think your mother has good advice." They were still sitting very close, so she started to notice minute things about him, like how carefully he'd trimmed his sideburns. "What's stopping you from publishing your music?"

He lifted a shoulder. "I'm not much for playing in front of an audience, and once my music is published, I'd probably receive requests to play it."

"Perhaps you can bribe your audiences for something you want in return."

His smile really was nice. Genuine, and not accompanied by flowery statements.

"Such as with Christmas trees and wassail?" he asked.

"That's a good start. You could probably secure a yule log out of it, and perhaps a set of candles for the tree."

"I'd also insist on silver bells."

Cora laughed. "You *will* be driving a hard bargain for your future audiences. But silver bells it is."

Cora didn't know if her heart could take it any longer; Lucien was still smiling at her. She needed some time alone to turn her mind back to rational thinking and away from thoughts of what it would have felt like if she *hadn't* pulled away from Lucien's almost-kiss.

She made a move to rise, and Lucien stood and helped her to her feet. The heat of his hand shot straight into her skin. She drew her hand away quickly, hoping he wouldn't notice how affected she was.

"Are you not going to play?" Lucien asked. "I thought that was part of our bargain."

He stood too close. Much too close. Cora needed some extremely cold air to clear her head. "I will play for you after supper. If we're to find a tree, we should take advantage of the light."

"All right." Lucien led the way to the door and held it open for her. In the entryway, he helped her with her coat, then asked the butler to send the stable boy to the gardens, where they'd meet him. "And tell him to bring an axe." Lucien shrugged on his own coat and grabbed his hat.

As they stepped outside, Cora pulled on her warmest gloves, solely for appearance's sake; her hands were certainly warm enough without them.

Lucien held out his arm. "Shall we?"

Cora couldn't stop the smile rising to her face. If a year ago she'd have seen this future moment, she wouldn't have believed it: that by the end of the year, she'd be married, pregnant, and widowed—and then walking on the arm of a handsome and caring man to look for a tree to cut for Christmas.

They didn't walk far. The stable boy, Jeffrey, met them at the edge of the gardens, carrying an axe. Cora greeted him. "Thank you for bringing the axe. We won't be going far. There are plenty of trees nearby."

Lucien thanked the boy as well and took the axe in his left hand, keeping Cora's arm linked through his right. They left the gardens and walked toward the line of trees. They passed several pines, their branches dusted with snow that had fallen a few days ago.

"Let's go inside the forest a few paces so we can find a tree that isn't too wind-beaten."

"All right," Cora said, enjoying the slow walk even though the temperature continued to fall with the approaching evening. "You're the one who gets to drag it back to the house."

Lucien chuckled and seemed to draw closer to her. Or maybe it was Cora's imagination, and she'd just become more aware of the warmth of his arm beneath her hand.

"Bryson and I did this once," Cora said, suddenly remembering the snowy day they'd wandered around her parents' property.

"Who is Bryson?"

Too late, Cora had already mentioned him. "Major Bryson was my fiancé before I met Will. He was killed in a battle in Tibet."

Lucien nodded. "I knew you'd lost a fiancé, but I didn't know his name." He looked at her. "I'm very sorry, Cora."

She lifted a shoulder, ignoring the lump in her throat as they entered the thicker trees, where the winter sunlight dappled the ground. "I suppose I'm cursed. My fiancé and my husband are both gone. It's a good thing I didn't agree to your proposal. You'd be on your way to an early demise." She laughed at her dark teasing.

But Lucien didn't laugh. He stopped, urging her to a

stop with him, causing her to release his arm. When she looked up at him, his brown eyes held no humor.

"Please accept my apologies," Cora hastened to say. "It was a terribly insensitive joke."

"I hope you don't believe you're actually cursed," Lucien said in a quiet tone. Even though he spoke just above a whisper, Cora heard his words clearly because the forest around them was absolutely silent. It was as if they were the only two living creatures in the entire world. Nothing moved, and the only sound was her own breathing.

"I don't believe I'm cursed, not truly," Cora said, "but I have wondered at times. Do you blame me after I've failed twice? Every man in the county should be afraid to be with a woman like me. Not that I intend to marry again, of course." She drew her arm from his and looked away, very aware both of how alone they were and how handsome Lucien appeared in his wool overcoat and angled hat.

"If you ever changed your mind, you wouldn't be able to hold back the line of suitors at your door," Lucien said.

Cora had to laugh; her heart was pounding too hard for her to do anything else. "Only if they were interested in living in the house."

"Cora," he said, hand brushing hers. Before she realized it, Lucien had intertwined their fingers. Even though they both wore gloves, the intimacy was undeniable. "That's not why men would line up at your door."

His mouth turned up slightly, and Cora was relieved his humor had returned.

"Then perhaps it would be because they know about Will's wine cellar," she said, glad this conversation had turned from a dark suggestion to teasing.

Lucien's mouth twitched. "I disagree there, too."

He was still holding her hand. Why was he holding her hand?

"You're right," she said. "It would be because they couldn't resist the chance to own Will's fine stallions. They're purebreds, you know . . ." Her voice trailed off as Lucien leaned closer to her.

"I know, but that's not it either."

She arched a brow. "Then pray tell *why* would they come? Tell me, Lucien, since you have all the answers."

He smiled. "I will after you have played the piano for me." He released her hand and stepped away. "It looks like we've stopped in the right spot. That tree is perfect."

Cora turned to see where he was pointing. A tree, just taller than Cora, stood out from the rest. Lucien was right; it was perfectly formed and would look beautiful inside the house. "It's almost too beautiful to cut."

"We should only have the best this Christmas." Lucien walked toward the tree and inspected it.

Cora watched him, not quite believing that she'd agreed to spend Christmas with this man or that they were cutting down a tree to trim.

What would he insist on next?

Nine

Lucien relaxed against the settee as Cora played piece after piece on the piano. Mrs. Evans had finally joined them, and she sat quite close to the fire, with a blanket covering her lap. From time to time, she dozed. With the combination of the fire and the sweet music, Lucien couldn't blame her.

Once Cora had played one melody, it wasn't difficult to talk her into playing more. He smiled to himself, though he knew his time was running out. Tomorrow was Christmas Eve, when they'd decorate the tree. Then Christmas. And after that . . . he'd be out of excuses to stay.

And with no more excuses, he'd have to return to London. How could he convince Cora from such a distance that it would be a good idea to marry him? Even with her being in mourning for a year, it would be difficult to come up with excuse after excuse to see her. As godfather of her child, he could certainly attend the christening, but then what?

He shook his head slightly at his grand notions. When Cora had listed off reasons that men would want to marry her, he'd disagreed with all of them. Because none of them were why he wanted to marry her.

Yes, Will had pleaded with him, and that's why Lucien had approached Cora with the topic in the first place. Yet the more time Lucien spent with Cora, the less he wanted to leave. He had tried to leave once but hadn't made it very far at all. It was strange to be falling in love with his best friend's widow. If Will had survived, would Lucien have had these thoughts at all?

He glanced over at Mrs. Evans, feeling a bit guilty about his thoughts. But her eyes were closed again, her mouth pulled into a faint smile. It seemed she hadn't decoded a thing he was thinking.

Cora finished her current piece, then started a new one after casting a smile at him over her shoulder. Lucien's heart inexplicably tugged. He'd interacted with Cora on a number of occasions while Will was alive, of course, and Lucien had always enjoyed her company, but he'd never considered her as anything other than someone else's wife. Perhaps that was the reason he felt differently now. At least, he hoped he wouldn't have developed these feelings if Will had lived. But how could he convince Cora that what he felt toward her now wasn't because of her late husband's request?

Cora's music ended in a grand crescendo, and she turned to look at him.

Lucien clapped. "Bravo! Another?"

She smiled, her brows lifting. "Are you not tired from dragging that tree to the house?" she said, lowering her voice, her gaze flitting toward her mother. "And you did eat quite a bit at supper. I'd have thought you'd be nodding off by now like Mother."

He shrugged, trying to keep his expression unaffected. "Who do you take me for? An elderly gentleman?"

Cora laughed—a sound more beautiful than her piano playing. She clapped her hand over her mouth and looked over at her mother, but the woman still slept. "I don't think you so old," she said in a quieter tone. "I'm just surprised that my music has kept you alert." She rose and crossed to him, a playful look on her face.

She stopped and held out her hand. "Come, it's your turn. Play me another of your compositions."

Lucien was definitely getting too comfortable around her, because it took no more persuading before he was on his feet and taking his place on the piano bench. She didn't sit by him but walked over to the fireplace and remained standing.

He placed his hands on the keys, sorting through what he might play. "This one is not original, but a rendition of *Silent Night, Holy Night*."

Cora's smile was quick. "Sounds lovely."

And that's how he started playing a round of Christmas caroles, improvising as he went. Cora clapped softly after each one, and eventually she came to sit in a chair close to the piano. When the clock chimed eleven, Lucien couldn't believe how much time they'd spent playing the piano.

"Goodness," Mrs. Evans said, finally opening her eyes. "Is that the time?" Her gaze was a bit bleary as she took in the scene. "I'm sorry if I've slept through the performances."

Cora crossed to her mother and reached for her hand. "We'll play more tomorrow. Let's get you to bed." She looked over at Lucien. "You should get some sleep as well." Arm in arm with her mother, she crossed the room, but not before Lucien noticed her blush.

"Good night, Mrs. Evans, Mrs. Griffiths," he said.

"Good night," Mrs. Evans said, and Cora repeated it. Her voice was soft; then she opened the door and departed.

Lucien was slower rising to his feet than Cora. He moved to the windows to look out at the black sky, giving

Cora enough time to get her mother settled and make her way to her room. He didn't want it to seem that he was following her through the house at such a late hour.

Cold seeped through the windowpanes, and Lucien decided that the moon must be hidden behind a dark cloud because he couldn't even make out the drive or the tops of the trees. He should have been tired; instead, he was wide awake. Everything in the house was absolutely quiet, so he made his way to Will's study, where he'd previously organized all of the estate papers so Cora could look over them when she was ready. It had been a simple task, really, since Will was more organized than one might have thought.

The study didn't remind Lucien of Will as much as it reminded him of the elder Mr. Griffiths. The colors were dark and the furniture heavy. Lucien was surprised that his friend hadn't remodeled with the lighter wood Will was so fond of. Perhaps he wanted the memory of his father preserved.

Lucien sat in the chair next to the credenza, remembering the last time he'd seen Will in this room. Will had been going on about a new stallion he'd purchased. Lucien smiled to himself. If there was one thing that could get Will excited, it was a new horse.

And a new woman. The thought floated through Lucien's mind, but he shoved it away.

It was hard to believe that Will had been unfaithful to his wife, especially since Lucien had spent a delightful few days with her. Cora was unassuming and quick to forgive— she was remarkable, really. The more he thought about her virtues, the more disappointed he felt in Will's behavior.

In life, Lucien had never envied Will, but when it came to Cora, Lucien was starting to envy his best friend. Which was ridiculous; Will was dead.

But he'd had the love and devotion of an angel, and he'd thrown it away.

Lucien's gaze strayed to the credenza, along its elegant

lines, finally stopping at the lowest drawer on the right side. There was a key hole in it—something he hadn't ever noticed. The drawer was open just a smidge, plainly not locked. Lucien crossed to close the drawer, but as he did so, a flash of pink caught his eye.

On impulse, Lucien opened the drawer. Various envelopes were stacked haphazardly inside. They all appeared to be addressed to "Will" or "William." Lucien moved to shut the drawer, not wanting to know what a single one said, but then he hesitated. It wasn't difficult to deduce that the letters were from Will's female acquaintances. The envelopes were in different colors, and the handwriting upon them varied.

And he'd kept the letters in a locked drawer . . . which wasn't locked now. Did that mean Cora had read them? He shut the drawer, unease spreading through him at the thought of Cora discovering the letters and reading even one of them.

Lucien walked to the window, where he stared into the black nothingness. The panes reflected the single lamp in the room, the rest of the room in shadows. He closed his eyes for a moment, mind reeling from all that had happened in the past few weeks, from all that was happening now.

He turned and walked back to the drawer, from which he took out a single letter and read the first three lines. It was enough to convince him of his next course of action.

He scooped up all of the letters, then strode out of the office and back to the drawing room, where the fire glowed an amber orange. One by one he tossed the letters into the fire, making the flames leap to life again. Lucien supposed he should have had misgivings about burning letters that didn't belong to him while a guest in another person's home, but he couldn't stand the thought of Cora reading them—or reading them again if she already had.

He tossed the last letter into the fire and watched it catch fire and burn. He realized that he hadn't given up the role of covering Will's tracks after all. He was doing it again, but with a completely different person's welfare in mind.

Ten

Cora laughed as the tree tipped again. Lucien had nearly cursed the first time. "Let me help you," she said, and finally Lucien relented.

Within moments, the tree was righted, and Lucien had secured the trunk to the metal stand. He backed away from it, brushing his hands together. "Not too bad after all," he said. "Thanks for your help."

Cora crossed to him and plucked a pine needle from his hair. "Did you lose something?"

He smiled and took the needle, his hand brushing against hers. "Thank you. I was looking for that."

A moment passed as their gazes held. His brown eyes were warm, his expression inviting, his mouth curved just so. Cora wanted to take one more step forward and grasp his hand, or perhaps run her fingers along his shoulders, or his jawline.

"It looks very regal," Cora's mother said, coming into the room. "What will you decorate it with?"

Cora blinked, bringing herself back to the moment at hand. She exhaled, willing her heart rate to calm.

Lucien turned to Cora, his expression questioning. "What do you think?"

"There are boxes of decorations stored in the attic."

"I can bring them down," Lucien said.

Her mother clasped her hands together. "Would you?" she said. "That would be lovely."

But Cora didn't know what to think of his sorting through the things in the attic. It might take him ages to find the right boxes. "We'll come with you. We won't need much for the tree, but we will need an oil lamp. There aren't any electric lights up there."

"I don't want to go up those narrow stairs," her mother said. "You two go, and I'll be sure to give you an expert opinion when you return."

Lucien laughed. "I could use it." He extended his arm, and Cora took it, realizing how natural it felt. She was becoming increasingly comfortable around this man.

They took the stairs to the first landing, then turned down the hallway and walked to the door at the far end. Lucien opened the door and motioned Cora to go through. At the base of the stairs, an oil lamp stood on a table. Cora lit the lamp, and Lucien picked it up. The staircase was only wide enough for one person at a time, so Cora went up the stairs ahead of Lucien.

As they reached the attic, Cora could almost taste the dust in the air. She'd come up here once with Will when they were first married and looked through some things from his childhood, but she hadn't been up since. At the time, she'd noticed crates labeled as Christmas decorations. She didn't know exactly what was in them.

It didn't take long to locate the crates, and she knelt

down in front of the first while Lucien held the lamp overhead, dispelling the shadows.

A collection of miniature silver candleholders the size of her smallest finger twinkled up at her with the glow from the lamp. "I hope there are candles to fit these," she said, sorting through the crate. She set aside bolts of ribbon until she reached a box. She opened it to find rows of tiny candles. "Perfect. Will's mother must have had enough made up for many years to come."

Lucien helped her remove the candleholders and candles, then reached into the crate and pulled out a set of silver bells. They rang softly at the movement. "These will be festive."

Cora smiled. "Mother will love them."

"I'll carry everything if you take the lamp and lead the way," Lucien said.

He gathered the boxes of candles and candlesticks; then, once he had those balanced in his left arm, he picked up the silver bells. "Thank you for this, Lucien," she said.

He looked over at her, his gaze soft and subdued in the near darkness. She hadn't realized how close they were standing, not to mention the fact that they were completely alone. She scanned his handsome face and felt her heart race as she wondered again what it would be like to kiss him.

But it was too soon. Too much. She'd been in love once, had been married once, and now she had a child on the way. She couldn't trust her emotions.

She stepped back, then turned and made her way around the furniture and other crates in the attic, with Lucien following behind. When she reached the top of the stairs, Lucien said, "Wait a moment."

She looked behind her.

"I have a confession to make," he said.

Cora turned, her heart pounding even faster.

"Last night, I found some letters in Will's office . . . letters from other—"

"Women. Yes, I've seen them."

"You've . . . seen them?" At her nod, he continued, "But that's not my entire confession. I burned them."

Cora let that sink in. "Why would you do that?"

He shifted the candles in his arms and stepped closer. "I know it wasn't my place, or my property, so I understand if you're upset. Please accept my apologies."

She continued to study his face, but it was difficult to read his expression with such little light. "Why did you burn them?"

"I didn't want them to be a reminder that might hurt you again."

Tears burned in Cora's eyes, and she blinked rapidly. Lucien was a caring man. "I'm quite past it all."

"Are you?" Lucien asked.

"I am," she said, trying to keep her voice steady. "There's nothing that can be changed now, so it doesn't matter any longer." She offered up a tremulous smile. "I think you need a rest from cleaning up after Will, though I do appreciate that I don't have to worry about coming across those letters again."

"I didn't do it for Will," Lucien said.

Cora stared at him for a moment. Then, without thinking, she stepped toward him, lifted up on her feet, and kissed his cheek.

Eleven

Lucien opened his eyes as the first bits of light entered his bed chamber. A smile tugged at his mouth, and he sat up in bed. It was Christmas morning, and he'd come up with the perfect gift for Cora. It had only taken a short trip to the village last night to procure it.

After she'd kissed his cheek in the attic, rendering him absolutely speechless, they'd spent a cozy few hours with her mother, trimming the tree and then singing caroles while Lucien played.

As mother and daughter, Cora and Mrs. Evans harmonized well, and Lucien rounded it out as tenor. He couldn't recall having spent a more pleasant Christmas Eve. Now, he could smell something baking; perhaps a spice cake or a bread pudding was in the works.

He rose and dressed for the morning meal. He was usually much earlier than Cora or her mother, but this morning, it appeared he'd slept late; the sun was already well on its way up the sky. Sure enough, when he went downstairs, both women were at the table in the morning room.

They looked up and smiled as he entered. Lucien greeted them, thinking he could easily get used to Cora's smile each morning. They chatted about the weather and which train Lucien would be taking in the morning. What Cora said next surprised him.

"Mr. and Mrs. Christensen are coming over for Christmas supper. I also invited Miss Bender, but I haven't received a reply."

"You sent the invitation out quite late last night," Mrs. Evans said to her daughter.

Cora gave a nod. "You're right. So there's time yet for them to send a reply."

Cora was celebrating Christmas by inviting guests over. This gave Lucien plenty of hope that his gift would be well received. Thinking about what he'd purchased for Cora reminded him that he should probably give her the gift before the guests arrived.

"I have a gift for you," Lucien blurted. There wasn't really any other way to say it.

Her eyes widened. "Oh?" Her face flushed as she glanced over at her mother. "I didn't know we'd planned to exchange gifts."

"We haven't, but I wanted to get you something . . . as my hostess," he finished lamely.

Mrs. Evans' attention had focused on him, but he couldn't tell if her expression was approving or disapproving.

"Shall I bring it down before the guests arrive?"

Cora opened her mouth to answer, but her mother cut in. "Why don't you take it to the sitting room? Cora can meet you there. I've a mind to finish my meal, and I'll join you later."

Lucien looked over at Cora, and at her slight nod, he rose and left the room.

By the time he arrived in the sitting room, Cora was looking out the massive windows. She turned as he entered, her gaze alighting on the wrapped parcel. "Really, Mr. Baxter, you shouldn't have."

"It's rather simple, truly," he said, crossing to meet her at the windows. "And I'd rather you called me Lucien."

"All right then, *Lucien*." She offered a small smile and took the package from his outstretched hand, then sat on the nearest sofa.

"Does your mother want us to wait for her?"

Cora shook her head and patted the sofa next to her. "Mother is giving us a few moments alone."

Lucien's breath fled for a moment.

Cora laughed. "She may seem a bit distant, but she's not dense." Her eyes were impossibly blue as she peered up at him. "Sit down; you're making me nervous."

He sat. He didn't need to be commanded a third time.

"I told her about your proposal," Cora said in a soft voice.

Lucien felt as if his heart had jumped into his throat. Whether from dismay or from hope, he didn't know. If Cora had told her mother, did that mean Cora was reconsidering?

She was smiling at him as his thoughts tumbled against each other, moving in all directions. "Don't you want to know what she said?"

"Yes," Lucien managed to get out, and then his body went cold all over. What if the women had laughed at him?

"She said nothing," Cora said. "But she didn't seem displeased."

Lucien swallowed against the sudden dryness in his throat. "And . . . how does that make you feel?"

"Your proposal never displeased me, Lucien," Cora said. "But as you know, my life is very complicated right now."

"I know," Lucien said, loving that she was calling him by his first name. Mrs. Evans wasn't completely against the idea; at least he hoped he was understanding her correctly. "That's why I bought you this."

Her gaze fell to the package in her hands. She untied the string, and then she removed the wrapper, revealing a long box. She opened it, and nestled inside was a silver letter opener with an intricately designed handle.

She looked up at him with a smile. "It's beautiful." But her eyes were questioning.

"It's to open the letters I will send you each week."

Her gaze held his, her blue eyes nearly violet. "Thank you," Cora said. "I regret that I didn't get you a gift." She was still watching him, and he could not help but touch her.

"I didn't expect one." He placed his hand on top of hers. When she didn't pull away, his heart soared. She hadn't questioned why he'd be writing to her. The fact that she seemed to accept the information sent hope through him as never before.

"You've helped me so much these past weeks," she said, her gaze dropping to their hands. "I should have gotten a gift for you."

He lowered his head until his forehead was almost touching hers. "There is one thing you can give me," he said in a low voice.

She blinked up at him, and he wished he could know her true thoughts. "Write to me too," he said. He laced his fingers with hers, his heart pounding, worrying if he was about to scare her away. He would be leaving in the morning, and there would be no other chance to tell her how he felt in person. "Next Christmas, I hope you'll accept my hand in marriage."

"Lucien . . ." Her eyes filled with tears.

He'd gone too far. He was an idiot for thinking she could ever love him. With a heavy exhale, he pulled his hand away, but she wouldn't let it go. Surprised, he felt his heart thump with renewed hope, and when Cora moved forward and wrapped her arms around him, that hope bloomed.

He recovered quickly and encircled her with his arms. Inhaling her rose-scent, he closed his eyes, knowing that if nothing else good happened in his life, he could die happy remembering this moment. In Cora's arms, there was no past, no future, just the present.

"I will write to you, Lucien," she said, her breath warming his neck. "And I'll look forward to that day."

He hardly dared believe her words. In fact, he didn't move at first, for fear that he might wake up from this delicious dream to find that having Cora's body brushed against his, and her arms wrapped around him, were only in his imagination.

"You are too good, Lucien," she continued in that voice he'd grown to love. "Sometimes I wonder if you're real."

"I've wondered the same about you," he said.

When she drew away slightly, his head was still spinning with a hundred thoughts and possibilities.

"I have one more gift for you," she said, looking up at him.

He was about to protest that she'd done enough, that she'd given him plenty, when she placed her hands on each side of his face and drew him toward her.

Her kiss wasn't anything he could have prepared for. It shot fiery heat through him and turned his heart into a thunderstorm of emotion. And it wasn't brief. She kissed him once, then twice, lingering, and he lingered even more.

When he finally had the sense to catch his breath, she drew away, smiling up at him. "Merry Christmas, Lucien."

Twelve

Twelve Months and Six Days Later

Cora laid her forehead against the windowpane of the second-story bedroom and smiled as she watched Lucien climb into the car below. Another car was waiting to drive her to the church, following after him.

The wedding guests were already at the church. Her parents had also left, taking three-month-old Robert William with them, so she could have a few moments to herself for final touches.

Today was her wedding day. She was about to be married to a wonderful, kind man, one who'd loved her son upon first meeting him. A man who'd written faithfully each week for an entire year and visited in between when time permitted. They'd always met with company around, keeping their interactions casual between them and hadn't announced their engagement until Christmas Eve, just a week ago.

Cora had taken her parents into her confidence, and their opinion was the only one she cared about. As the car pulled away, moving along the front drive, then toward the village church, Cora smoothed the skirt of her dress and turned to face the mirror a final time. Her dark hair had been expertly arranged, and small winter flowers dotted the pin curls.

She wore a soft blue dress, nothing too excessive, but definitely a change from widow's black. She'd been wearing varying shades of gray the past week, so blue was a nice change. That, and it was her wedding dress. Her shape from before carrying Robert William had returned for the most part, and she was nearly back to her pre-pregnancy self. She'd never be the same shape, of course. Carrying a child and giving birth had softened her angles and widened her curves. But she didn't mind. Lucien had frequently told her how he loved her glow of health.

It was time to descend the stairs and climb into the waiting car, but first, she picked up Lucien's most recent letter. He'd given it to her that morning, saying it was the last he'd write before she became his wife. Carefully she opened it, not wanting to bend a corner or wrinkle an edge.

> *Dear Cora,*
>
> *The sun is just rising on the morning of our wedding day. To say I've been looking forward to this day for a long time is an understatement. Although circumstances weren't ideal in bringing us together, I feel blessed that you were given another chance at love—and that I am the recipient of it. Most days, it seems as if I live in a dream, thinking that you and Robert William are too good to be true. You told me once that life was far from a fairytale, but I believe*

I've found a fairytale life with you. I love you both with all my heart, and I can't wait to make our family official.

Love,
Lucien

Cora's heart swelled as she read the words once, then twice. Did Lucien really believe in fairytales? Perhaps they could create one together. She exhaled slowly, then placed the letter in her bureau drawer, along with the other fifty-one. After glancing in the mirror once more, she left her bedroom and descended the stairs. She walked through the hallway and entrance, her step quickening with each stride.

The year's wait had felt too long at times, and at others, not enough. But as she walked out into the crisp New Year Eve's afternoon, she knew she was ready to begin the next chapter of life. Her son would grow up surrounded by love. And Cora had more in Lucien than she could have ever hoped for. Instead of facing a quiet widowhood for the rest of her life, reflecting on her lost love and her short, tragic marriage, she had a new future with Lucien.

The chauffeur opened the car door, and the brief ride gave her heart time to settle down. When the church came into sight, with her father outside waiting for her, Cora blinked back tears. He looked formal in his dark suit, but his face was wreathed in warmth.

"Cora," he said, holding out his hands as she stepped out of the car. "You look beautiful."

She smiled at her father, hardly daring to believe that a year and three months ago, her father had given her to Will. This time, her marriage would be different. Nothing had been rushed, and nothing had been hidden. A year of letters had proven that.

Cora slipped her arm into her father's, and they entered the church together. The scent of winter roses reached her first, and then she saw the congregation with their smiling faces. Cora had insisted on no gifts, that the presence of friends was all she needed. Seeing everyone was enough.

And then, at the end of the aisle, she saw Lucien waiting for her. His smile made her heart leap, and the intensity of his gaze shivered through her. In moments, they would finally be married. Her father led her down the aisle, and with each step, her heart pounded harder.

Her parents sat on the front row, holding little Robert William. Behind them were Lucien's parents. Other relatives, as well as several neighbors and friends, dotted the benches. A small gathering compared to her wedding with Will, but it was perfect for her and Lucien.

When she reached Lucien's side, he whispered, "You came."

"Why wouldn't I?" she asked.

He winked, and then they turned to the minister, who began the vow recitations.

Before Cora knew it, the minister was pronouncing them husband and wife. Lucien slid his hands around her waist and leaned down, giving her a soft, yet lingering, kiss. Cora wanted to pull him closer, to kiss him harder, but they were in a church full of people.

The church bells rang, and congratulations sounded. She and Lucien walked down the aisle together and accepted embraces and warm wishes. Cora smiled and thanked everyone but found herself wanting to be alone with her new husband. His hand slipped into hers and squeezed. She squeezed back, and Lucien leaned down.

"Soon it will be just us," he said.

It was as if he'd read her mind.

Her mother appeared at her side. "Come, the meal is served in the church hall."

Cora and Lucien followed her mother outside and into the adjacent building that served as a church hall. Long tables had been arranged in the hall and set with a delicious array of food. They took their seats as the honorary couple.

Lucien asked her mother, "Where's Robert William?"

"He's with my sister, but the nanny will take him back to the house soon."

"Let him stay a bit longer," Lucien said.

Cora's heart warmed at the words as she realized that no other man could love her son more. Lucien had been a true friend to Will, and he'd do right by his son. Moments later, as the first course was served, her mother brought over Robert William. Lucien immediately took him in his arms.

"Will you be all right while I take your mother on a honeymoon?" he asked in a quiet voice, his gaze serious.

Robert William gurgled and smiled at Lucien.

"Yes? You'll have to be the man of the house while we're gone. Can you manage that?"

Another smile.

Cora laughed. Robert William turned toward her, stretching his arms out.

"All right, son," Lucien said. "You may kiss your mother once more, but then we have to eat our meal."

Cora took her baby and cradled him against her neck, breathing in his baby scent and reveling in how Lucien had called him *son*.

"Would you like a little brother or sister?" Lucien whispered to Robert William.

Cora flushed and elbowed Lucien. "He's too young to hear of such things." Her face had to be flaming by now. She was no innocent, but someone might overhear their conversation. "Where did you say you're taking me again?" she said, changing the topic.

"I didn't say," Lucien said, his smile growing wide. "We can leave now if you're that curious."

This topic wasn't any safer. The next hour passed by too slowly, however, and Cora's head was starting to drum. When Robert William was taken home, and the food was properly consumed, Lucien rose to his feet. Holding up his wine glass, he offered one more toast to the wedding guests in gratitude, wishing them good health. After another round of congratulations and embraces, Cora and Lucien made it outside, where a car was waiting. Lucien helped her into the front seat.

"Are *you* driving?" Cora asked.

"If only the two of us know where we go, we will have more privacy," he said.

Cora laughed. "Is it really that secret?"

Lucien shook his head. "My parents and your parents know, but let's pretend it's only us."

"All right," Cora said, settling back into the seat. "I assume it's not far if we're taking the car."

Lucien only smiled and started driving. He turned in the direction of the estate, surprising Cora. Just before reaching the road leading to the house, he veered onto a smaller road that led toward the back of the property. He stopped in front of a cottage that had once belonged to the estate manager before everything was centralized in the village.

Cora climbed out. "This old place?" She turned to Lucien, sure that he must be fooling her.

"Come inside and see it." He grasped her hand and led her toward the front door.

As they drew closer, Cora started noticing little things about the place. She'd seen it several times while out riding, of course, but it was plain that many improvements had been made to the exterior. The door was new, and the windowpanes shone clean and sturdy. It was then she noticed smoke coming from the chimney, white against the violet and pink sunset.

"What did you do to this place, Lucien? And when?"

He flung the door open, and Cora took in her surroundings as she walked inside. The interior looked like a new cottage. The hardwood floors had been stripped and refinished, the furniture reupholstered, walls repapered and freshly painted. A cheery fire glowed beneath the mantel, and the kitchen shone like a newly minted coin. In the corner was a pianoforte—which could have only been Lucien's doing.

Cora spun around, disbelief pulsing through her. In addition to the remodeling, nearly every surface held a vase with winter roses, making the place smell heavenly. She walked slowly through the rest of the rooms, then came to a stop at the master suite. The four-poster bed was piled high with downy blankets. Silk hangings adorned the walls, making it look like a fairyland.

"Do you like it?" Lucien asked, leaning against the doorframe and watching her.

She couldn't speak at first, but then she found her voice and crossed to Lucien. "I love it," she said, throwing her arms around him. "It looks straight out of a fairytale."

He chuckled and pulled her tightly against him. Warmth spread through her, both at the full-body embrace and at the thought that now they were married—and at that they were completely alone in this out-of-the-way cottage for their wedding night.

"I have one more surprise," Lucien said, drawing her back to the front parlor.

Cora was a bit disappointed that he hadn't kissed her, but she followed, and when he led her to the pianoforte, her heart rate doubled.

"I wrote you a song," Lucien said.

She settled beside him on the bench, her eyes stinging with emotion.

As Lucien played, Cora leaned her head on his shoulder and closed her eyes. The music started softly, hesitantly, then grew to become a soaring melody. The only way Cora could describe it was pure love.

When Lucien played the last note, Cora didn't move, letting the final sounds sink into her memory.

"Thank you," she whispered. Then she opened her eyes and lifted her head.

Lucien was watching, his eyes full of everything the song had said and more. Cora reached up and touched his cheek.

"Thank you, dear Lucien. I love you."

"I love you too," he whispered.

Then, at last, he was kissing her. Slowly at first, just like the song he'd written for her. When the kiss started to soar, he picked her up in his arms and carried her into the fairytale bedroom.

As the door shut quietly behind them, Cora knew her fairytale was just beginning.

ABOUT HEATHER B. MOORE

Heather B. Moore is a *USA Today* bestselling author. She writes historical thrillers under the pen name H.B. Moore; her latest is *Finding Sheba*. Under Heather B. Moore, she writes romance and women's fiction. She's one of the coauthors of The Newport Ladies Book Club series. Other works include *Heart of the Ocean, The Fortune Café*, the Aliso Creek series, and the Amazon bestselling Timeless Romance Anthology series.

For book updates, sign up for Heather's email list: http://hbmoore.com/contact
Website: www.hbmoore.com
Facebook: Fans of H.B. Moore
Blog: http://mywriterslair.blogspot.com
Twitter: @HeatherBMoore

A Fezziwig Christmas
by Lu Ann Brobst Staheli

One

London—1790

Dick Wilkins had hunched over the ledger for hours, and the crick in his neck told him that the workday would soon draw to an end. He could hardly wait to climb from the tall stool, where he was perched at his desk. He'd never surmised why accounting clerks sat at such uncomfortable contraptions, but those were the accommodations given to him and his best friend, Ebenezer Scrooge, who sat to his left.

Even his mentor, Old Fezziwig, who sat to his right, teetered upon a stool, its spindly legs appearing uncertain at the mass of weight balanced upon them. The minute hand continued a steady click-click-click toward the hour, and the scratching sounds of quill upon paper matched the rhythm as the men worked without conversation, as they did every day, until a resounding *dong* indicated that at last the hour of seven had arrived.

Fezziwig looked toward the clock. Dick directed his gaze there as well. Twelve long hours had passed since his arrival, when he and Ebenezer had come from their shared room in the back of the counting house and had taken their spots upon their uncomfortable stools. Today had seemed no different from any other, except that it was—tonight was Christmas Eve, and Fezziwig was hosting his annual holiday party.

Dick had anticipated this night for weeks. Once again, he would see Pricilla Fezziwig, the second-eldest daughter of his mentor. How well he remembered the silly girl she had once been, but at Fezziwig's summer picnic six months ago, she was much changed. The vivaciousness of her laughter had been as jovial as that of her father. Her beauty matched that of her mother and elder sister, Annabelle. The kindness she had toward the children had shown that she would one day be a wonderful mother herself. In short, she'd grown up, and Dick cherished the glimpses of the woman she had become.

The lilt of her voice had echoed through his memory since he'd seen her last. He only hoped she remembered him fondly in the time that had passed. Of course, his niggling worry was that she wouldn't remember him at all. Yet he was certain he was falling in love.

Fezziwig adjusted his waistcoat. His rich laughter rang out for a moment, and then so did his jovial voice. "Yo-ho, there, my boys."

Dick and Ebenezer set down their pens and directed their gaze toward Fezziwig, awaiting his signal that indeed the day was done.

"No more work tonight. It's Christmas Eve." If Fezziwig's Welsh wig been two inches taller, his head would have hit the ceiling.

"Christmas Eve." Ebenezer stood and rolled his

A Fezziwig Christmas

shoulders, working the stiff muscles that had developed during the long day.

Dick followed suit, taking a deep breath in an effort to remove the kinks from his back. "Christmas Eve," Dick said, his tone matching the lilt of his employer's.

"We've a party to prepare for, boys!" Fezziwig said, clapping his hands.

Dick jumped to his feet. "To the street."

"To the street," Ebenezer agreed.

In a clatter of commotion, they scurried across the wooden floor, through the heavy door, and onto the cobbled street that passed before Fezziwig's Counting House. Together they opened the shutters that lined the outside of the business, then barred and pinned them into place. Had it not been a winter day, the shutters would have stood wide the time the business was open, but the brisk wind seeped in through the glass to such an extent that the men within could have frozen to death at their desks, pens in hand.

"Fezziwig must be planning on burning the coal tonight," Ebenezer said.

"No expense is too great for his annual holiday fest." Dick brushed soot from his hands, hoping to avoid soiling his clothes. "Come. There is much to do before the ladies arrive."

"Ah, yes, the ladies," Ebenezer said. "Another evening to spend with Belle."

"I can only hope my evening turns out to be as fine as yours," Dick said.

He was aware that Ebenezer had stopped just short of the door and had turned to look at him. "And what of you, Dick? Is this an evening of dancing your way through a bevy of young ladies? Or perhaps you have a single fair maiden in mind."

"I . . . there . . . I . . ."

"Come, lad," Ebenezer said as he gave a playful punch against Dick's right arm. "Tell me."

Dick ducked his head, suddenly embarrassed to be sharing his thoughts with Ebenezer, no matter how close the two of them had grown through their shared schooling and apprenticeship. "Well, I am hoping to have at least one dance with Pricilla."

"Pricilla Fezziwig?"

His incredulous tone stabbed Dick's heart. What if Cilla thought him too forward? Was he prepared to make a fool of himself at this party? And would Fezziwig himself approve? Dick reached into his collar with a sudden need to adjust its position as he cleared his throat. "Um, yes, that Pricilla."

"You and Pricilla Fezziwig. I never would have guessed." A roaring laugh burst forth from Ebenezer as he slapped his friend across the shoulder. "A fine choice, Dick, a fine choice, indeed. Perhaps tonight you will lose your heart."

"I believe I already have," Dick said.

Now if he could convince Cilla, as he'd come to call her in his heart, then perhaps his next six months would turn out to be even more agreeable than his dreaming of seeing her again had been. He buffed his fingers against his vest, removing a cloud of dust and hoping that the worn fabric would not speak ill of his present meager circumstances. As an apprentice, he did not have the means to buy fine clothing, but he hoped that would not push Cilla away from him. Would she understand that someday he would have a counting house of his own, just like her father?

"Have you spoken with her?" Ebenezer asked, his voice hushed as though he, too, was embarrassed.

"No."

"I see. Then tonight is all the more important. Not only must you win the lady's heart, but you must also woo her mother."

"Wha . . . ?" Dick didn't know what to say. Win her mother's heart? Surely Ebenezer must be mistaken, but then, he had been courting Cilla's sister Belle. Perhaps he knew something more than Dick did. Could he learn the way to Cilla's heart by following the pattern of his friend? He glanced at Ebenezer, who was busily arranging a wreath on the doorframe.

Last Christmas, Ebenezer had fallen in love with Belle, and Mrs. Fezziwig had taken a liking to him, inviting him to their home on visiting days for tea and allowing him to sit near Belle so they could engage in conversation. Ebenezer had spoken about occasions when he had taken a bouquet to the mistress to "brighten the parlor during our visit." But more recently, he had given the flowers to Belle, hoping she understood that the arrangement of bindweed, orchids, and exotic tiger lilies were meant to show her the feelings he could not verbalize.

Dick wondered at the combination and its meaning. The idea of including bindweed in the arrangement did not seem romantic at all, but Ebenezer had more experience at these things than he did. Dick could only hope that this year, it would be him that Mrs. Fezziwig favored to court her next eldest daughter, Cilla. He assured himself he would choose a flower much more enticing than bindweed for the bouquets he would bring to her door.

"You seem to be an expert at this, my friend," Dick said. "I'm ready to listen and learn."

Ebenezer admired his work, his mouth spread into a wide grin. "The key is in first winning the *mother's* heart. She's the one who will give final approval for the fellow seated in her parlor to steal a private moment with one of her daughters."

"I would have thought that approval would come from Fezziwig himself," Dick said. "Isn't it the father who must be approached to request the daughter's hand in marriage?"

"True, true. But unless Mrs. Fezziwig approves, you will get no farther than a single dance at tonight's party, and only then if she doesn't already have a dance card filled with suitable matches for her daughter."

"And what does Mrs. Fezziwig look for in a future husband for her daughters? You seem to have qualified." Dick gave a nod to let Ebenezer know he did not doubt his qualifications.

"A future, my boy," Ebenezer said. He tapped a finger against the top of Dick's head. "And a brain that carries potential in business to support the lass." He tapped Dick's shoulder. "Strong limbs to support her, even if doing so requires physical labor." He tapped Dick a third time, this time upon his breast. "And a heart filled with love to carry the two of them through whatever trials and difficulties may come their way."

"And if a suitor has all of these traits?" Dick leaned forward in anticipation.

"Then he must prove it." A moment of silence passed between the two before Ebenezer spoke again. "What say you to standing up with me at my wedding? Tonight I plan to ask Old Fezziwig for Belle's hand in marriage."

"Well, done, man. Well done." Dick moved forward to offer Ebenezer a slap on the back.

This time Ebenezer's laugh was accompanied by a blush upon his cheek. The two of them scurried back into the warmth of the counting house, ready to tackle their next assignment.

Despite the dreariness of their daily work, Fezziwig was a pleasant man to work for, far better than the taskmasters Dick had feared in his early years at the blacking factory, the place where he and Ebenezer had first met. Would he retain that pleasantness if Dick someday married his second eldest daughter? He could only hope.

"Hilli-ho!" Fezziwig said as he hopped from his stool. "Clear everything away. We need to open space for the dancing."

For the next few minutes, Dick and Ebenezer packed off every movable item from the office floor, hiding them away. Dick brought a broom and water pail from storage, and he began sweeping and watering the floor as though his very life depended on it.

"Ebenezer, bring the coal," Fezziwig called as he trimmed the lamps.

Ebenezer did as instructed, heaping fuel upon the fire. Within minutes, the warehouse was snug and warm, the floor dry, and the evening light from outside the shutters helping to make it a bright ballroom despite the winter's night.

"Only a few minutes before the revelers arrive," Fezziwig added. "We want to be ready, and my wife and lovely daughters will be here any moment."

At the mention of Fezziwig's daughters, Dick and Ebenezer exchanged a smile and a nod. Indeed, they both were looking forward to that. Dick held hope that if all went well tonight, then in six months or a year, he, too, would be able to approach Fezziwig to ask for the hand of his daughter. And the two of them—Dick and Ebenezer—would be brothers, with the two most beautiful brides in all of London.

Two

"Who do you think will be there, Belle? Who will come to Father's Christmas party?" Priscilla Fezziwig stretched her leg as though engaged in a complicated arabesque from a quadrille, watching her own reflection in the mirror that hung upon her bedroom wall.

This would be her first Christmas party since her coming out, and although she had attended several parties before and since then, she anticipated this one to be special. She had already met a few men she wanted to know better, and with luck, some of them would be in attendance.

"I expect a double-dozen men or more, all wanting to spend the evening dancing with you." Annabelle stood before the mirror, giving a stern look meant for her younger sister, but the smile upon her lips was proof she was not upset.

A Fezziwig Christmas

Cilla stopped posing long enough to give Belle a smile of her own. "And you will be greatly disappointed if Ebenezer Scrooge is not there to dance with you."

"Out with you," Belle said, swatting the air toward her sister in mock playfulness, as though Cilla were nothing more than a pesky fly as she continued her measured dance. The blush upon Belle's cheek stood as proof the statement was true. "Ebenezer and Dick will both be in attendance. As apprentices in Father's counting house, they are likely working to make that dull office into a grand ballroom as we speak."

"Dick Wilkins?" Cilla stopped dancing and tilted her head as though trying to read a name written upon the wall before her. "I've met so many young men recently that I can *hardly* remember what father's second apprentice looks like."

Her sister scoffed, as though she knew the statement to be untrue.

Cilla let her eyes drift toward Belle. "Of course, I cannot forget the visage of Ebenezer Scrooge. All the hours he has spent fighting for your attention amidst your other beaus, who drape themselves on the couches of our parlor."

"They do not drape themselves across the couches," Belle said as she arranged a final curl upon her forehead. "Soon enough, you will have suitors coming to court you."

Cilla stepped to her sister's side and gently placed her hand on Belle's arm. "Do you think Father will allow any of them to court me?"

Belle laughed and shook her head. "You've only just had your coming out. I'm sure you already have a half dozen men you'd like to spend this evening dancing with."

"A dozen." Cilla laughed as well. "I suppose I am a little too hurried in my desire to find a beau."

Belle pulled her into her arms. "I'd certainly say so. What a silly goose you are, ready to tie yourself down so soon."

"Do you think you made *your* choice too soon, Belle?"

"No, and tonight I will tell . . . Ebenezer . . . that he has won my heart." Belle placed her hand against her breast.

Cilla noticed the hesitation in her sister's voice as she said his name. She could only hope that she, too, would discover someone who, with the mere mention of his name, would make her suck in her breath the same way. "If only there is someone for me," Cilla said, a sigh releasing from her.

"A double dozen will line up to take your hand and lead you around the room, hoping beyond hope that there will be a moment to pause in a quiet corner and drink in your presence," Belle said.

"Do you really think so?" Cilla could feel her heart pound with the headiness of the suggestion. She allowed herself a moment to reflect upon those she might hope would attend, one among them being Dick Wilkins, whom she did remember after all.

"Where else in all of London can single young men find a spread of fine foods such as Mother will place upon the tables, plus lively music that will keep their toes tapping, and a girl as lovely as you to dance with on Christmas Eve?"

Cilla pulled away from her sister just far enough to look into her eyes. "I'm sure many parties offer similar fare."

"But none will have *you*. Now, on with you." Belle patted Cilla's hair. "We have much to do before either of us will be allowed to attend Father's party."

Despite her questioning, Cilla knew Belle was right about one thing—the party would have a gathering of fine young men. The part she wasn't so sure about was whether she would find one she was most interested in, one she might think of as her *beau*. But perhaps she was not yet ready for such a commitment after all.

Perhaps she needed to dance and flirt and converse with the finest young men her father's party could bring. And there were so many other things she wanted to do in her life besides marriage. Her love of children went beyond those she someday hoped to have herself. Perhaps one day, she would work at a school. London had so many needy children that it might be her calling to work among them. But tonight was the Christmas Eve party.

"Pricilla! Annabelle! Mother needs your help in the pantry." Elizabeth, the youngest Fezziwig daughter, stood at the door, her hands clasped together as they always were when she was excited. "The guests will arrive soon, and food must be transported to the party."

"Tell Mother we are coming," Belle said. She reached for Cilla, and they clasped hands. "Are you ready to meet your match?"

"I'm ready to meet a double dozen," Cilla replied as she and Belle followed Lizzy.

When Cilla Fezziwig entered the warehouse, she decided that her father had outdone himself this year. The counting house had been transformed into a scene more elaborate, more festive, and more welcoming than ever before. Garlands hung from the work tables, which lined the edges of the room, and the stools had been placed for convenience at the edge of the area opened for dancing purposes.

In came a fiddler with a music book, who went up to her father's desk and set to tuning his instrument. The sound was dreadful, and Cilla could only hope the music would improve by the time the guests arrived.

"Surely that noise is not to accompany the dancing this evening," Cilla said, her face twisting in response to the screeching of the fiddler, who seemed oblivious to the pain he was inflicting upon her ears.

Belle chuckled. "By the time he is through, you will think an orchestra has come to perform at the ball. Besides, you will be so consumed with dancing and conversing with the young men who have come to steal your heart that a little off-key music will not spoil your evening."

Mrs. Fezziwig stepped lively past them. "Have you ever heard such a lovely tune?"

In response, Lizzy, who followed along at her mother's skirts, slapped her hands against her ears. Belle and Cilla both laughed, nodding in agreement with their younger sister rather than with their mother.

"Hurry along, girls," their mother said. "The time is short, and the food is waiting."

Cilla and her sisters made trip after trip from the carriage outside, their hands filled with dishes their mother had prepared. They lined the platters fit for a king along the sideboards that usually served for counting money. Succulent roast beef, turkey stuffed with gingerbread dressing, bread and cranberry sauces, parsnips and swede, roasted chestnuts, and figgy pudding awaited the guests, as well as the Fezziwig family.

"Ah, my wife." Fezziwig waddled in from the back storage, arms outstretched. Mrs. Fezziwig handed a platter heaped with meats into his care, but the look upon his face made it evident that he'd been after something other than becoming part of the food procession.

"None of that until the food is all arranged, sir," Mrs. Fezziwig said, tapping her palm gently against her husband's cheek as a sign of affection.

Cilla herself had received the same gesture from both parents on many occasions. She hoped to someday share the same endearment with her husband, and this night would take her one step closer. She had already attended not only her own debutant party, but also those of four of her friends, and at each, Cilla had met young men who might attend the Christmas party.

As she carried a set of cream pies, one in each hand, to the dessert table, she thought of Percy Ainsworth, a gentleman from York who had spent the majority of an evening entertaining Cilla and her friend Sarah Miller at the latter's home. His sense of humor was delightful and his manners impeccable. She dreamed of waltzing around the floor held in his arms but was startled from her reverie by a *bump* and an *oof.*

"Cilla! What on earth are you doing?" Lizzy stood before her, hands on her hips in the same gesture Cilla had seen from her mother on more than one occasion. The girl huffed as though waiting for a response from her older sister.

"Sorry," Cilla said. "I guess I was daydreaming."

"Probably about the suitors you hope to gather tonight," Lizzy said, her voice as indignant as her stance.

"Leave her alone, Liz," Belle said, coming to Cilla's rescue. "There will come a time when you, too, dream of the fine young gentlemen who will come to call."

"Harrumph!" Lizzy went to find where her mother had gone with the last of the food.

Belle smiled toward Cilla. "And who were you dreaming about this time?"

Cilla thought she seemed genuinely interested, despite the fact that she was arranging the plates in a more attractive display. "A gentleman I met while visiting Sarah." She ran the tip of her finger around the edge of a pie tin, then licked the cream that had gathered there, something her mother would have scolded her for had she seen it. "He's from York, so I doubt he will be in attendance tonight."

Belle took hold of Cilla's arm to move her away from the confections. "You never know. Father has clients from all over the country. He's an honest man, and his reputation has spread far and wide. What is the gentleman's name? I'll keep an eye open."

"Percy Ainsworth," Cilla said. "But there's really nothing to come of it."

"All the same." Belle glanced once more over the preparations and, apparently satisfied, started to lead Cilla toward the door, in search of their mother. "Anyone else I should be aware of who might be coming?"

Cilla blushed before stating, "Phillip Henley, George Butterfield, William Byron, and Fitzhugh Morgan."

"And how many hearts do you intend to break?"

"No, no. I don't want to break any hearts," Cilla said, clasping her hand around her sister's forearm. "I only want to entertain the best of the best when it comes to finding my beau."

"Something I understand completely," Belle said as she heard someone call her name. "Ebenezer." She held out her hand toward *her* beau, the one she had chosen.

"Belle," he said before turning to his companion. "And I'm sure you remember my fellow apprentice, Dick Wilkins."

Dick bowed to each of the young women, but it was Cilla to whom he spoke. "Miss Fezziwig, it is so nice to see you once again."

Cilla couldn't hide the blush that rushed across her cheek. Perhaps there *was* one more name she needed to ensure remained on her list.

"Nice to see you, as well," Cilla said before she turned and walked away, out the front door of the counting house.

"We need to go home to change into our finery for the party," Belle explained. She smiled at Dick, then turned her full attention to Ebenezer, reaching out to place her palm upon his hand. "If you will excuse us. We can't have the owner's daughters looking like ragamuffins at his annual Christmas party, can we?"

"It would be a travesty, to say the least," Ebenezer said before placing his lips gently against the back of her hand. "You will return shortly?"

"You will hardly know we have gone." Belle removed her hand from his and waved before departing.

Three

Pricilla. Dick loved the name the Fezziwigs had given their second daughter, despite the fact it often referred to *one who is ancient or venerable*. She certainly wasn't old, and her wisdom was growing with age. The name *Pricilla* seemed to fit this daughter perfectly. Who would not want for a wife who was passionate and compassionate, romantic and generous? Cilla drew Dick toward her like a moth to a flame.

"Ah, I can hardly wait for this evening to be over," Ebenezer said. "Then I will know if Fezziwig will give his blessing for my quest to move forward."

"And I will embark on my quest," Dick said.

"Remember, win the heart of her mother, and you will do fine."

Dick had worked at the counting house for three full years, and every year, the festivities were more elaborate and more attended. Of course, he and Ebenezer had played a significant role in that, for it had been they who'd moved the furniture, hung the holly boughs, and lit the candles, while Fezziwig, his Welsh wig slightly askew, directed their every move from a chair, like a conductor might lead a Beethoven symphony.

Mrs. Fezziwig had been responsible for the bounty of food, but Dick was certain that Belle, Cilla, and perhaps even young Lizzy had been of assistance to their mother. The aromas wafting from the laden table were heaven to Dick, who could not resist snitching a taste from the plate of roasted gammon.

"Here to ya now," Mrs. Fezziwig said when she caught him. "Enough time for that after the other guests arrive." She hurried out the door, likely on her way to join her daughters.

Dick felt duly chastised. He was supposed to impress Mrs. Fezziwig so she would not hesitate to allow him to call upon Cilla, but he'd drawn her attention in a negative way before the festivities had even begun. He climbed upon his usual stool to wait for the guests, mulling the way he hoped the evening would progress.

However, Ebenezer danced around the bare floor as if the fiddler were playing music instead of still tuning his fiddle.

True to her word, Belle and her family were back in no time. Mrs. Fezziwig wore a broad smile unmatched by any Dick had ever seen. Next came her daughters—Belle, Cilla, and Lizzy—all in various ages of the beauty of womanhood. And right behind them, six potential suitors who seemed to be attaching themselves to Belle and Cilla.

They can't be, Dick thought. *Surely they know that Belle is already called for? And Cilla is meant to be mine.* But he had no right to claim any kind of commitments when it came to Pricilla. As much as he'd thought about her all these months, the fact that she'd hardly greeted him earlier indicated that she had done none of the same thinking about him.

A bustle of people burst into the counting-house-turned-ballroom, and soon Dick lost track of Cilla in the mêlée of music and laughter. More young men and women who were employed by Master Fezziwig arrived, including the housemaid and her cousin the baker, plus the cook with the milkman. Each greeted Dick as though he were the one in charge. In came the boy from over the way, who was suspected of not having food enough from his master and likely hoped to snatch a morsel or two from the bounty Mrs. Fezziwig had laid out. The lad tried to hide himself behind the girl from next door. Anxious to the point of losing their manners, the crowd pushed and pulled until all were in and the dancing had begun.

The fiddler had at last found his tune, and the reel that came was lively. Dick himself was pulled into the throng as twenty couples took hands into a half round, then back again the other way, down the middle, round and round. He had no clear idea with whom he was partnered, and he didn't really care. His eyes searched the crowd, hoping to settle upon Cilla, but she was nowhere to be found. The dance became more and more disorganized as the fiddler played. The top couple ended up in the wrong place, so a new top couple started off.

Fezziwig clapped and called out, "Well done. Well done!"

When the music ended, the dancers came to a halt, and the fiddler drank from a pot of port placed at his side as a means to cool off. Then he started off again.

Stumbling to the sidelines with dizziness from the reel, Dick continued to scan the crowd, hoping for a glance of Cilla. Ebenezer and Belle stood in the corner by the punch. Lizzy was talking with the boy Dick had suspected of sneaking in for the food. The two stood next to the desserts, taking generous samplings from the various treats. Fezziwig and his wife stood to the side of the room, fanning themselves in an effort to regain their breath after the vicious reel they had all just been flung through.

At last, Dick saw her. Her blue satin dress and fair curls tied away from her face with bows, Cilla daintily sipped punch on the opposite side of the room. But she was not alone—she was with Percy Ainsworth. His accounts were among the most coveted at the counting house. For a young man, he had done well for himself, and if he was in pursuit of Cilla Fezziwig's hand, then Dick knew that he, a poor apprentice, had no hope at winning the heart of the girl he so wanted, let alone winning the approval of her mother, and eventually her father, as a suitor.

"Have you taken a turn around the floor with her yet?" Ebenezer suddenly stood at his elbow.

"It seems she is previously engaged." He pointed toward where Pricilla stood with Percy.

"Don't let something as minor as that stop you from asking," Ebenezer said.

"Minor? Have you seen the size of his bank account?"

"And have you tried to have a conversation with him? *Boring* is not a strong enough word," Ebenezer said. "Cilla will thank you for taking her away from his pompousness."

"You really think so?" Dick asked, unsure whether he had the nerves to even try.

"I *know* so," Ebenezer assured him. "Now get after it. I'm on my way to find Old Fezziwig to see if I can move forward to the next stage in the game of love."

Four

Cilla attempted to carry on a conversation with Percy Ainsworth, but the gentleman she had found so fascinating at her friend's house had turned into a bore, his sense of humor lost in self-aggrandizement. He'd done nothing but go on about his investments and how the trustworthiness of her father had led him to this counting house, and eventually, to this party.

Not once had he asked about her, how she fared after the wild dance he had led her on, or if she wished to find a cushioned chair upon which to rest. An offer of refreshment would have been welcomed, but Percy seemed unaware that it was his place to care more for the needs of the lady than to prattle on about himself. Not once did he ask for her opinions or thoughts. No, his entire delivery had been about himself and what he thought and felt.

Her patience worn thin, Cilla looked around the room. Surely one of the other young men she'd set her cap on the past few months was in attendance. Phillip, George, William, or Fitzhugh—would one of them come to her rescue? But such was not her luck. The six young men who had followed her and her sisters into the gala had all partnered up with other young ladies. Most of the other revelers were the age of her parents or the very elderly.

Not willing to give up, she checked the room again. Perhaps she would find Belle. Even if she was with Ebenezer, there was no reason Cilla couldn't attach herself to their party for a few moments at least, long enough to escape dull Percy, who continued to drone on as though he believed she was paying attention.

She caught a glimpse of Ebenezer as he exited the room and allowed her eyes to trace where she assumed he'd come from. To her surprise, she did not find Belle, but Dick Wilkins. The apprentice might not have been much to look at, and he certainly didn't have the wealth Percy did, but money might not be everything, especially if it meant not having to listen to Percy continue to talk about nothing but himself.

She remembered a brief conversation with Dick at the summer party. He'd seemed to be a likeable chap. He'd been interested in her thoughts about education in the London schools and her desire to improve the lives of the poor children. But she could think of no gracious way to break from Percy. Cilla knew she couldn't simply walk away, then saunter up to Dick, hoping he would ask her to dance.

As she pondered her situation, fate solved the problem for her. Dick took a swift drink from his glass, then set it on a tray as he passed a waiter. Purposeful in his stride, he headed toward her.

Oh, thank heavens, Cilla thought. Her heart fluttered in a way she had never experienced. *Please let my wish come true. Let Dick Wilkins ask me to dance.*

A Fezziwig Christmas

Certain that Percy was completely unaware of her, Cilla offered Dick her most charming smile as he approached. For a second, he hesitated, and she thought she'd been mistaken. Was there someone else, a different lady he was moving toward? But no, he regained his assurance and moved closer. She allowed her eyes to rest upon Dick and only Dick, willing him forward with her smile. He stumbled briefly, then regained himself and smiled at her in return.

When at last he reached her, Cilla put out her hand. "Mr. Wilkins, how nice to see you again."

"I . . . um . . ." Dick stammered, as though unable to form a response.

She needed rescuing, and Mr. Wilkins seemed to be her only hope, if only he could speak.

"Miss Fezziwig," Dick said at last, bringing a halt to Percy's soliloquy, "your loveliness has drawn me across the room as though mesmerized. I simply had to be near you."

Percy drew back, seemingly shocked at the boldness of Dick's statement, but Cilla felt a thrill pass through her entire body. Never had Mr. Ainsworth spoken such words of endearment to her, and she expected he never would.

"Mr. Wilkins?" Percy's voice carried a question, but Cilla didn't care what he thought. If Dick asked her to dance, then she would be away with him and pray that this would be the last she would see of Percy Ainsworth.

"Mr. Ainsworth, I hope I am not disrupting your conversation with Miss Fezziwig," Dick said.

"Don't be silly," Cilla interrupted. "Mr. Ainsworth and I have had a lovely time, but I'm sure he will not mind my sharing a few minutes with you." She looked toward Percy and batted her eyes before continuing. "You've been telling me such fascinating things about your business, Percy, but wouldn't you care for a beverage from the refreshment tables? My mother has served several blends of tea and liquor and such delicacies as you can't imagine. Go along and enjoy yourself. Mr. Wilkins will take fine care of me while you rest your voice."

Percy looked confused by her words, but his glance toward the food told her she had hit the mark.

"Well, if you're certain . . ."

"Positively." Cilla hoped her relief did not show in her tone.

Before Percy could move away, the fiddler began to play a new piece, having recovered from the frenzy of the earlier reels. This time his choice of tunes was more stately and dignified, and Cilla was even more relieved.

Dick offered his elbow to Cilla. "May I have the pleasure?"

She looked at it for only a moment, glanced at Percy as he headed toward the food, then placed her hand against Dick's arm. "The pleasure would be mine."

Percy's quick retreat toward the food tables indicated it would also be his pleasure, and Cilla was glad to have him gone.

Five

Dick was enamored with the way Cilla held her head, her dancing curls framing delicate cheeks, the music of her laughter, and the gentle tones of her voice. Her hand in his caused such riotous behavior in his heart that he was unsure at first if he could even speak. He could not rush anything, because he could hardly maintain his breath. Besides, she was still young and inexperienced, as her conversation showed.

"I am so pleased that you asked me to dance, Mr. Wilkins," Cilla said when they were a distance away. "Mr. Ainsworth had more than tired me."

Dick chuckled at her boldness. "Well, let's hope I do not soon do the same."

Yet what if he did? Would he be able to tell if she'd grown tired and frustrated by his dancing, his lack of conversational skills, or if she simply did not wish to spend a portion of her evening dancing with a poor apprentice?

But that was not the least of his worries. Cilla had not noticed, but Dick had seen Percy leaving the table of delicacies, after having partaken of a generous portion, and he was now headed toward Mrs. Fezziwig, who was taking a moment's breath away from the desperate dancing her husband had been whirling her through every chance he got, almost since the party had begun. Certainly, Old Fezziwig intended to spend as much of his time dancing as possible.

What if Percy was going to ask Mrs. Fezziwig about courting Cilla? What could he do? If Percy did ask Mrs. Fezziwig for permission to court her second daughter and she granted his request, would she also grant permission to Dick? Would she think a wealthy man was a more acceptable suitor than a mere apprentice in her husband's counting house? Mrs. Fezziwig had always been friendly to both Dick and Ebenezer whenever she stopped in to visit with her husband. But friendliness did not necessarily mean she would welcome another apprentice as a suitor for a second daughter.

Yet, she *had* welcomed Ebenezer as a suitor for Belle, and at this very moment, Ebenezer might be speaking with Fezziwig about the possibility of moving from suitor to betrothed. Dick glanced around the room, hoping to catch sight of his friend to see how the conversation had gone.

"Mr. Wilkins?" Clearly, Cilla was trying to get his attention now that the dance was finished. How had he let his eyes stray from her even for a moment? "Are you bored, then, with my company?" The girl was certainly bold. One would always know where he stood with her if he but took the moment to listen.

"Bored? No, never with you, Cilla." Once again, Dick drank in her beauty.

"Good, because I was beginning to think that perhaps . . ." Cilla put a smile upon her face, and the two of them took off again across the floor as the fiddler struck up a lively tune.

A Fezziwig Christmas

Conversation was not easy with the tempo of the reel, but Dick wanted to ensure that Cilla knew he was pleased to be with her. "You must tell me more about your work with the school children." He assured himself that he'd find a moment to speak to Mrs. Fezziwig and that all would be well concerning Percy Ainsworth.

Cilla had already said she found Mr. Ainsworth a bore, so there should have been no need for Dick to worry when it came to the competition Ainsworth offered. But he still did. All his wealth. And the number of reels he had claimed from Cilla. Yet, Percy was not the only gentleman at the Christmas ball, and soon another came to tap Dick on the shoulder.

"Mind if I cut in?"

Dick would have loved to say that yes, he did mind, then waltz with Cilla across the room, far from the new rival, but he feared being as bold in his actions as she was with her words. He wouldn't dare frighten her off like a skittish rabbit.

"Miss Fezziwig?" Dick asked, hoping beyond hope that her answer would be no, but she gave him a smile, then removed her hand from his and placed it gently into the palm of the waiting gentleman.

"We will continue our conversation later about the school children," she said, directing her gaze toward Dick. And off she went.

A promise of more conversation was enough to satisfy him for the moment, and of course, there would be more dances, and more forfeits, both his own and those with others giving up their partners. .

Dick managed to escort Cilla around the floor several more times. He danced with a dozen other fine ladies in between, but none caught his heart the way he felt when he listened to Cilla's laughter and bold conversation. He stopped to enjoy cake, cold roast, and boiled mincemeat pie, and plenty of beer.

The grand event of the evening came when the fiddler

struck up "Sir Roger de Coverly," and Old Fezziwig stood once more to dance with Mrs. Fezziwig as the top couple. Some twenty pair had gathered to join them. Dick was in sore need of a partner, and while Cilla stood not more than a few feet away, unfortunately, Percy was a similar distance on her other side. Could he get to her before Percy did?

A second line of couples began to form just as Dick reached her. "Miss Fezziwig?"

And a second voice also called out her name. "Miss Fezziwig?"

At first she was confused. Percy stood to her left, his gloved hand outstretched. Dick stood at her right, his hand also extended and waiting for a response. She looked from one to the other, uncertain what to do. But the music would not wait, and apparently, neither would Percy.

He snatched her hand, nodded toward Dick, and said, "Better luck next time, sir," then escorted a bewildered Cilla into the line, making the two of them the head couple.

Dick had no choice but to move out of the way. More couples joined the formation. The Old Fezziwig and his wife were a match for them, even though many were younger. Dick hoped that the same could one day be said about himself and Pricilla. As it stood now, Percy did not appear to be up to the quality of the dancing. His stiff back and prudish mouth did not allow his appearance to demonstrate the same joy the elder Fezziwigs had written upon their faces.

The dance continued—the couples advanced and retired, both hands to their partners, bows and curtseys, corkscrew, thread-the-needle, and back again to their place. Fezziwig and his wife were outstanding dancers indeed.

Dick couldn't help but smile at Percy's attempt to mirror his hosts' agility—a rousing failure at best, and one that could fully wedge itself into Cilla's mind as another reason to avoid the company of Percy Ainsworth.

Before the final note was through, Dick felt a hand upon his shoulder. "Missed the final reel it seems," Ebenezer said.

A Fezziwig Christmas

"Yes, but that performance might have been worth it," Dick said, indicating the mess that was Percy and the satisfying look of horror on Cilla's face.

"Have you spoken to her mother?"

"No." Dick's expression shifted from humor to concern. "But it looks as if Ainsworth might have."

"Don't let that stop you," Ebenezer said. "Get it done before Mrs. Fezziwig leaves. Better now than later."

Dick couldn't agree more; it was time to strike while the memory of Percy and the disastrous encounters Cilla had suffered from him this evening were fresh upon her mind. Hopefully they would make their way into the ear of her mother.

Six

The chords of the final reel hung in the air as the great clock in the counting house struck the hour of eleven. Cilla couldn't have been more pleased; the end of the ball had come at last. No more would she be forced to engage with the wildly poor dancing of Percy or suffer the boredom of listening to him droning on about himself as though he were the King of England.

"I must join my parents in greeting their guests as they leave," Cilla explained as she tore her hand from Percy's and rushed to leave him behind.

Mr. and Mrs. Fezziwig stood, one at either side of the door, and shook hands with every person leaving. Cilla, Belle, and Lizzy lined up next to their mother, each repeating the chorus "Happy Christmas" as the guests departed and climbed into the waiting carriages on either side of the street.

As Percy approached, he gave a tip of his hat to Fezziwig before stopping in front of Cilla. Once again, he took her hand. "It's been a pleasure, Miss Fezziwig. One I hope to repeat soon."

Not if I can help it, Mr. Ainsworth. Cilla made an effort to smile politely as she withdrew her hand. She nodded her head the same way he had toward her father. Glad to have him gone, from in front of her Cilla turned toward the next departing guest, but as she passed the couple off to Belle, she realized that Percy had not progressed yet beyond her mother. She leaned slightly to hear their conversation.

"On Sunday next then, Mrs. Fezziwig. I look forward to seeing you and your lovely daughters again." He paused for a moment, looking toward Cilla, whose mouth was agape. "Shall we say around seven?"

Cilla frantically shook her head, her curls moving wildly. Surely her mother would not allow Percy Ainsworth to come calling, not without asking her permission.

"Seven will be fine, Mr. Ainsworth," her mother said, unaware of her daughter's reaction.

Then Percy was gone.

Cilla had lost all ability to speak to the remaining guests as she shook hands and watched them depart.

How could Mother do this to me?

Had Belle had a say in who was invited to court her before she decided upon Ebenezer? He had not been the only one to come for such purposes. Had anyone else spoken to her mother tonight about coming to court? She doubted it. Other than Dick Wilkins, none of the other gentlemen had seemed interested enough to even ask for a second dance. Cilla was disappointed that Percy was the only one from her previous flirtations at other balls who had attended this one. But that did not mean that others could not gain her mother's favor. Only time was necessary, a commodity Cilla feared she did not have at the moment. Would her mother's invitation to Mr. Ainsworth mean her future was already settled?

If Percy had been an utter bore at the ball, she could expect nothing better at their home. A stuffy and formal meeting, where she and Percy would be expected to get acquainted while sitting in the presence of both her parents did not seem a likely scenario for romance. She suddenly realized she was still young and needed to flirt, not to be tied down to a man more in love with his wealth and position than seeing that she was having a wonderful time at the party. She didn't want Percy to be among those who were allowed to call, but her mother's permission had already been granted. What could she do?

"Miss Fezziwig?" Dick Wilkins stood before her, hand offered in the customary greeting.

Dick Wilkins, who had made every effort to spend time with her tonight. Granted, he was only an apprentice, but so was Ebenezer, and her mother had welcomed him into their home as a suitable beau for Belle. Surely she would also allow Dick to call. Cilla had enjoyed their dances and their few minutes of conversation. He had seemed truly interested in her thoughts about educating the poor children of London. Perhaps his presence on Sunday next would stave off further advances from Percy. Dick had saved her once on this dreadful night. And here he was, hopefully to do so again.

"Mr. Wilkins." Cilla clasped his hand like the lifesaver he seemed. "Dick." She batted her eyes and gave him her widest smile. "I had such a lovely time tonight, and the reasons are all due to you."

Dick sputtered for a moment. When at last he regained his composure, he said, "Why, Miss Fezziwig—Pricilla—it was my pleasure."

She moved in closer to him, ready to whisper her request. "Are you available Sunday next, at, say, seven o'clock? My mother is hosting a few guests, and I would love to have you among them."

A Fezziwig Christmas

"Why, I am flattered that you would think to include me, Miss . . . Cilla." Dick's cheeks suddenly flushed.

Cilla wasn't sure what that meant, but he had accepted the invitation. She would not have to endure Percy alone for an hour or more. Dick was a pleasant fellow. Surely, she could make conversation with him. And doing so would show her mother that she could make decisions and arrangements of her own.

"I will be pleased to see you there," Cilla said. "But let's keep this our little secret. Mother doesn't yet need to know."

"Oh." Dick nodded as though he understood, although Cilla was quite sure he did not.

Dick might not be the most stellar of choices, but he had already proven himself to be more useful and entertaining than Percy Ainsworth. In the meantime, she would make arrangements to visit Sarah Miller and perhaps discover why Phillip, George, William, and Fitzhugh hadn't made an appearance at her father's party.

Imagine, missing what many considered the ball of the year. Belle had promised that a double dozen men would dance with her. The party had certainly been well attended, but not by the gentlemen of her set. Only a few elderly acquaintances of her father's, two lads not much older than Lizzy, the four other gentlemen who had followed them in, plus Ebenezer and Dick Wilkins, who, like Ebenezer, was practically bound to attend. And, of course, Percy Ainsworth, the man from York who had not turned out to be quite as fascinating as she had expected.

A waste of a perfectly good evening and a lovely gown.

Her plan was set. Dick was coming, and she hoped that Sarah would find others to do the same. After a final curtsy toward Dick and Ebenezer, who remained behind to close the doors, Lizzy, Belle, and Cilla headed out the door before their parents.

Seven

With the final guests gone, and the Fezziwigs having said their own goodnights, the counting house felt as empty as any evening Dick and Ebenezer spent there. Only the leftovers, which Mrs. Fezziwig would remove in the morning, and the sagging decorations, which no longer looked fresh and welcoming, remained behind to keep the two apprentices company.

"It was quite the party, wasn't it, Ebenezer?" Dick said as he doused the last candle. Only the final embers smoldered in the fireplace.

"Indeed it was," Ebenezer said. "Indeed it was." He stood before the fire, a poker in his hand. "Do you suppose Old Fezziwig means for us to tamp this out?"

"There can't be more than a half penny's burn left. Let it put itself out," Dick said. "We can enjoy a minute more of warmth. 'Tis back to the cold tomorrow, I expect."

A Fezziwig Christmas

"I'd say you're right." Ebenezer pulled a stool away from the wall, where they had been all evening. "Let's have a sit. My feet have not had but a moment's rest the entire night."

"Belle kept you busy, eh?"

"Belle and the dancing and trying to keep everyone happy. Lizzy thought she should get as many dances as Belle, so when she couldn't find a partner, I was asked to dance with her." Ebenezer had taken off a shoe and was rubbing his foot. "How did your evening turn out? Did you find a chance to dance with Pricilla?"

"Indeed," Dick said. "And . . ."

Ebenezer looked up as though trying to read the silence. "And what?"

"Cilla asked me to come to her house the evening of Sunday next."

Ebenezer dropped his shoe in his haste to stand, and grabbed Dick's arm. "That's wonderful. Why do you sound worried? Did you not have an enjoyable time? Was she not the girl you dreamed her to be?"

"Of course she is; Cilla was wonderful. She is a delightful dancer, her sense of humor is superb, and none was as beautiful as she, her older sister excepted." Dick chuckled at that.

Ebenezer joined in the laughter. "So what is the problem?"

Dick stood and paced the floor. "What do you know of Percy Ainsworth?"

"Other than that he's one of the biggest investors in London and that he keeps his money at Fezziwig's counting house?"

Dick's concern grew even greater. "Would he be the kind of man Mrs. Fezziwig would approve of to court her daughter?"

The sound Ebenezer involuntarily made did more to solidify Dick's worries than to alleviate them.

"It's hopeless," Dick said. "Why would Cilla want a man like me, when she could have someone as wealthy as Percy?"

"Wealth isn't everything," Ebenezer said.

Dick gave his friend a teasing glance. "I guess you're right, or else you would not be courting Belle." A smile crossed his face. "You're certainly not wealthy, and perhaps on a road never to be."

"Hey, now. Have on ya!" Ebenezer said, pretending to toss his newly retrieved shoe at Dick's head before setting it back down.

"Percy received the same invitation," Dick said. "But his came from Mrs. Fezziwig."

"And yours came from Cilla," Ebenezer said. "Seems to me that yours is the more valuable invitation in the end, coming from the lady herself, and all."

"Standing against the gentleman may prove awkward, though, especially if Cilla has not informed her mother that I am also on the guest list." Dick stroked his chin as though he had a beard. His brows heavy with thought, he resumed pacing the emptied room. "I suppose you're right. Pricilla Fezziwig is the woman I want, and if I intend to have her, I must be ready to stand against any other suitor who wants the same. I'll go to this soirée and hope for the best."

"*Work* toward the best." Ebenezer placed his hands upon Dick's shoulders, stopping him from his forward motion. "You will work to win the lady's heart, and Percy Ainsworth will be left in the cold. She will choose you. You are the better man, and anyone with half a brain will see that." A teasing tone crept into his voice. "Now, if there are to be other suitors whom you must go up against . . ."

"Stop!" Dick playfully punched his best friend's arm, and both of them laughed. "I forgot to ask, how did your tête-à-tête go with Old Fezziwig? Do you have permission to pursue Belle's hand?"

"Yes, and I will see her Sunday next." Ebenezer couldn't help but smile. "So there will be more than one beau sitting in the parlor, trying to win the heart of a Fezziwig daughter and keeping her mother impressed at the same time."

"I'm glad you are not among my competition, sir."

"That would be a terrible thing." Ebenezer stirred the coals a final time.

Both men watched the diminishing flickers of light.

Dick felt no more assured of his situation with Cilla than he had before, but the final ember died, leaving the place pitch dark and ready for the cold to seep in. "Time for us to hit the covers before we freeze to death and neither one of us gets the girl we love."

They moved into the storage room in the back, where they had been sleeping since they first came to apprentice for Fezziwig.

Ebenezer was the first to slip into his bunk, a mattress under a counter in the back of the shop. "Good night, Dick. In the end, all will work out for the best."

"I hope for whatever is best for Cilla, and I hope that the best is for her to choose me," Dick said. "Good night, my good friend."

Eight

The next three days, as much as Cilla worried about the meeting her mother had arranged with Percy, she feared mentioning the event. She still hadn't told her mother she had invited Dick to attend. Cilla needed him there to give her someone to talk with other than Percy. How had she been so naive as to think that someone like Mr. Ainsworth would be the man of her dreams? He had seemed sophisticated at first, suitable and pleasant to be with. A pompous ass was more what he turned out to be. Nothing at all like Dick Wilkins, who had been charming and who had rescued her at the party, and who would hopefully be doing the same at her mother's tea.

The previous evening with Belle, she had attempted to broach the subject of Percy's invitation, which accomplished nothing. Belle's mind was too filled with romance of her own. Besides, Belle had reminded her, Percy was not the only one invited to spend Sunday evening with the Fezziwig

A Fezziwig Christmas

family. She had invited Mr. Wilkins herself, and Ebenezer Scrooge had received the blessing of their mother, and their father as well, it seemed.

Did that mean... Of course it did. Ebenezer was Belle's only beau now and was likely ready to ask for her hand in marriage. Although Cilla couldn't have been more pleased, it meant that conversations about her own worries fell on Belle's tone-deaf ears.

"Cilla, you are a romantic. You fall in love too easily, and someday you will find someone too, a man as wonderful as my Ebenezer," Belle said, her encouragement doing little to ease Cilla's concerns. "Once Mother sees the two of you together without all the commotion of a ball, she will recognize that, and Percy will never again be offered an invitation to call."

"Are you sure?"

"I know so," she said. "Don't you remember when Gordon Nelson was determined to win my heart? Mother invited him over for weeks on end, until at last I convinced her that he was not the man for me."

"And how did you do that?"

Belle smiled, then quickly covered her lips with one hand, as though she were embarrassed. "I provoked him time and again until his temper got the better of him. No matter how high his station in life, Mother did not want to see her daughter married to a brute."

"And look what it got you: a handsome man in Ebenezer Scrooge."

"Yes, and one who will one day own a counting house of his own, just like Father." She gave Cilla a hug and promised, "And the same will happen someday for you, too."

"Do you mean Mr. Wilkins?"

"Only if you want, my dear sister. He is a good man, and it would be nice to have your husband and mine be best friends. You could do worse."

Cilla nodded. "And Percy Ainsworth is at the top of the list."

And that's as much as she would say about him. Cilla didn't need to tell everything she had in mind. She would do what she could to overwhelm Percy and hopefully drive him away as a result. Again she chastised herself for even thinking that he would be the man she wanted to spend the rest of her life with. If only she were not such a romantic dreamer as her sister said she was. Despite the misjudgment about Percy, the name of Dick Wilkins stayed in her mind, and he seemed a very real possibility as someone to get to know better.

At the stroke of one, the doorbell rang, and Cilla ran to open it. "Mother, my carriage is here. I'm off to have tea with Sarah. I'll be home in time for supper."

"Fine, dear," her mother called as the door closed behind Cilla.

Cilla climbed into the carriage and gave the driver her destination. For the next while, she was able to breathe, not allowing herself to worry about Sunday night, Percy Ainsworth, or even Dick Wilkins.

When the carriage arrived at Sarah's, Cilla was more relaxed and hopeful than she had been since Christmas. The housemaid ushered her into a sitting room. Moments later, Sarah swept into the room with an air of self-confidence Cilla had not noticed previously.

Standing to greet her friend, Cilla said, "Sarah, what has happened to you? You simply glow. Have you been to the country and not told me, or has something else wonderful happened?"

"Something wonderful." Sarah said indicating for Cilla to sit. "But first, tell me about the ball. I wish I could have attended, but soon enough you will know the reason I was not there."

Cilla settled in, prepared to share her tale about how awful Percy had been but also hoping Sarah would have

A Fezziwig Christmas

other options for her. "I hoped that several of the gentlemen I've met in the last few months would make an appearance at the ball and that it would be a grand time. Unfortunately, that was not to be."

"Oh no. My dear Cilla," Sarah said as she reached forward to pat Pricilla's hand. "What happened?"

"The only one among our mutual acquaintances who came was Percy Ainsworth."

"Oh but he's so handsome and wealthy. Wasn't he charming?"

"A stuffy bore is more like it." Cilla's voice had taken on a tone of frustration. "He talked about nothing but himself and his money the entire evening. Had my father's apprentice, Dick Wilkins, not been there to save me, I might have perished from the experience."

"How dreadful," Sarah said. The maid appeared at the door with a tray. "Would you care for a cup, Cilla?"

"Yes, thank you." Once the tea was served and the maid exited, Cilla continued. "But boredom is not the worst part." She leaned toward her hostess to share her secret. "He has approached Mother, and she has given him permission to come courting on Sunday evening. Oh, Sarah! What am I ever to do about Mr. Ainsworth?"

"Will anyone else be there?"

"Belle and Mr. Scrooge. I've invited Mr. Wilkins as well, something my mother does not yet know."

"The same Wilkins who came to your rescue at the ball? Do you like him? "

"Like him?" The tingle that passed through her at the mention of his name suddenly made her wonder. Did she care for him? "He's a nice gentleman, and he came to my aid at the worst of times, but I'd never considered him as one to come courting." *Until now.* Of course she had no feelings for Dick Wilkins. She hardly knew him. Or maybe she did.

"Any port in the storm, as they say." Sarah took a sip of her tea. "What help may I afford?"

"You know many fine gentlemen; several of them I've met at parties with you. I thought that perhaps you could tell me why they would not have attended my father's ball. How I could get them to show an interest so my mother would not try to pair me with Percy, especially since I know he is not one who I could ever bear to be with?"

"Do you have someone in mind?"

"Yes, of course. How about Phillip Henley?"

"Gone to the south of France to escape the winter cold."

"George Butterfield or William Byron?"

"George has set sail for America, although I can't imagine why, and William has decided it's more important to spend his time caring for an ailing grandmother. If you ask me, he's doing so in the hopes that when she dies, she will deed her estate to him."

Cilla's face and heart fell as her hopes were extinguished. "And Fitzhugh Morgan?"

The smile that burst upon Sarah's face told the story. "And that's the news I have to tell. Fitzhugh and I are engaged to be married."

"It's hardly been six months since you met, yet you're already engaged?" Cilla made herself stop talking before she offended her friend.

"He's absolutely wonderful," Sarah said. "Someday the same will happen for you. But for now, Fitzhugh has a friend, Ethan Horrick, who's coming from Yorkshire this week. I'll see if a meeting can be arranged, perhaps if you asked us to your home on Sunday evening? But I can't promise."

"I understand. Thank you for trying to help." Cilla took a final sip of tea, then set the cup onto the tray again. "And my absolute best to you and Fitzhugh." She stood and hugged her friend to show her sincerity. "I've taken enough of your time today. I'm sure you have much to do in light of your coming wedding."

Sarah walked her to the door. "Good luck to you,"

Cilla settled into her seat in her waiting carriage and

gave her friend a final wave. *Yes, good luck to me, for without it, I could be stuck with Percy for the rest of my life.*

"No," she whispered as the carriage drove on. "That just won't do."

Nine

"Ebenezer, I don't know what to do." Once again Dick paced the storage room that he and Ebenezer shared as living quarters. "Percy seemed to always be at her side at the ball, but she tells me he's a bore. Then her mother has accepted Percy's request to call this evening, and neither of her parents know that Pricilla has also invited me. How can I court the girl with another suitor in attendance?"

"Whether Mrs. Fezziwig knows you are coming or not, you know she has always been gracious to us." Ebenezer stood in front of Dick, and the pacing ceased. "Pricilla has invited you, and you will accompany me. I am definitely invited. Mrs. Fezziwig would never cause a scene about your being in attendance, whether Percy is there or not. Get through tonight, and there will be many others, I assure you."

A Fezziwig Christmas

"But what if Cilla finds me to be a bore, the same as Percy?" Dick rubbed his hands together, feeling the dampness that had gathered there.

"You're not a bore, and besides, she turned to you when Percy proved too much. That must count for something."

"I was surprised she even knew my name."

"Well, she did, and she's invited you to her home." Ebenezer shrugged on his waistcoat. "Now get ready. We don't want to keep the ladies waiting. This should be an interesting evening for us."

Within minutes, they left and completed the brisk walk to the Fezziwigs' house, a stately brick flat in the middle of one of the finer districts.

"One day I will own a home like this," Ebenezer said. "It is my plan to start a counting house before Belle and I marry. She is used to finery that I can offer only when I am an equal to her father, not as an apprentice."

"And how soon do you think you can do that?" Dick wasn't certain he wanted to know. Even at a few months, it meant that Ebenezer would be leaving the shop and becoming a married man. They had been close over their shared years as apprentices, but even before that, when they were both lads. Having Ebenezer leave would be devastating. Who would Dick discuss life with?

"We're here." Ebenezer climbed the steps and rang the bell.

A maid opened the door, gave them a curtsy, and led them into the parlor, where Mrs. Fezziwig sat with Belle and Cilla. Percy Ainsworth sat stiffly on a chair a short distance from Pricilla, who seemed to visibly relax when she saw the new visitors.

She stood and offered her hand, as she had done at the ball. "Dick, it's so good to see you. Thank you for coming."

For a moment, Mrs. Fezziwig looked startled, but then she shook her head as though to clear her mind and again became the perfect hostess. "Mr. Wilkins and Mr. Scrooge.

Welcome. Please have a seat. Would you care for tea and biscuits?"

Ebenezer took the chair closest to Belle, but Dick looked around, not sure where he should be seated. He imagined that the overstuffed armchair on the opposite side of the room was reserved for Old Fezziwig, should he join them. No other chair seemed convenient to the conversation.

Before he could broach the decision regarding both a chair and refreshments, the chimes rang again, indicating yet another visitor's arrival.

The maid was on her way before Mrs. Fezziwig could speak. Dick went to the window and chose a chair from the side of the lamp table and carried it directly across from Cilla. His proximity was perhaps not what he would have managed had they arrived earlier, but at least this way, every time she looked up, she would first see him.

Sarah Miller entered the room with Fitzhugh Morgan, her hand tucked into his right elbow, and another gentleman to her left, a gentleman Dick did not recognize.

"Mrs. Fezziwig," Sarah said. "How I've missed seeing you these few months." She released her hand from Fitzhugh and walked toward the mistress of the house, arms wide open.

Mrs. Fezziwig stood and embraced the young woman, then turned her attention to the men who had accompanied her. "Gentlemen." She offered a hand as Sarah made the formal introductions.

"Mrs. Fezziwig, this is Fitzhugh Morgan, my fiancé."

"Oooh, such a pleasure," Mrs. Fezziwig said. "A fiancé," then she looked toward Percy Ainsworth with a nod.

Does this mean she has already decided on Percy? Dick wondered, but one glance at Cilla told him she was focused on the other gentleman who had accompanied Sarah.

"And this," Sarah continued, "Is Ethan Horricks, a great friend of Fitzhugh's down for a short visit from Yorkshire."

A Fezziwig Christmas

"So nice to meet you," Mrs. Fezziwig said, and her daughters echoed the sentiment.

Was Cilla's welcome perhaps a little more enthusiastic than Belle's had been?

"Anna," Mrs. Fezziwig said to the maid. "We are in need of more chairs and extra settings for tea."

Now that yet another potential suitor had joined them, Dick took the initiative and grabbed a fine spot for himself. One glance at Cilla, and he knew she was pleased with the additional visitors. Did she already know Mr. Horricks and was glad to see him, or was just the presence of more people enough to relieve her of having to entertain Percy for the entire evening while finding him a bore?

Ebenezer was right. Cilla had invited Dick, and that meant something more than Percy's invitation, which was solely from her mother. One more suitor shouldn't cause concern, especially since Percy had already lost the race when it came to Cilla's liking him.

Ten

Cilla had thought that the presence of Sarah, Fitzhugh, and one of his friends would help the evening along, but it did not take long before Percy began expounding upon everything he knew about business and money, especially his own. Her father had joined the gathering not long after Sarah's entourage arrived, and even his attendance did not stop Percy's adulation of himself.

"Mr. Ainsworth, which of the fine arts do you enjoy?" her mother asked, obviously attempting to change the course of conversation.

Percy halted his lecture long enough to look shocked by her interruption. "Enjoy? None. Tolerate? Many." He looked toward Cilla. "I expect my future wife to make every attempt to change my mind. Perhaps we could start the process this evening. Miss Fezziwig, would you do me the honor of playing the piano?" He nodded his head toward the corner.

A Fezziwig Christmas

The piano sat almost in hiding because it was there entirely for show. Neither she nor Belle played, although Lizzy seemed to have an ear for music and could pick out a tune. "I'm afraid that whatever I would attempt would not be pleasing to your ear, sir, so I will decline."

"Then perhaps your elder sister could accompany as you sing?"

"No, I'm not one to sing anywhere where others might hear me," Cilla said. "I know well enough that my voice would be cause for offense." She placed a smile upon her lips and gave her shoulders a shrug, hoping to stop Percy from further questioning without making herself seem like a complete dunce. She had done her best at her studies, but perhaps her best was not good enough. No matter to her that Percy might think so, and she was not sure whether it mattered to Mr. Horricks, or if she cared that it might. This was their first encounter, and although he was friends with Fitzhugh, whom she had adored, Horricks didn't seem to have the same charming personality. He was only here as a distraction from Percy, anyway. She looked toward Dick, and the smile he gave her in return spoke to her heart. Clearly, her inadequacies with the musical arts did not matter to him.

But Percy was not to be deterred. "What sort of education have you been given, Miss Fezziwig? Surely your parents prepared you to be the wife of a fine gentleman." He looked at Ebenezer, his nose wrinkling as though he smelled something foul. "Or, perhaps not."

"What are you trying to say, sir?" Ebenezer half rose from his seat, but Belle placed a hand against his forearm to hold him down.

"Not now, dear."

Old Fezziwig himself jumped up, but no words were forthcoming, only a smattering of indistinguishable sounds, sputtering and spitting, as though he were in such a rage he could not speak. When at last he spoke, he managed only,

"I'll have you know—" before Percy continued his berating, this time addressed toward Cilla herself.

"I am disappointed, Miss Fezziwig. I expected you to be a better match. I was hoping for an accomplished lady who spoke several languages, played the piano, and sang, yet you have none of these traits. How is your education so incomplete? Do you paint with watercolors and oils, at least? Do needlepoint, perhaps?"

How dare he! Yet, Cilla couldn't allow herself to say the words. Percy was giving her exactly the fodder she needed. His comments would be enough to break any possible match in the eyes of her mother.

"I would venture that you don't know the names of the monarchy, let alone those of the peerage and gentry. Can you recite the names of the royal family, or even your own? And what of the study of history and geography?" Percy had moved to tower over her, something her mother would never allow.

Mrs. Fezziwig rose from her chair and started to advance toward Mr. Ainsworth, the anger rising with the color of her cheeks.

Apparently, Dick could stand it no longer either. He stood and faced Percy. "Enough! You, sir, are a brute."

Cilla placed her hand against her breast and had a look of pleasant surprise upon her face. Once again, Mr. Wilkins was coming to her rescue. But he was not yet through.

Turning toward her mother, Dick said, "If you'll pardon my boldness, Mrs. Fezziwig, I believe it's time Mr. Ainsworth leaves." Then Dick again faced Percy. "You have worn out your welcome, sir."

"Agreed!" Mrs. Fezziwig said, as she too turned to meet Percy face-to-face, her finger pointed directly at his nose. "You *are* a brute, and I will not stand here and have my daughter insulted by such as you. I don't care who you are, you are no longer welcome in our home."

A Fezziwig Christmas

"And my business with your husband?" Percy said with a threatening tone.

"My husband's business has nothing to do with what happens in my home," Mrs. Fezziwig said. "Mr. Fezziwig is an honest man, and if he spends his days counting money for men as pious as you, I'd prefer he lose a hundred such customers. I will see you to the door. I'll not have you saying that I have been anything less than a proper hostess, although there is plenty to be said about the poor manners of a *gentleman* like you."

"Mr. Ainsworth, the dissolution of our business will be taken care of in the morning," Mr. Fezziwig said, finally able to speak.

Only Mrs. Fezziwig's control of the door kept Percy Ainsworth from closing it with a bang behind him.

Cilla had not intended for the dissolution of her father's business arrangement to happen, and she hoped it did not hurt his accounts too badly, but perhaps it was for the best. The severing of Percy's ties with her father's business would guarantee that she would never have to face him again. She would not be pressed to settle for boring Percy, who thought only of himself.

Dick still stood in front of her, like a man protecting his wife. She wasn't sure what had gotten into him. He had always seemed so shy. But he had challenged Percy in a way she would never have expected. Once again, he had come to her rescue where Percy was concerned, and Dick's value rose considerably in both her mind and heart. She would do her best not to underestimate him again.

"We should go as well," Sarah said, her hand placed against her chest as though she was flustered by the recent conversation, her fiancé at her side. Mr. Horricks stood, and the look on his face seemed like an animal that couldn't wait to escape from its pen.

"Thank you for coming," Cilla said, hurrying to Sarah to give her a hug. "I'm so sorry the evening ended like this."

"None of it was your fault," Sarah said, then stood and leaned forward to whisper in Cilla's ear. "Mr. Wilkins would make a wonderful catch. Don't lose him."

Cilla's breath caught in her throat. Was Dick really the best man for her, after all? Had she done the right thing by inviting him here? Could he be a perfect suitor someday? Thank goodness she had him here tonight. She looked toward him in what he must have taken as a signal, as he moved to her side—Dick Wilkins, the poor apprentice who worked for her father. The plain man who had always been so kind. The man who had come to her rescue every needed moment since their first dance at her father's Christmas ball. The only man who cared about the things that were important to her. And now, here he stood, not in the least worried about the terrible things Percy had claimed about her lack of preparation to be a wife.

"Mr. Wilkins." Mrs. Fezziwig, her arms crossed, looked directly at Dick.

Cilla blanched. What could her mother have to say? Would she ask Dick Wilkins to leave too?

"Y-yes?" Dick looked afraid of what her mother might say.

"I hope to see you next week for tea," Mrs. Fezziwig said, her hand fluttering about as though she didn't know where to place it.

"Why yes, I'd be honored," Dick said. He looked at Cilla, who was smiling.

Was it possible that Dick Wilkins was the one with whom she could fall in love? Or did she feel that way only because he proved to be an escape from Percy Ainsworth? No, Dick had qualities she wanted in a husband. She leaned toward his arm, hoping he could forget that she had done her best to make him believe they were friends and nothing more. But she couldn't brush him off or turn him away any longer.

"Dick?" If only she could step back in time; then she would change the way she had treated him to let him know she did indeed care.

"Yes, Cilla? My sweet?"

Eleven

Dick couldn't believe he had said it: *My sweet.* And she hadn't moved away from him. If anything, she had moved closer. Was it possible that she could feel the same? He didn't know how, but he would find a way to help her learn to love him back.

Now that Percy was gone and Mr. Horricks seemed to be only a one-time guest, no one stood in Dick's way. Ebenezer was right; Dick was worthy of someone like Cilla, and he believed she felt the same.

With the other guests gone, there was no need for them to continue to stand. "Shall we sit?" Mr. Fezziwig said.

Dick waited for Cilla's cue as to which chair to occupy, not surprised when she arranged the chair Percy had occupied closer to herself.

"I think this will do," she said.

Ebenezer and Belle had already taken their seats, and

A Fezziwig Christmas

Mr. and Mrs. Fezziwig were on the way to theirs when Lizzy came into the room. "Did I miss something?"

"Nothing we care to discuss, Lizzy," her father said. "Instead, we have much happier business this evening. Ebenezer?"

Ebenezer suddenly seemed nervous, with his face blushing red and beads of sweat appearing across his brow. "Uh, yes, sir . . . Mr. Fezziwig." Ebenezer stood, then turned and dropped to one knee before Belle. He reached for her hand and placed a tender kiss upon the back and then the palm before he proceeded. Her sisters and mother drew in a deep breath.

"Belle Fezziwig, I have come this evening to ask you to be my bride." Ebenezer said. Tears formed in Belle's eyes. "I love you, Belle. Will you be my wife?"

As though he had no control over his own person, Dick looked across the short distance to Cilla. All his fears vanished regarding the direction his own courtship might take. He knew he would grow to love her more each day, just as Ebenezer and Belle had grown to love each other.

Belle's answer was so quiet that Dick almost missed it as she whispered, "Yes."

Ebenezer let out a shout of joy such as Dick had never heard from his friend. He jumped to his feet and pulled Belle to hers, his arms closing tightly around her. "Belle, Belle, Belle," he repeated over and over as he danced her around the room.

"Gracious!" Mrs. Fezziwig cried, the joy in her voice matching Ebenezer's enthusiasm, and her husband added the word a few times himself yet did nothing to break Ebenezer's enthusiasm away from his daughter.

At last Ebenezer stopped moving about the room long enough to look at the woman who was to be his wife. "Belle Fezziwig, I love you will all my heart. I love you more than all the gold in the world. Nothing will ever pull us apart."

He pulled her into the corner near the piano, where

only Dick could see what was happening.

The kiss Ebenezer gave Belle seemed proof enough.

Never had Cilla witnessed a more romantic moment. She could only hope that someday her own engagement would come as sweetly.

"Now that Ebenezer and Belle are engaged, I have a question of my own," Dick said, looking first at Cilla, then at her mother, and back again to Cilla. "Is it possible that I may have permission to court your daughter, Pricilla?"

Cilla could hardly believe it, but her heart sang at the idea of courting Dick. What a wonderful man he had turned out to be. And someone who seemed to understand her.

"That sounds like a fine plan," her mother said.

"I agree wholeheartedly," her father said.

Dick returned his gaze toward Cilla "Do you approve? I will do everything in my power to never be a bore."

She giggled at his reference to Percy, the man who had opened the door for Dick to come into her life. All confusion was wiped from her mind. No longer did she question who was to be her beau. She supposed she had known all along; Dick Wilkins would always be at her side.

Cilla remembered the comfort of being in Dick's arms as they danced for what seemed brief moments.

She placed her fingers onto the back of his hand and said, "Yes."

Then Dick Wilkins let out a whoop of his own.

ABOUT LU ANN BROBST STAHELI

Lu Ann Brobst Staheli got her start as a celebrity paparazzi-stalker-chick, which led to an award-winning career as a ghostwriter of celebrity memoirs. A masochist at heart, she taught junior high-school English for 33 years before moving to the school library. She once spent two weeks' summer vacation backpacking through Europe with 15 of her students. She has won three of Utah's Best of State Medals—two for writing and one for teaching—but refuses to wear them all at the same time because she'd hate to be known as a showoff.

Website: LuAnn's Library
Facebook: Lu Ann Brobst Staheli
Twitter: @LuannStaheli

A Taste of Home
by Annette Lyon

One

Overland Route Rail Line—December 23, 1913

Frost framed the window, which looked out onto the snowy landscape whizzing past the train. Every second brought Claire Jennings closer to home for Christmas and farther from San Francisco, where she worked as a maid and nanny. Soon she'd arrive at the Salt Lake City depot, where her father would be waiting to drive her and her traveling companion, William Rhodes, down to Spanish Fork. They'd ride in the family buckboard, not in an automobile like the ones she'd been around since spring.

Claire breathed a happy sigh. Snow on the ground and the Rockies in the distance were signs that she'd left California behind. *This* was the landscape she'd grown up in. She'd missed the changing seasons. And she was almost home. She could hardly wait to see her family again and pass out the gifts she'd bought for them in California.

She'd found a brooch for her mother and a handmade pipe for her father. She'd bought two parasols for her little sisters and a set of toy metal cars for her little brother. She imagined her family members opening their presents and hearing of her adventures. How on Christmas Eve they would trim the tree, fresh cut from Mr. Burton's land up the canyon, then sip herbal tea by the fire as Mother read the Christmas story from the book of Luke. After listening to the scripture account, the family would carol through neighboring streets, then return home for a taste of Mother's special holiday bedtime snack: walnut-covered toffee, something she made only for Christmas. Claire began craving toffee the moment the leaves began to change color every year.

Except in San Francisco, December's weather was only a bit cooler than June's. The leaves didn't go through the same changes. The "winter" Claire had left behind had felt more like a Utah spring, nothing like a proper winter. Seeing Christmas wreaths on house doors and tinsel and lights lining the city shops had seemed odd. Quite frankly, it hadn't *felt* like Christmas in California.

Nothing would feel like Christmas until Claire walked in the front door, hugged her family, and smelled Mother's toffee. At the thought, a ripple of anticipation went through Claire. She could hardly wait to hug her parents, to feel her father's mustache brush against her cheek, to hear her mother's sweet voice sing carols while making orange rolls, even as Claire herself scolded her younger siblings to stop sliding on the wood floor in their bare stockings—they'd tear.

Claire laughed to herself, eager even for that.

"What's so funny?" Beside her, William opened an eye.

"Oh, nothing," Claire said. "I'm eager to get home, is all." She turned back to the window, hoping Will would go back to sleep. He'd gone west to work as well, although only to Sacramento. Claire and Will had grown up a block apart, so traveling home together for the holiday had made sense. Her father had insisted on it for her safety. Not that she felt particularly safe with Will Rhodes, of all people.

But Claire hadn't had the heart to tell her parents what she really thought of the Rhodes boy. How could she like him? He'd always been a mischievous horror. One day at school when she and Will were about ten, he'd dumped her into a large trash bin behind the schoolhouse. He'd been ridiculously tall and strong for his age even then, so no amount of putting up a fight from her had done any good. She'd been stuck in that trash can for fifteen solid minutes before her teacher, Miss O'Brien, had marched out to find her. Claire's boots had been permanently stained from the garbage. Every time she'd looked at them for the next year and a half—until they wore out and her feet were too big for them—she'd wished curses on Will's head.

And that was only one instance of a thousand.

Claire no longer feared Will in the same way. With age, he had learned to behave in public. He wouldn't again dip the ends of her braids in white paint, as he had when she was eleven. Her mother had cut three inches off of her hair after that. She still hadn't forgiven Will for giving her the shortest hair in the entire school.

At thirteen, in an attempt to scare her with a flame, he'd held a candle close to her. Claire had refused to scream and run, but Will didn't give up—at least, not until the candle tipped and wax dripped onto her favorite apron. *Then* she screamed. Her favorite apron was ruined.

By the time she'd turned fifteen, he'd also locked her in the school coat closet and had exchanged the pie in her lunch pail for a paper sack of worms.

At twenty-one, Will no longer pulled those types of pranks—to her knowledge. Yet the boy—man?—still enjoyed a good "joke," so she'd been on edge ever since they'd boarded the train.

Will hadn't tried anything aggravating or foolish on the

trip so far, unless one counted a few sarcastic comments about fellow passengers as they'd boarded. Claire wasn't sure whether to take his tameness as a sign that she had nothing to worry about or as a clue that she should be on guard even more because if Will hadn't pulled any pranks yet, he was bound to at any moment. All the more reason to wish him back asleep.

Will again lowered his chin toward his crossed arms, shifted positions, and grunted.

How gentlemanly, Claire thought with a shake of her head.

"How much longer?" Will asked.

He'd asked the same thing ten minutes ago. Claire didn't know the answer then, and she didn't know now. She tamped down a thread of annoyance so it wouldn't show in her voice. "I don't know."

Maybe he'd doze off and sleep the rest of the way. Another grunt from beside her.

"Snow," Will said. "It was sure nice living without it."

She gaped at what she could only call heresy. "But it's not Christmas without snow-covered mountains and seeing your breath in the cold." She gestured toward the landscape outside. "This is a start—it's finally starting to look like December—but it won't truly be Christmas until I'm with my family."

Will said nothing in reply. His hat drooped over his face a bit, which annoyed Claire even more. The least he could do was have the manners to conduct a proper conversation. She reached over and lifted the brim of his hat. His right eye popped open again, and he grimaced as if the light in the train car was hurting him somehow.

"What?" he asked.

"Are you so unsentimental that you don't even care that you're going home for Christmas?"

"I care." He snatched his hat from her fingers and sat up. "I just don't like my fingers and toes going numb while milking cows. I'd be quite happy living where it never froze. Snow is beautiful; I'll grant you that. But dealing with it is not so great."

"Oh. I hadn't thought of that." Claire thought of other aspects of winter that she hadn't missed, like facing the outhouse on January nights or getting out of bed in the morning only to step onto a freezing-cold floor, the water bottle she'd brought to bed with her having gone cold hours before.

She suddenly felt bad for judging him so harshly. Of course he cared about something other than his next prank. He had to have emotions beyond glee at another's expense. Just as she wasn't exactly the same girl who'd been in that trash bin, he wasn't the boy who had put her there. The boy had been replaced by broad shoulders and a narrow waist. His shirt was tight across his chest, thanks to all the physical labor he'd done recently. Claire's heart thumped curiously, and she felt her cheeks warm.

She swallowed and tried not to admire how handsome Will had become. Now that she'd noticed it, she couldn't believe she'd been blind to the obvious. When they'd boarded the train, she'd seen only what she'd expected to— the mischievous boy who'd always caused her trouble. Now, instead of being the perpetually disheveled mop it had once been, his hair was trimmed and neatly combed, with a small bit out of place by the cowlick at his right temple. Deliberately not looking at that spot, she dropped her eyes to her clasped hands and attempted to speak in a softer, more compassionate manner.

"Do you look forward to any particular family traditions?"

He turned to look at her. "Like what?"

"For example, my mother has a special toffee recipe she makes only at Christmastime. The house fills with the smell of toffee. She makes several kinds, but my favorite has crushed walnuts on top. For me, it's not Christmas until I smell Mother's toffee."

Will nodded thoughtfully. "I like ham at Christmas dinner. And my mother makes delicious rolls." His tone said that he wasn't quite sure if his answer was what Claire was looking for. "Of course, we have ham other times. Rolls, too."

"I—I can see how you would like those things," Claire said, doing her best to validate his offering. Will seemed sincere, which was more than she'd expected. Claire tried a different tack. "Does your family have a tree?"

A few seconds passed. Will looked into her eyes, and she could have sworn she saw sadness in them. Then he simply shook his head. "No tree." He picked at a callus on his left palm. "Just a wreath on the door made of cuttings from the Johnsons' tree." He glanced up. "But we have stockings."

"There you are," Claire said. "Stockings are a wonderful tradition."

Will nodded and continued to worry the callus. Claire wanted to reach over and make him stop; it was as if he were picking at a scab *inside* him. But that was silly. This was Will Rhodes, for heaven's sake. The boy didn't have a sentimental bone in his six-foot, muscled body. She flushed at the thought of his muscles, then licked her lips and cleared her throat as if fellow passengers could hear what she'd been thinking.

What if Will was genuinely sad but hiding it? Curious, her eyes moved to his face, then quickly away before he could notice. Sure enough, the corners of his lips were turned down, and a furrow creased his brow. Claire wanted to reach over with her thumb to smooth it out.

"We'll be home soon," she said, hoping that would help.

He nodded, saying nothing. Something in her chest twisted in a strange way, telling her that perhaps there was something more to William Rhodes. Perhaps he wasn't all jester any longer.

A Taste of Home

When they reached the Salt Lake depot, Will looked up, seeing the city and signs out the window, and immediately became animated, the sadness melting away. The sight made her smile. As the train squealed to a stop, Claire wondered at her reaction. Had she really just hoped Will would be happy?

Something must be terribly wrong, she thought with a chuckle. *Perhaps I'm catching a cold.*

Two

Will hopped off the train quickly, eager to escape the stuffy confines of the railcar. As he breathed in the crisp winter air, it bit his lungs in a familiar, pleasant way. His work boots crunched the snow on the platform. After months in California, he felt as if he'd stepped into another world—a familiar one, yes, but one that he'd lived in long ago.

One he didn't particularly want to return to.

Not with Mr. Roberts living at the house now. Will would never be able to call him Father, Stepfather, or even George; loyalty to his late father prevented it. Will should have been grateful that his mother had found a new husband so she wouldn't be alone. But Will couldn't help but think that Mr. Roberts had simply seen Mother as a way to get room and board in addition to a great cook, an immaculate housekeeper, and someone to warm his bed at night—all at no cost to himself save speaking a few words before the minister. As always, the thought made Will grind his teeth and want to punch something. Over the last few months, he'd taken out his frustrations with a hammer as he'd shingled roofs. As soon as he got home, he would have to stay silent so he wouldn't explode and ruin the holiday for Mother.

Will might have been able to accept a stepfather if he'd been prepared for it. But his mother and George Roberts courted and were married all while Will was away. The first he'd known of it was in a telegram from his younger brother Henry, informing him that the nuptials had taken place.

And Will was supposed to pretend that all was well? The Roberts children were living at the house. Had they displaced his siblings from their beds? Would Christmas dinner be a ham with rolls, humble as the tradition was? Or would Mr. Roberts insist on a turkey or some other food? Would they have stockings and a wreath on the door or entirely new "traditions" foisted upon the Rhodes household?

Except it isn't the Rhodes household any longer. It's the Roberts household. A horrid thought dawned on Will with a shudder: *Mother is Mrs. Roberts.*

Will would rather have stayed in California for Christmas. He would have been content to hole up in the bunkhouse above the Curtis family barn while the family celebrated. But then he'd heard that if he didn't go home for Christmas, Claire would be traveling alone.

As he stood on the platform, Will was vaguely aware of people milling about. He stared at the snow clinging to the eaves of the train station. Only when Claire touched his sleeve did he shake his head and return to the present.

"Are you well?" Claire asked. "You look a bit peaked."

"Right as rain," he said, putting on a grin.

She eyed him for a moment, as if she didn't quite believe him. Eventually she looked around. "Do you see my father anywhere? He's never late, but I don't see him."

She walked off and beckoned for Will to follow, although he wasn't in nearly the same rush. She'd proven to be a more-than-pleasant traveling companion. She was even prettier than she'd been as a young girl. And she'd always been the prettiest girl at school. Why he still remembered the blue ribbons tied at the ends of her braids, he didn't know. But for pretty much his entire life, he'd tried to get Claire to notice him. That had once meant teasing her; he'd loved seeing those cheeks turn bright red with indignation as she stomped her foot and yelled, "I hate you, William Rhodes!"

She'd noticed him. *Yelled* at him. He'd had happy, satisfied dreams those nights. Then, when she was about fifteen, she'd begun ignoring him. No amount of taunting could make her look his way. Until the rail ride.

Will followed Claire about ten feet behind, purposely thinking of her instead of how life at home had changed in his absence. He was traveling with the girl he'd always had his eye on. During the trip, she'd talked to him—and hadn't said she hated him even once. As soon as they found her father, it would be over.

She stopped and put a hand on her hip, head cocked to one side. "Can't a strapping young man like yourself walk faster?"

Claire Jennings was teasing him?

Unable to hold back a grin, Will sauntered over and rocked back on his heels, thumbs hooked in his pockets. "I suppose I could move faster, but quite frankly, the view from back here is far nicer." He waited for her reaction.

Her cheeks, pink from the nip in the air, colored further—whether out of flattery, fury, or shock, he didn't know. He wasn't particularly certain he cared either. "Well, I never." She shook her head and laughed. "I should punish you for that remark."

"But?" he prompted.

She laughed again; the sound was like tinkling crystal. "It wouldn't do any good." She tipped her head toward the main doors. "My father's not here. Let's wait inside. And you walk beside me this time."

"Yes, ma'am," he said, tipping his hat, just as happy to walk at Miss Jennings's side. People would see them together.

Inside, she went ahead, straight toward a bench, so Will hurried to catch up. Before sitting on it, she turned around, and so suddenly that Will nearly ran into her. "What if something is wrong?"

"What do you mean?" Will asked, taking a step back—not that he wanted to, but he did it to give her a little space.

"What if my father had an accident on the road? Or what if my letter didn't arrive, and he doesn't know to come today?"

"He knows. He replied by telegram, remember?"

Claire nodded but bit the edge of her lip. "I suppose so." She sat on the front edge of the bench, clearly worried.

"How about I see if anyone sent a message ahead?" Will asked.

"You'd do that?"

"Of course."

"Thank you." Claire nodded, clearly pleased with the idea. "Just don't go buying me a ticket to Chicago or anything."

Will mock gasped and put a hand to his chest. "I'm wounded. I would never do such a thing." As he turned to move away, he said, "Seattle, maybe. Never Chicago." Behind him, Claire laughed aloud. He couldn't help but grin as he hurried to the ticket counter, not knowing where else to inquire.

He had to wait in line a few minutes, but soon he reached the front of the line, where an elderly gentleman sat behind the counter. "Where to?"

"Actually, I'm Will Rhodes, and I'm traveling with a Miss Claire Jennings. Her father was supposed to meet us here. We just arrived on the San Francisco train—"

The man nodded his bushy, white head. "Rhodes, you say? And Miss Jennings? Miss Claire Jennings?"

"Yes," Will said eagerly. "That's right."

"I have something for you. One moment." The old man walked away, shuffling to a table at his right and muttering something Will couldn't make out. The gentleman paused here and there to read, then shook his head and moved around more papers until he nodded and returned with a small, yellow page clutched in one hand. "You're Will Rhodes, you say?"

"I am," Will said, wondering if the paper was something to worry over.

The man blinked several times, moving the page closer and then farther away in an effort to read it. "Clifford in the back took the message. Came in on the telephone this morning."

Will held out his hand. "May I read it? Please?"

"I suppose so," the old man said with a shrug and handed the paper over slower than molasses.

Will had to clench his teeth, forcing a polite smile onto his face, as he waited for the paper to be within reach. At last the elderly, shaky hand was close enough, and Will took the page.

No sooner had Will turned his attention to the few lines of text than the next person in line stepped forward and asked for a ticket to Ogden, effectively shoving Will to the side. He read the short note, and his stomach dropped.

Call from Mr. Jennings. Message for Claire Jennings traveling with Wm Rhodes. Joey has measles. House under quarantine through the new year. Claire to call when she can.

Will returned to the bench with a slow stride, not wanting to deliver the message—not when he knew how much Claire had looked forward to going home. At last he reached the bench and sat down heavily.

"What is it?" Claire's tone was wary. She turned to him. "What's in that note? Is something wrong?"

In the few seconds he took to try to find the words, Claire took the note from him and read it. She sat back in dismay. "Quarantine? Oh no."

"I'm sure Joey will be fine," Will said, wanting to ease her distress.

"It's not that. I mean, sure, I worry about him, but . . . it's the other part."

"I know," Will said softly.

Her chin lowered, and she twisted a handkerchief instead of wiping the tears that had just tumbled down her cheeks. "I can't go home. If I do, I won't be able to leave for weeks—maybe a month—and I'll lose my position. If I go home, I may as well telegraph the Hudsons to replace me. My family is close to losing the farm, and the money I earn may be the only thing to hold the bank off."

She sniffed and looked at Will. He wanted to hold her and wipe away her tears, assure her that everything would work out. But he couldn't do that, of course. His second urge was to make a joke, but he squelched that idea too; he wasn't that person anymore.

"Will, what am I to do? I can't go back to Sacramento now. The Hudsons have plans that most certainly do not include me. And I can't go home either. I'm stuck."

A few more tears fell. Will put a hand on her shoulder; it was all he dared do. "I'm so sorry," he said.

She had to be thinking of all the things she'd miss out on, all of the things her family would do without her. Being away from home at Christmas would be as hard for her as going home was going to be for him.

With a sudden flash of insight, Will knew what to do. "How about we let a couple of rooms in a hotel and spend Christmas here in the city?"

"I can't afford it."

His mind searched for a convincing argument. "I made more money than I'd expected to—lots of work after hours—so I can easily cover your room." It was true, to a point. He had earned more than expected, although his original plan had been to save the money so he could buy land of his own—far from Mr. Roberts.

"I can't allow you to—"

"I insist. Besides, where else would you go?" He held his breath, hoping she'd agree. Staying in a hotel here provided the perfect excuse to stay away from Mr. Roberts. A gentleman didn't abandon a young lady in a big city.

Claire shook her head dully. "You must be mad." She dabbed her eyes with the handkerchief, then stood and walked out of the depot toward the luggage area. She looked for her trunk, spotted it, and walked toward it. Will followed and reached her as she sat atop her trunk.

"It will be an adventure," Will said, taking a seat beside her. "Christmas cheer must be everywhere in the city. We'll seek it out and have a merry time doing it."

She eyed him skeptically, one eyebrow raised. "Is this a joke?"

"Of course not." Yet he couldn't blame her for thinking he would be teasing.

"What is all of this talk of *we*? Go hire a coach. I'll find a hotel room and stay there until I can go back to Sacramento." She sniffed and straightened her back as if trying to be strong. "I imagine a hotel costs less here than in California." She closed her eyes turned her head as if she didn't want him to see her crying.

Will reached out and put an arm all the way around her shoulders. Miraculously, she didn't pull away. She even turned toward him, though her eyes were down. Will chose his words carefully.

"I won't leave you here alone. To be honest, I'd rather not greet my stepfather over Christmas ham. I'd rather be here . . . with you."

He meant the last part more than the rest. He was only starting to admit that the long-time infatuation he'd had for the eldest Jennings girl had become something more. If he could, he would take care of her and protect her, make sure no pranksters—like he'd been—ever bothered her again. He couldn't bear to see her sad. For the foreseeable future, reversing that frown was his only objective.

Claire raised her gaze to his. "You'd do that for me?"

"For me too," he said, trying to make his voice light. "You're a lot easier on the eyes than Mr. Roberts."

She laughed through her tears, then wiped them with the back of one hand—one cheek and then the other. "You've convinced me, Mr. Rhodes. Lead on."

"Excellent!" He stood and moved to ask a porter for directions to a nice hotel, but then he stopped and turned around. "You want *me* to lead on? Eager for the view, eh?"

Still sitting on her trunk, Claire laughed so hard she rocked back and forth, crying tears of mirth. A flood of warmth went through Will. He'd made her smile and laugh if only for a moment. The success was intoxicating. He knew he'd do anything to make her happy again—for longer and longer.

He held out his arm for her. "We'll find a hotel and have your trunk and my bag delivered. There has to be one nearby, don't you think?"

"Definitely." Smiling wide, she stood and put her arm through his. "Shall we, Mr. Rhodes?"

"Miss Jennings, it would be a pure delight." He tipped his hat, and they were off.

Three

Will and Claire learned of a highly recommended hotel within walking distance that was frequented by rail passengers—the Peery. After arranging to have their luggage delivered there, they walked along the wide, busy streets of Salt Lake City. Carriages and buggies were joined by some automobiles, all moving along the bustling streets.

Claire had her hand resting in the crook of Will's arm. She liked how being escorted by a handsome young man made her feel—fancy and metropolitan. They passed store windows decorated for the season. Fluffy white batting used as snow. Nutcrackers. Red and green bobbles. Small trees covered in tinsel. Blinking electrical lights, and more. When they passed the displays at the ZCMI department store, Claire couldn't help but stop and gaze at the elegant designs and products—china, tablecloths, and gleaming pans in one window. Another window had clothing: silk scarves, a tailored wool coat, ladies boots of supple leather, and a jaunty hat.

Will didn't seem particularly excited about kitchenware or women's clothing, of course, so Claire didn't linger. "Let's find the hotel," she told him. "I can come back later."

"After we get our rooms and contact the train station about your trunk," Will said as they continued down the street, "we should probably send word to our families."

"Definitely," Claire agreed. "And let my family know where I'm staying. I hope the hotel has a telephone or telegraph." She hoped that sending the message would be quick; the sooner she could think of something other than missing her family, the better.

They waited for a break in traffic before crossing to the next block, then continued walking past several more city blocks, with Will leading the way. He'd spent time in Salt Lake before, living with his aunt and uncle while working at some orchards, so he knew where Broadway Street—an address that didn't follow the grid addresses most of the city did—was located. They headed west, with the low winter sun ahead and to the left. They'd already passed Temple Square, with its dome-shaped tabernacle and its huge temple with six towering spires. Claire was eager to see what else the city held and happy to let Will guide the way.

Eventually, Will paused and nodded to the right, toward a building. "Look. Maybe something for tomorrow?"

Craning her head back, Claire took in the grand building. According to the marquee, this was the Capitol Theatre. Thanks to incandescent lights inside, she could tell that the interior was grand, with lush carpets and sweeping staircases flanking the lobby.

"Or," Will said, interrupting her thoughts, "we could see a motion picture."

"Both sound lovely," Claire said as they continued to walk. "I wonder if we could find a dance to attend. I so love a good dance."

"Too bad we aren't stuck here during warmer weather." Will adjusted his hat. "In the summer when it's hot, there's nothing nicer than taking the open-air train out to the lake—"

"*The* lake? As in the Great Salt Lake?"

"Yep," Will said. "You can bathe in the water, but you can't sink. There's so much salt that you float."

"I can't imagine." Claire had heard about how enormous the Great Salt Lake was, and she felt a twinge of regret that she wouldn't be visiting it. She imagined that Will would look quite nice in a bathing suit. But there was no point in dwelling on lost summertime activities in December. "What made you think of the lake?"

Bathing in a massive salty lake didn't seem to have much to do with her comment about wanting to dance.

"I was thinking of Saltair."

"I've heard of that. Someone called it the Coney Island of the West, but I don't really know what that means."

"Me neither. The pavilion is open air and built right on the water. The summer I spent here, I went there often. Everyone does—young people and their parents on the same floor."

"I'd like to see it sometime."

"Maybe we can come back in the summer and spend a whole day at Saltair. There's more than bathing and dancing—there's food and entertainment. There's even a roller coaster."

A warm tingle went through Claire from the tip of her head down her spine and into her toes. Will was thinking about spending time with her—a whole day with her—months and months from now. She found her heart rate speeding up a bit and was grateful for the layers between their arms—his shirt, her blouse, two coats—preventing him from feeling her increased pulse.

"What else have I missed?" she asked as they stopped at another corner.

Will's mouth scrunched up in thought, and then he pointed to his left. "Well, a few years ago, the Salt Palace burned down. It was a few blocks down that way and was built, in part, from big blocks of salt from the lake. The building used to house bike races, fairs, and exhibits. It had hundreds of electric lights, so from a distance, it looked as if it had a glowing dome on top of it."

"That sounds almost poetic." Claire looked up at Will. "Too bad I didn't get stuck here a few years ago."

Will flushed slightly at the compliment, then pointed to a dark brick building across the way. "There it is," he said. "The Peery Hotel."

The name was emblazoned on a sign on the top of the hotel overlooking the street corner. As Claire and Will crossed the street and approached the three-story building, Claire took it in. The brick was a purple so dark it was almost brown. The windows and doors had bright white edging that made the building look sharp, like a man who had just put on a freshly pressed suit. The second story had three separate sections, connected at the back, with gaps between them.

Claire tilted her head. "Interesting shape." She remembered what the porter who'd recommended the Peery had said about it. "I see what the porter meant about the E-shaped upstairs. Every room *would* have natural light. Clever."

Will opened the door for her. She stepped inside and caught her breath. The lobby was narrow and long—and beautiful. Her entire childhood home could have fit inside the lobby, with room to spare. Perhaps two houses could have fit. The walkway she and Will stood on was flanked by carpet, on which several couches and end tables stood. About halfway down the walkway on the right, a fire crackled in a fireplace, and beyond that stood an upright piano. To the left, at the far end of the lobby, was the registration desk.

In the center of the lobby, directly ahead, a staircase went straight up to a landing and then turned left. Claire could imagine walking down the stairs, wearing a ball gown and jewels, to meet her beau below. She hadn't expected a stopping place for rail travelers to be this nice. It probably wasn't as sophisticated as she'd heard the Hotel Utah was, but the Peery was easily the most beautiful building she'd ever entered.

"Are you sure you can afford it?" Claire asked. "It looks awfully expensive."

"I'll check, but I'm quite sure the cost won't be a problem." Will looked over and asked, "Are you all right?"

She nodded. "I'm fine. It's just that—this is like a dream." Such glamorous surroundings would certainly ease the ache of missing Christmas.

Will led the way to the registration desk. Claire admired the electric grand chandelier and the elaborate designs on the banisters. Moments later, Will handed Claire a key, and they walked up the staircase to find their rooms. Will had requested that their rooms be in the same corridor but not next door. That way he would be close if Claire needed help with anything but far enough away to satisfy anyone questioning propriety.

They found his room, the first at the corner of one of the *E*'s arms. Claire walked along the hallway, checking the room numbers, until she reached the last door on the left. The hallway ended with a big window looking out on the street in front of the hotel. As she slipped her key into the lock, she wondered how much the city was lit up by electric lights and if she'd be able to see them from her windows after dark.

The lock clicked, and she turned the knob and then stopped and called toward Will at the other end of the hall. "Did you get the right key?"

"Sure did." He was closing the door behind him, apparently having already looked over his room in the time she'd taken to find her room. "Would you like to rest or freshen up? Or—"

"I'm ravenous, actually," Claire said.

"You're in luck," he said. "As soon as we make telephone calls home, we'll eat. I happen to know that a nearby café has an excellent mutton."

Four

Will spent much of the first night staring at the crown molding and thinking about where he would take Claire the next day—Christmas Eve. And what would they do for Christmas Day? Surely they could find a restaurant open, at the hotel if nowhere else. They could attend a mass at the Cathedral of the Madeleine. Neither he nor Claire was Catholic, but he imagined that going to mass would be a good experience and very Christmassy.

He was up shortly after dawn, not because he wasn't tired but because after working so many early mornings in California, he couldn't sleep past five thirty or six o'clock anymore. The sun had yet to rise, but he couldn't lie there any longer, so he got up and turned on the lamp by his bed. The sudden glow, made with the barest of efforts, made him smile. It was so unlike lighting a fire, lantern, or candle.

A Taste of Home

I could get used to this.

He quickly washed and dressed and then wrote a note to Claire, which he slipped under her door.

I'm in the lobby. Come down when you're ready, and we'll get some breakfast.

With that, he made sure he had his key and then headed down to the lobby. The lights gave the lobby a warm glow that contrasted the darkness just beyond the doors. Will found a spot on an empty couch and picked up an abandoned copy of the local newspaper, the *Deseret News*. He read the entire issue without comprehending a word. His mind was entirely preoccupied with the possibilities of entertaining Claire today. He racked his memory for every interesting place he'd ever visited in Salt Lake, grateful that his aunt had insisted that he visit someplace new every Saturday and write home about it. Three months of such experiences had left him with a lot to choose from.

He'd outlined several possible activities depending on Claire's preferences, including a Christmas Eve dance at the Hotel Utah. She'd asked to go to a dance, so he assumed she had a formal dress packed. He'd have to stop by the department store for new shoes and trousers at the least, or he wouldn't be at all presentable for a ball. Normally, he didn't care about dressing to fit an occasion, but something about the prospect of attending a dance with Claire—about being seen with her and wanting her to be proud to be on his arm—changed his attitude.

If he and Claire managed to do half of what was on his itinerary, he wouldn't have much left from his salary by the time they headed back to California. He'd been saving up to buy a cow for his mother. Now that Mr. Roberts had brought along his old cow, the family's need for milk was satisfied. Money for buying his own land could wait. Will figured he had no need to feel guilty for using his hard-earned money elsewhere.

For someone else.

"Will?" came a voice behind him.

He jumped to his feet and whirled around to see Claire approaching. Her hair was up in a simple bun, with curls at the sides of her face. She wore a simple, blue dress that made the blue of her eyes look deep. *A man could get lost in those eyes.*

"Will?" she said again, and only then did he realize he hadn't answered her.

I must look like a fool, standing here speechless.

He cleared his throat and smoothed his worn trousers, then smiled. "Good morning. Sleep well?"

"Like a dream. I've never slept in such a luxurious bed before."

Glad someone was able to rest. Will had spent more time directly with Claire Jennings in the last two days than he had over the rest of their lives put together—silent hours in the schoolhouse and church meetings didn't count. He'd become more eager for his time with her to never end.

Yesterday there had been moments when he thought she might feel the same—from a look, a laugh, a tone. But at other times, he'd caught her rolling her eyes or otherwise seeming to view him as the silly boy of their youth. He couldn't exactly blame her for that, yet he planned to do his best to win her over.

He held out one arm. "I know a delightful place a few blocks from here. They serve the best biscuits."

"Sounds delicious." Claire slipped her hand into the crook of his arm, and they walked onto the street, which was just lightening as the sun peered over the mountaintops.

Breakfast was lovely. Will managed to remember his manners—for the most part. His mother wouldn't have been *too* embarrassed had she seen him. And Claire couldn't stop talking about the delicious biscuits. He ordered a second basket of them just for her.

After eating, they meandered about the city streets, or so he hoped it appeared. He wanted the day to feel spontaneous and fun rather than planned out. By ten o'clock, the streets were busy, and people were about their daily activities. Will and Claire walked past a large park, noting groups of people walking about, children playing, and mothers pushing their babies in prams.

"I didn't know the city had such a place in the middle of so many big buildings," Claire said, slowing her step. "Look at all the trees. It's lovely."

"Yes, it is," Will said. He wasn't looking at the trees but rather at her brown lashes and thinking of how her profile looked almost fairy-like.

From the park, Will led Claire on a loop north to the Cathedral of the Madeleine and, from there, west to Temple Square. The temple was visible from quite a distance, but as they approached the building, Claire's step slowed. At the base of the temple on the west side, Claire gazed upward at the giant spires, her head tilted all the way back, her mouth open in awe.

"Took forty years to build it," Will said. "And most of that was the exterior."

"It's beautiful. I've never seen anything like it. I mean, I saw the spires as we walked yesterday, but being right here . . ."

Will looked behind them and noted that one of the many exterior doors of the domed tabernacle was ajar. Sounds of choir singing floated on the air, and when Claire shivered and wrapped her arms around herself, he had an idea. "Let's go in there to listen."

"Are they holding a concert right now, in the middle of the day?" Claire asked, turning around. Her voice sounded skeptical, but her face had lit up with anticipation.

"I have no idea," Will said. "But I imagine we can slip inside, warm up a bit, and listen from one of the back benches." He'd done as much during the time he'd lived with his aunt, coming here to hear the Mormon Tabernacle Choir practicing. He had never gone to a concert, although the choir held them regularly, often on Sundays. From time to time, he'd found himself in need of spiritual nourishment, and he'd been able to find it on weekdays. Aunt Rhoda's husband, Uncle Gentry, wasn't religious, and he frowned on anyone attending services or even talking about religion. By attending weekday practices, Will could hear the choir without his uncle ever knowing.

Will and Claire strolled to the open door and peered in. Sure enough, at one end of the tabernacle, the choir members sat in their seats before the grand organ. Throughout the rest of the building, a few people were scattered about the benches.

"Amazing acoustics," Will said. "They say you can hear a pin drop from the other side—when it's otherwise silent, of course."

When Claire didn't reply right away, he looked over to make sure she was all right. She wore a faint smile.

"Claire?" he whispered.

"It's beautiful," she said, then shook her head. "I keep saying that, but it's true. And I mean the building and the music both."

Will pulled the door open farther and beckoned for Claire to come inside. She stomped her boots free of snow, then stepped in, her face lifting as she took in the sight of the interior: the organ, the balcony, the choir, the benches. Will saw the building with new eyes and remembered his own first impression—how amazing the place had seemed the first time.

Will took Claire's hand and led her to a bench. Without releasing his hand, she sat and scooted over, making room for him. He lowered to the seat, hotly aware of her small, delicate hand in his big, rough one. He ventured a quick peek at his fingers but looked away just as fast, annoyed with himself for not cleaning his fingernails better; elegant Claire would think less of him. Hopefully she wouldn't notice.

Somehow, having Claire's good opinion mattered. Will wished he could go back in time and tell his younger self not to do so many of the awful things he'd done in an attempt to get her attention. Perhaps then she would see him as more than the pesky boy from home.

Claire looked over, warming Will inside. She gently squeezed his hand with hers—and looked down at their joined hands. Of course, she'd see his dirty nails and be disgusted with them. Will flushed. As Claire returned her attention to the choir, Will watched her from the corner of his eye. She didn't *look* disgusted.

That's something, at least. But not enough. He didn't want to be only not-disgusting in her eyes. He wanted to be worthy of her attention. Someone she could *admire*.

They stayed in the tabernacle for four songs, after which the choir appeared to be adjourning, so Will and Claire decided to leave. As they stepped outside, Claire hugged herself against the cold. "It was much warmer in there, wasn't it?" she said with a laugh.

"Shall we find a restaurant? I imagine you're famished. Breakfast was hours ago."

"After eating two baskets of biscuits, I shouldn't be hungry."

"Oh, I ate my fair share," Will interjected.

"Be that as it may, I *am* hungry."

They walked along, looking at various restaurants, when they noticed several storefronts with the same paper in the window—a notice of some kind. Curious, they walked over to read the notice in the window of a sweets shop.

Christmas Eve Dance
7 in the evening until midnight
Hotel Utah

The very dance to which Will had hoped to take Claire. After walking for so much of the day, would she prefer to stay in her hotel room and rest? The event would be fancy; he hadn't packed anything appropriate to wear.

The thought had scarcely crossed his mind when Claire cried, "A dance! Oh, Will, we should go."

"Really?" Will asked, pleased. "I'd heard of the dance, but I wasn't sure—"

"I *adore* dancing." She tilted her head, and her eyes looked him over, up and down. "I'd wager you're quite good at it."

You'd lose that wager. But he wasn't about to admit being a sorry dancer. He'd fake his way around the dance floor, doing his best not to step on her toes—or anyone else's—if it meant he got to spend the evening with Claire Jennings.

"Let's go. I'll need to buy some trousers first, but I've needed new ones for some time anyway."

"Oh, we have plenty of time for that," Claire said. "I might even use some of the money I've saved to buy a comb for my hair." She marched on in the exact direction of the department store.

"I didn't expect you to learn the city so quickly," he said. "Or is it just the locations of clothing stores you memorize so easily?"

She laughed and pointed up and across the street, where large letters proclaimed ZCMI. "I'm terrible at directions, but I *can* read." She laughed but then ran four steps ahead of him, as if she feared retaliation of some sort. He just might have tried to tease her had she not hurried out of reach.

Five

With the promise of shopping, Claire forgot about eating until she and Will emerged from ZCMI an hour later. At that point, they were both beyond famished. Claire could have eaten several baskets of biscuits if they had been laid before her. They carried their parcels to a café with a wreath on the door. Bells on a ribbon jingled as they pushed the door open, and for a moment, Claire felt a pang of homesickness.

What would her family tree look like? She glanced at Will, wondering if the wreath made him miss home too—and wondering what his family's wreath looked like.

Neither of them would ever know. She hoped he wouldn't regret staying in the city with her.

Inside the café, they ate sandwiches and sliced apples as a late lunch and early supper. Then they headed back to the hotel, each carrying a parcel wrapped in brown paper, neither letting the other see inside. As they walked, Claire eyed Will's package, which was large enough that he carried it with both hands. She suspected that he'd bought a shirt in addition to trousers. Maybe shoes too. Possibly more.

Her package contained a pearl-edged comb and a beautiful shawl with several shades of violet, like the color of the mountains before dawn. She imagined that knitting the wispy lace must have taken some time. At the thought of wearing the comb and shawl that night while dancing with Will, a giddy thrill shot through her.

Inside the hotel, as they crossed the lobby to the stairs, neither spoke. Will walked past his door and escorted Claire to her room first. They'd spent most of the return walk in pleasant silence, something she wouldn't have guessed possible with Will Rhodes. But their stroll through the snowy city streets had been nice.

When she opened her clutch purse to find her key, Will spoke.

He checked the time on his pocket watch. "It's half past five. If we leave in an hour for the dance, we'll be right on time. Is that enough time for you to get ready?"

"Absolutely. Now where is my key?" She would have to hurry if she hoped to not look a fright within sixty minutes, but she didn't want to look like those girls who spent their lives before a mirror. "I'll meet you in the lobby at half past six."

Victorious, she withdrew her key and looked up to find Will gazing at her intently with hazel eyes. She couldn't look away. Something in her middle flipped and flopped deliciously, and she had to remind herself to breathe.

But it's Will, the boy who put a spider in your lunch pail.

It was no use. He was also a grown man who had lost all traces of a boyish face and who now looked strong enough to rip a tree right out of the ground. And he was looking at her as if she were the only woman in the world. The cover of his pocket watch snapped closed, ending the moment with a jolt. Will cleared his throat.

"One hour, then." His eyes seemed unable to determine where to focus—her face, the wall, the carpet, his hands. A distinctive shade of pink appeared on his neck and climbed to his face. Was he self-conscious because she'd caught him staring at her? The thought made Claire bite her lip with pleasure and turn to hide a smile.

Will cleared his throat yet again and opened his mouth to speak. "So. An hour," he said again. "Um . . . Should be a fun distraction, eh?" He took one step backward and then another but bumped into the wall, then nearly tripped altogether. He righted himself, flushing red, then raised a hand in a wave and turned to go to his room.

Claire slipped inside her room, closed the door, and leaned against it, reliving the moment, committing it to memory. She might never experience such a thing again—especially from a man such as William Rhodes—so she was determined to save the memory as a cherished letter. She'd tuck it away into a special spot of her mind from which she could pull it out and relive it at any time she wished.

When her heart had regained its usual pace—or almost, anyway—she turned her attention to getting ready for the dance. Fortunately, she had packed a formal gown. It was a gift from the Hudsons' daughter, who had determined that it was several seasons too old for her to wear. Yet the pale pink gown was several seasons newer, and far nicer, than any gown Claire owned. She'd planned to bring it home for safe keeping, but using it tonight would be even better.

Seventy minutes later, she dabbed rose water under her ears and on her wrists, checked her hair—and the new comb—one last time and admired the shawl. She wasn't positive, but she was almost sure that it made her blue eyes look almost violet, and she quite liked the effect.

I hope he likes it too.

Giddy butterflies again. She placed a hand on her middle to calm the fluttering. She vowed to enjoy the evening without worrying that Will probably saw her as an entertaining dalliance. After all, he'd called the evening a distraction.

Tonight isn't about the heart, she thought as she flounced to the door. *It is about distraction—about having a delightful time.*

She hurried toward the staircase, then slowed at the top step so she wouldn't stumble. One step at a time, she walked down the first set of steps to the landing and then turned to the left and went down the second set, which brought her to the final landing facing the lobby. Claire caught her image in the mirror on the landing; she was beautiful tonight. She couldn't hold back a smile.

She didn't spot Will until he stood from a sofa. He looked so different: his hair was slicked back, and he was wearing an entirely new suit that emphasized his broad shoulders. She had half a moment to wonder if he'd had the suit delivered—and if, by some miracle, it hadn't needed tailoring—before he reached the foot of the stairs and put out his hand.

Claire carefully stepped down the last of the stairs, holding the banister until she took Will's hand.

"You're beautiful," he said softly, then drew her close. Before she could reply, he gestured toward the doors. "I've hired a carriage so you don't have to ruin your dress in the snow."

The ride was short but cozy. Claire would have been quite happy to spend an hour riding beside Will, who had his arm about her shoulders. The moment seemed unreal. She wasn't the kind of girl who let any man get close or pretend that they were in a relationship. Yet here she was sitting next to Will Rhodes in a manner she would have never thought possible unless they'd been courting for some time.

Yet I've known him for years, she reminded herself.

A Taste of Home

But the boy you thought you knew no longer exists, another voice argued.

Before she could fret over the paradox, the carriage had stopped. Will got out and helped her onto the icy sidewalk, and together they entered the Hotel Utah, where they were quickly enveloped by the crowd in the enormous lobby-turned-ballroom. Claire tried not to look too much like a bumbling, inexperienced girl from the country, but she couldn't help gaping at the marble floors, the elegant columns, and the exquisite balcony that looked over the main floor. A staircase far grander than the one at the Peery went up to the next floor, where she was certain that more elegance awaited.

Will led her to the side of the room as they waited for a set to end. A small group of musicians with stringed instruments were gathered in one corner, playing cheerful holiday music. When the set ended, a waltz was announced, and Will did not delay a moment in leading Claire to the floor and taking her into dance position. The touch of his hand at the small of her back was warm and made her want to draw closer to him than was proper. She rested her left hand on his right shoulder and placed her other hand in his outstretched one.

The music began, and Claire and Will whirled about the room to the rhythm, around and around. The world seemed to fall away, leaving the two of them gazing into each other's eyes, locked in a moment Claire wished could go on forever. They danced for hours, stopping occasionally for refreshment and to step outside for a breath of air. It all felt like a dream. When outside, however, the crisp winter chill woke Claire up, making her very conscious of the fact that she really was here dancing with Will after spending an entire day with him.

"Ready to go back in?" Will asked after a few minutes.

She nodded. "I could use another cup of punch before dancing again, though." Her toes were feeling pinched, but she didn't want to ruin the evening by saying so. They could turn purple and bleed for all she cared, and she wouldn't say a word.

Inside, they walked the edge of the floor to the refreshment table. Claire stopped beside a column and watched the dancers, fully expecting Will to fetch her a cup of punch as he had before. When he didn't move right away, she looked up expectantly, thinking that perhaps she'd missed something he'd said.

"Hmm?" she said.

Will's gaze became the steady, intense look from before. She felt ready to melt into the floor, and the feeling had nothing to do with the heat of the room. "I can hardly believe I've spent the day with *the* Claire Jennings. It's been a dream come true."

For a flash, a burst of joy filled Claire's heart, but just as quickly, she pushed it away. Will Rhodes was a jester, a prankster. He didn't have a serious bone in his body.

No matter how handsome his face or how serious the expression on it.

"Careful now," she said, keeping her tone light and teasing. "You could make a girl think you're serious when you talk like that."

A look of confusion—disappointment?—crossed Will's face. "You think—" He shook his head. "Come here." Without further explanation, Will took her hand and led her, not to the dance floor and not to the refreshment table, but up the staircase—and so quickly that she had to lift her skirts and practically run to keep up.

"Is something wrong?" she called over the orchestra.

He didn't answer, just kept going. When they reached the second floor, he looked side to side as if searching for something, then pulled her toward a door to the right. They ducked inside what looked like a chapel—a room with rows of pews and, on the other side, a podium and choir seats. The room, like the rest of the building, was beautiful, but Claire didn't have time to admire it. Will led her to one of the pews and urged her to sit beside him.

"What?" she said and then tried to catch her breath.

Will took both of her hands in his and looked at her, all traces of teasing or lightheartedness gone. "I was serious back there." His eyes seemed to grow a bit glassy as they searched her face.

"I don't know what you mean . . ."

"I think you do," Will said earnestly. "Look, I know we weren't exactly the best of friends growing up."

Quite an understatement.

She shook her head and closed her eyes tight for a moment. When she spoke, she avoided his eyes. "You made my life rather miserable."

"I know. But you must believe me—the boy who did those horrible things did so because he cared." When her eyes widened in disbelief, he rushed on. "A boy doesn't know how to get the attention of a girl who has his heart in her hands."

Claire's brow furrowed. She couldn't make heads or tails of her feelings and Will's words.

"For a long time, I've dreamed that one day, I'd have a chance . . . with you." He looked at their joined hands. "I understand if you still think I'm nothing more than a pest. I do. But I'd like to think that after the time we've spent together the last two days, that I could have a chance. Just a small one." His thumbs gently stroked the tops of her hands, sending little zips of energy up her arms. "May I have that chance?"

She found herself nodding and hoping against hope that doing so wasn't an utterly foolish thing to do—that she wouldn't find her boots strung up on a telegraph pole. Will must have sensed her trepidation because he didn't speak right away. Instead, he raised her hands to his lips and kissed her knuckles, first those of her right hand and then those of her left. She never wanted him to let go, never wanted this moment to end.

But of course, it must.

Will released one of her hands, then reached up to adjust her shawl around her shoulders. "The color brings out your eyes."

She couldn't hold back a smile at that.

Together they walked, silently, out of the chapel, down the stairs, and around the dance floor to the outside doors. Will hailed a buggy, and they rode back to the hotel, still in silence but this time holding hands in addition to Will having his arm around Claire's shoulders.

When they stepped out of the carriage, a group of carolers stopped by the hotel doors and joyfully sang "God Rest Ye Merry Gentlemen," one of her father's favorites. After spending most of Christmas Eve focused on other things—in spite of the trimmed evergreens at the dance—Claire could no longer forget what day it would be in a couple of hours.

At home, her family had likely already gone caroling. With the quarantine, they might have gathered around Joey's bed and sung carols there instead. Mother would be passing around pieces of her special toffee with chopped walnuts. When Claire had been little, sprinkling on the walnuts had been her job.

Now she stood there outside the hotel, listening to carolers, and a wave of sadness washed over her. How would she survive tomorrow? Most businesses would be closed for Christmas Day, so Will couldn't distract her with activities. *Perhaps I'll stay in my room and cry the day away.*

"Claire?" Will said, his voice suddenly filled with concern. "Are you all right?"

His question only made things worse. Tears filled her eyes, and she couldn't speak without them tumbling down her cheeks, so she simply shook her head. But that action sent the tears rolling anyway, so she ventured a short answer. "It's Christmas in a few hours. And I'm not home."

"I'm so sorry." Will pulled her close and held her. With her ear pressed to his chest, she heard the steady, even thumping of his heart, and somehow the strength and constancy were soothing.

He gently urged her toward the hotel doors, for which she was thankful: she couldn't have walked away from the carolers on her own volition. Together they went upstairs, and again Will brought her to her door. This time he found her key and let her in, but of course, he stayed in the hall after she'd stepped across the threshold.

"I'm sorry you're not home," he said quietly.

"I know." Claire turned around and managed a half smile. "And thank you. For everything."

He nodded and closed the door, clicking it shut.

She whispered, "Merry Christmas," then dropped into a chair by the window and cried into her hands. She would miss trimming the tree. She wouldn't be able to pass out the gifts she'd brought with her. She wouldn't see any of her family members until winter had passed and spring had come again.

The street outside was quiet, with few people and fewer vehicles. A faint glow from the electric street lights and some interior lighting revealed individual snowflakes, illuminated like falling halos. She leaned against the windowpane and gazed out onto the peaceful landscape, wishing she was home.

She didn't know how long she sat there staring, but suddenly she blinked at a movement on the street. A figure was walking through the snow—a man in regular work clothes. His hair was still slicked back, though, and she recognized his walk.

For some unknown reason, Will was trudging through the snow, hands in his pockets, head down, late at night on Christmas Eve.

Six

Will couldn't rest. The sadness that had so overcome Claire minutes ago haunted him. Sadness had overcome her after two days of him making her smile and laugh. He paced his room as he took off the suit, wearing a trail in the carpet, as his mother would say if she could see him. He unbuttoned his shirt and tossed it onto the bed beside the suit coat, still uneasy, still wanting to hold Claire in his arms, to find a way to make her happy again.

But he couldn't do it—and not for lack of trying. He'd diverted her for a time, but in the end, he wasn't her family, and Salt Lake wasn't her home. Instead of reaching for his nightclothes, he eyed his work pants and shirt, which were draped over the back of a chair. He needed air to clear his head and exercise so he could stop pacing the room. He put on his old clothes and coat, then grabbed his room key and headed down the stairs and out to Broadway Street, where he shoved his hands into his coat pockets and walked the dark streets of Salt Lake City. The light from electric streetlamps reflected off the snow, making the night brighter than it should have been for the hour.

Will walked several blocks east, north, west, and north again, paying no mind as to where he was going. Where he went didn't matter. What mattered was letting his mind work like a machine, like gears going round and round, trying to solve the problem of Claire's sadness. His chest ached at the memory of her teary eyes—she'd tried to hide her tears, but the music of the carolers had brought back the fact that it was Christmas and she wasn't home.

He wasn't her home. Will's ache increased. He wanted to be her home. Forget diverting her for a day or two; he wanted to be with Claire always.

He couldn't think on that, not while she was under a weight so heavy that all she felt was melancholy.

How can I lift her burden? That was what his focus needed to be. He didn't care what it took. He'd do anything to make her happy again. If she told him that embracing Mr. Roberts as his father would make her happy, he'd have done so in a blink. Somehow, forgiving the man who'd interloped on Will's family seemed far easier than making the sides of Claire's mouth turn up and her eyes light up again.

Will kicked a lump of snow and hunkered deeper into his coat, flipping the collar up. He thought of the conversation he and Claire had had on the train about family Christmas traditions. He knew that when morning came and she remembered anew what her family was doing without her, she'd crumble. When she didn't get a bite of her mother's walnut-covered toffee . . .

His head popped up, and his step came up short. Of course. He could give her at least one tradition. It wouldn't be her mother's toffee, but surely that sweet shop they'd passed earlier had something comparable. He hurried toward that part of town, trying to remember exactly where he'd seen the store. When he reached the shop, the interior was dark, and a sign that read *Closed* hung in the window. Even so, he reached for the door handle and pulled. Locked.

Of course the shop was closed. Like most reasonable people, the shop owners and their employees were with their families this late on a Christmas Eve. Once again, Will trudged onward, this time toward ZCMI, knowing full well its doors would almost surely be locked too. But he had to check. He needed to find a way to bring Claire some small measure of Christmas joy.

What about Aunt Rhoda? He shook his head at his own thought. His aunt lived in the Avenues neighborhood. By the time he walked over there, it would be well past midnight. At that hour, she'd be unlikely to open the door to a strange knock. Besides, what could he expect of his aunt—for her to call out for Santa, who would magically appear with a box of toffee?

After confirming that the department store was closed, Will had to admit that Aunt Rhoda seemed like his only option. She might have made some toffee for Christmas—or received some from a friend as a gift. Hopefully she wouldn't feel bad that he hadn't let her know he was in town.

He made his way to the Avenues, suddenly unsure of where his aunt's house stood. Everything looked different at night and in the winter, giving the streets a changed appearance from what he remembered. At last he spotted the lamppost with the hanging sign bearing Rhoda's married name, Jensen, written in black paint against a white background. He'd found the correct house.

Will stood before his aunt's house and debated again, even though he'd made the trek with every intention of knocking on the door. He looked upward. Trails of smoke spiraled from the chimney—the remains of the evening's fire. The windows were dark save for a small glow from a side window near the back—the kitchen, if memory served. The light was probably from a candle or small lantern. Someone was up.

Determining that he'd have better luck knocking on the back door, Will walked along the drive flanking the house, treading through two or three inches of snow. He was glad he'd worn his sturdy boots. As he reached the kitchen window, he slowed and peered inside, trying to make out who was still awake.

Aunt Rhoda, I hope.

The silhouette of a bun moved across the pane. Will reached into the flower beds, which were dead for the winter, and brushed aside enough snow to find a pebble. He flung it. The pebble pinged off the glass, and although it sounded loud in the quiet of the neighborhood, he wondered if it had made enough noise to be heard inside. Rhoda picked up a dishcloth and wiped the fogginess from the window and then peered out, shading her eyes to help her see.

Will waved his arms and called out, "Rhoda! Aunt Rhoda, it's me, Will!"

She startled, tossed the cloth to the side, and cranked the window open a couple of inches. "Will? What in tarnation are you doing in my yard so late on Christmas Eve?"

He stomped his feet to keep them from freezing. "Can I come in? I'll explain everything."

"Of course," she said. "Come around back. I'll let you right in."

She cranked the window closed, and Will headed for the back door. When it opened, Aunt Rhoda's face appeared with a bright smile in spite of tired eyes. Will was lucky she hadn't retired for the night. "Come in, come in," she said, standing aside.

He stamped the snow off his boots, then crossed the threshold, grateful for the coal stove still giving off heat. He hadn't realized how cold he'd gotten.

"Come sit down in the kitchen. You'll have to disregard

the dollhouse. Gentry got it into his head to make it for the girls for Christmas, and I've been spending the last few hours gluing on the final touches."

Will removed his coat and hat, hanging them on a wooden coat rack his father had made years ago. Then he followed Aunt Rhoda to the kitchen and sat at the table. The dollhouse was narrow and tall, with three stories and two staircases. Each room was decorated with real wallpaper and curtains that Rhoda had likely hand-sewn from fabric scraps. Curling wooden trim like wooden lace framed the roof edge.

"The girls will love it," he predicted.

"I hope so," Rhoda said, rubbing her eyes. "It's been far more work than we anticipated."

"What's left? Maybe I can help."

"I could use another set of hands, but first, tell me what brought you here in the middle of the night, with snow coming down, and after Christmas has officially begun." She pulled out the chair beside him and sat on it, waiting for his reply expectantly.

Will glanced at the clock hanging above the stove. Sure enough, it was a quarter past midnight. "I was traveling home for the holiday with Claire Jennings. She has a position as a housekeeper in California. You remember her?"

His aunt nodded. "I believe so. Pretty thing, fair, the oldest of several siblings? Her family lives down the road from your family."

"Right." Then Will launched into the crux of the situation—Joey's measles, the quarantine, and how Claire would have lost her job if she'd gone home for Christmas.

"How sad," Rhoda said. "I remember how her family always celebrated the holiday longer and bigger than anyone else in town."

Will leaned toward his aunt with his plea. "She's beside herself. I've spent every moment trying to keep her spirits up, but there is no changing the fact that it's Christmas, and that fact alone makes her cry."

Rhoda studied his face. "You love her," she said in wonder.

His head snapped up. "What?"

"Don't deny it. You're totally gone over her. I can tell. You're sad because she's sad. You want to fix it. And . . . your ears are turning bright pink."

Will suddenly wished he hadn't taken off his hat. "I, uh . . ." He fought the heat building in his face, but the more he tried to resist, the more the heat of the blush intensified. "I have an idea of what might lift her spirits. She misses her mother's Christmas toffee—homemade toffee with walnuts on top. I hoped to find some in a local store but didn't think of it until every store had closed. I don't suppose that . . . Do you have any toffee I could take off your hands? I'd replace it as soon as I can."

Rhoda's smile broadened. "To think that my nephew is so besotted over a girl that he tramped through inches of snow in hopes of procuring a bit of toffee. I never would have thought it of you. You've grown up, Will."

The compliment meant little at the moment. Will just wanted an answer. "Do you have any toffee?"

"No."

The single word cut to his heart. *Now what?*

"But," Rhoda went on, raising a finger, "I could make a batch if you're willing to wait. I'd need you to glue on the rest of the shingles, though, because I won't have the time."

"Consider it done," Will said, perking up. "I could glue shingles to a thousand toy houses."

"I think I'm getting the better end of the deal." With a laugh, Rhoda patted his shoulder and stood. "The supplies are on the other side of the table. Follow the pattern of the shingles already glued on. It's not hard—just time consuming. I'll be by the stove."

Will went to work, determined to do a perfect job to thank his aunt, who had started up the fire in the stove again and was bustling about, getting sugar and butter, boiling them and testing the temperature, chopping nuts, and preparing a metal tray with a layer of parchment. At last she deemed the buttery-smelling toffee ready to set. She poured it from the pan and smoothed it over the parchment. Then she sprinkled spoonfuls of chopped nuts onto the toffee and gently pressed the nuts into the toffee's surface with buttered fingers, which Will supposed helped her fingers to not get too sticky. He watched each step eagerly, but now that the toffee was in the tray, he wasn't sure what happened next.

"It needs to harden before we can break it into pieces," Rhoda said. "The fastest way to harden it is to put it outside in the cold."

Rhoda set the tray outside, then washed the newly dirtied dishes. Will placed the last few shingles on the house. His eyes had grown heavy, his body yearning for sleep. He rested his arms on the table and put his forehead against them—just to rest his eyes a moment. Or so he thought.

The next thing he knew, someone was jostling his shoulder, calling his name. He opened his eyes and looked about the dim kitchen, trying to orient himself. The room was light but not from the lantern—from the morning sun breaking over the mountains.

"Will, it's morning. The toffee is ready." His aunt's voice brought him back to consciousness.

It was Christmas morning. Everything came back in a flood—why he was in Salt Lake, why he'd come to Aunt Rhoda. Will sat up and turned to his aunt, who was freshly dressed, with her hair in a new, smooth bun instead of the wispy one from the night before. She held out a white box decorated with a cheerful red bow, two jingle bells, and a sprig from a fir tree. The package looked like Christmas itself, ready to be opened up and to spill its joy.

"It turned out?" Will asked, half afraid that if he touched the box, the night—the dance with Claire, his aunt, the box of toffee—would all prove to be a dream.

A Taste of Home

"Beautifully. I took a taste to be sure and saved a piece for you." Aunt Rhoda held in her other hand a piece of toffee—shiny and tan, with what Will thought looked to be the perfect amount of nuts.

Will took the toffee and bit off a chunk. The buttery sweetness engulfed his mouth, and he inadvertently groaned with pleasure. "Delicious."

"Glad you think so," Aunt Rhoda said, beaming with pride. "Now go. I've packed some muffins; you must be starving."

"Thank you," Will said, mouth already watering.

"I woke you now because I wasn't sure if you'd want to be around when the little ones wake up and run for their gifts."

Will didn't want to be around for Uncle Gentry to see either.

When Aunt Rhoda spoke next, it was in a whisper. "Your stepfather may not be the best man in the world," she said, as if she could read Will's mind. "In fact, he's far from the perfect man. In some ways, I think he's a scoundrel. But . . . your mother loves him, and she chose him. I have a feeling that soon, she'll need her family more than ever."

Will nodded, understanding with grudging acceptance. If Mr. Roberts proved to have the mettle that Will—and, apparently, Aunt Rhoda—suspected, then Mother would indeed need her older sister, Rhoda, and her eldest child, Will. He resolved to not let anything, not even Mr. Roberts, get in the way of his relationship with his mother.

He also resolved to treat Claire in such a way that those who knew him would know that she was happy and treated with respect and love. His throat tightened as he reached for the box, so beautifully wrapped.

His eyes connected with Aunt Rhoda's, and they smiled at each other knowingly. Mr. Roberts was a link they unwillingly shared, but they were on the same side of the war, fighting for his mother.

"Thank you for helping me, Aunt Rhoda. This all means so much." Footsteps sounded upstairs, and Will glanced upward. "I'd better go."

Rhoda nodded and followed him to the back door, where she held the box as he put on his coat and hat. After a hug, she pressed the box into his hands. She reached for a sack on the floor and gave it to him too. "Here. I put some ornaments inside. Take a branch from the yard. She needs a tree."

"Good idea," he said, taking the bag and the box.

She put a hand to his cheek in the same way Mother often did. "I hope Claire knows how lucky she is."

Looking into her eyes, he grappled with his emotions. "I hope so too."

Seven

Claire looked at herself in the mirror above the washbasin and grimaced. Red, blotchy skin. Bloodshot eyes. Hair wild and unkempt because she hadn't taken it down after the dance. All she'd done was remove the beautiful comb—something she'd treasure after such a wonderful night with Will—and her dress. But then her sadness over missing Christmas overcame her; she'd thrown herself onto her bed and cried herself to sleep.

Even a drunkard after an all-night drinking party would look better. She turned from the mirror, vowing to avoid it for the rest of the day. She could finish her hotel stay—finish Christmas—in this room. She'd order room service and see no one.

Least of all Will. If he'd thought her beautiful last night, he couldn't possibly think so this morning. Instead, if he were to see her now, he'd be liable to turn tail back to

California. She slipped the comb from the dressing table into her clutch, unwilling to look at it. Right now, it represented a man she cared for but who might not care for her so much after all. And it represented the most miserable Christmas of her life.

She sat on the bed and worked at taking the pins out of her hair, not for the sake of her appearance but because her scalp hurt and she wanted to brush out the last bit of evidence of the night before. Halfway through the job, a knock sounded on her door. She realized that she hadn't put out the placard requesting privacy. Hair half up, half down, Claire tiptoed to the door in the other room and waited to hear more from the person on the other side. Usually the housekeeper called out, and if she heard nothing from a guest, then entered to clean the room. But no one called out.

Claire wished she could see to the other side of the door. There was no knowing who was on the other side, so she didn't dare speak and reveal her presence. And she wanted to be left alone. A second set of knocks sounded—this set more insistent—followed by a voice she knew.

"Claire, are you all right? I know you're in there."

Why had Will come to her room now? Perhaps he wanted to go out for breakfast. They hadn't arranged anything for today. Why not use a note like before? Claire wore her robe, so she was decently covered, but she looked like a cat that had been fished from a pond. She pushed some hair out of her eyes and felt the rat's nest that was her hair.

Will *couldn't* see her this way. She wouldn't allow it. He would think he'd been mad to say she was pretty, and he'd have plenty of fodder for jokes to tell his friends about the Jennings girl. She couldn't bear the thought.

I can't speak to him. Not now. She'd be too likely to burst into tears again—another reason for Will to think her silly. Claire looked about frantically for a scrap of paper and found one with a pencil on the side table. She scrawled a quick note.

A Taste of Home

Woke unwell. Staying indoors to rest. —C

She should probably have included *Merry Christmas*, but the thought had sent her hand to trembling. The simple note would have to do. She slipped it under the door, then heard movement on the other side as Will picked up the paper.

"Claire, please open the door," he said. "I have something for you, and I want to see you, just for a moment, to wish you a Merry Christmas. Please?"

His pleading almost worked—until he mentioned what day it was. She shook her head and waited, silently, hoping to hear his footsteps move away yet, at the same time, hoping he'd stay.

"I'm not leaving. I'll stay out here all day," Will said. There was a gentle thud, as if his forehead rested against the door. "Just open up. Just for a minute."

A battle raged inside Claire. If she let him in, he'd see her at her worst. He might joke about the sight for years to come. Or . . . if he was earnest about the feelings he'd expressed last night, he might change his mind after seeing her this way. Or he might be the man she hoped he was and still care.

She analyzed her heart. What did *she* feel toward Will Rhodes—not the boy who had tortured her but the man she'd spent time with? Thoughts of his smile, his touch, his kindness all warmed her, spreading heat throughout her chest and making her smile.

That decides it.

This moment would tell her what Will's true character was. If the last two days had been nothing but entertainment for him, at least she would know. Just as she reached for the doorknob, bells rang out in the distance, playing "O Come, All Ye Faithful." Her heart ached anew, but she shook off the sadness and, without letting herself think beyond her next action, opened the door. In almost the same motion, she turned and walked to the couch. At least that way, he wouldn't see her face immediately. She sat on the sofa, keeping her face down. Will stepped into the room, and her heart fluttered in spite of herself.

"I brought you something."

Claire slowly raised her eyes. Will held a fir branch and a paper sack in one hand and a beautifully wrapped gift in the other. Her brows drew together. "I—I don't understand."

He stepped farther into the room. "This here will be your tree—our Christmas tree. It's not very big, but I imagine its size will make it easy to prop in the corner, seeing as we don't have any other way to hold it up."

"How sweet." Claire found herself smiling a little. The "tree" was quite pathetic, but truly, it was the thought that counted. He'd brought her a tree in the only way he could. And he hadn't commented on her face. *Maybe he hasn't noticed how awful I look.*

Will settled the tree in a corner by the window. "There. And this"—he held up the paper sack—"has a few ornaments with which to trim the tree. It's not a lot, but it's the best I could do on short notice."

Claire stood and crossed to him. She took the bag and peered inside. A single strand of homemade cranberry garland lay in the bottom with half a dozen gold balls. "You got me real ornaments," she said with wonder.

"It's all Santa's doing," he said, brushing her gratitude off with a wave. He gestured toward the tree, and Claire stepped forward with the paper bag. Transferring the contents to the tree took only moments, but when she stepped back, the result was quite pleasant.

"Hmm," Will said. "We're still missing something."

"Oh?" Claire glanced at him briefly, then returned to admiring her little tree. She still didn't want to face Will directly but watched him from the corner of her eye. Will stroked his chin dramatically as if in deep thought. His hair was utterly mussed, yet he was as handsome as he'd been last night, and she found him utterly irresistible this way. "So tell me," she said, hoping her voice was even. "What's missing?"

The floorboards creaked behind her—he'd stepped closer. She felt his hand on her shoulder, then swallowed nervously as he turned her about to face him. She almost protested, but the moment he'd touched her, she realized that she *wanted* to look into his hazel eyes even though her eyes were bloodshot and her skin was splotchy and her hair looked little better than a beaver's dam. She only hoped he'd try to look past all that. Maybe he could, if he felt as he claimed to last night.

They were standing toe to toe. She slowly raised her gaze from his work boots to his face. When their eyes met, she gulped and waited for him to speak.

"I couldn't sleep last night," he said. "I paced my room until I decided to pace outside."

"I saw you walk away," she said softly. "Where did you go?"

"Nowhere at first. I just wanted to find a way to make you smile again. It took me all night, but with a little help . . ." He held out the wrapped box. "Even though you can't be home, hopefully this will bring you a bit of Christmas."

Claire took the box and untied the ribbon. The bells and sprig fell to the ground unheeded as she removed the lid. Beneath the lid were a dozen or more pieces of toffee—walnut-covered toffee, just like Mother's. Her vision swam. "How? Will . . ."

"Taste it." He selected a piece and offered it to her.

Wordlessly, she bit it, enjoying the touch of his fingers as much as the toffee. She let the flavor consume her.

"Mmm." She closed her eyes to savor the taste. She leaned in, breathing the scent of the box. She swallowed the toffee, lowered the box, and grinned. *"Now* it's Christmas." Claire selected another piece of toffee and bit some off.

Another wave of Christmas magic brought her home for a moment.

Will stepped closer, his face showing a range of emotions. "Last night, I knew you were hurting, and that made me hurt."

He reached forward and cupped her face in his hands. The slightest turn of her head, and she could kiss his thumb. She forced herself not to but was growing lightheaded having him so close.

"Claire, I want to make you happy—to work at it for my whole life. Even when times get hard, I want to go through those times together."

One of his thumbs, once so close to her lips, now stroked her cheek. Claire felt heady and wondered if she should sit down, but she wouldn't move and lose this moment for a thousand pounds of toffee.

"No more practical jokes," Will said. "No more trash bins or spiders or scissors or—"

In a rush, Claire closed the distance between them and grasped Will's face with both of her hands. She pushed herself onto her toes to reach him but paused a fraction of an inch from his mouth—then wondered if she'd gone mad. Maybe this wasn't what he'd meant. Maybe . . .

Will grinned, then laughed as if he'd conquered the summit of the highest mountain, then kissed her. Had he not been holding her, she might have dropped to the floor in a puddle of warmth.

When Will and Claire broke apart, she knew that her future would hold many more stories about silly times, happy times, and serious times.

And toffee with walnuts. Every Christmas. Because toffee meant home.

ABOUT ANNETTE LYON

Annette Lyon is a Whitney Award winner, a two-time recipient of Utah's Best of State medal for fiction, and a four-time publication award winner from the League of Utah Writers, including the Silver Quill Award in 2013 for *Paige*. She's the author of more than a dozen novels, almost as many novellas, several nonfiction books, and over one hundred twenty magazine articles. Annette is a cum laude graduate from BYU with a degree in English. When she's not writing, knitting, or eating chocolate, she can be found mothering and avoiding the spots on the kitchen floor.

Sign up for her newsletter at:
http://annettelyon.com/contact

Find her online:
Website: http://AnnetteLyon.com
Blog: http://blog.AnnetteLyon.com
Twitter: @AnnetteLyon
Facebook: http://Facebook.com/AnnetteLyon
Pinterest: http://Pinterest.com/AnnetteLyon

My Modern Girl

by Becca Wilhite

One

1924

"Here's what I don't want. I don't want you to proclaim your undying love. Is that too much to ask?" Margie tried not to grin through her words as she tugged her skirt closer to her knees. She would never get used to this hemline.

Henry gave a solemn nod and didn't say a word. She went on.

"It's 1924, and I'm a modern girl, Henry. Undying love is so old-fashioned. Any girl on her way to the city to make her way knows that she can't leave home if she's all tied down."

Henry nodded again, and Margie felt her face heating. She no longer had to try not to grin; a grin was the last thing coming. Wasn't he going to say anything at all? Maybe she'd been too convincing. As she stepped closer, he moved back.

Not enough to be out of her reach, exactly, but certainly enough to make her drop her arm and her eyes.

She stared at the flowers beside her feet. The little garden that her father grew for Mama was bursting with color. June was the perfect time for growing too attached to this silly little garden. She turned away, staring instead at the road that skipped over the rolling hills, the road that would carry her away from this tiny life into the real world of New York City.

"All right, then. I'm going." She held out her hand as if to close a business deal.

Henry shook his head. "You may have changed, Margie, but you haven't changed that much." He took both of her hands in his and stepped closer. She had a moment to wonder how much he thought she'd changed before he closed the distance between them and wrapped her own arms behind her back, pulling her close. His kiss, tender and insistent, spoke the words he wouldn't—or couldn't—say. That he would miss her. He wanted her to stay. He wouldn't stand in the way of her dreams.

Margie didn't need to hear the words again. He'd hinted at them, in his quiet way, for the past several months as Margie had made her plans. But somehow, just now, Margie had a hard time focusing on those plans. She had trouble focusing on anything except his hands on her back and his mouth against hers. She felt a breeze play over the backs of her knees and remembered that she was a modern girl. Modern girls didn't get swoony in the oversized arms of coal workers. Modern girls found fun and giddy pleasure on dance floors and in clubs, with a long string of artistic young men in tailored suits and shiny shoes. She knew it. She read *Harper's* magazine.

Modern girls didn't sigh over handpicked wildflowers tied with knitting yarn, even when those flowers smelled like a perfect Western Pennsylvania summer. And they didn't admit to sentimentality. Nobody needed to know that

Margie packed the crooked, lumpy glass vase Henry had made her, with its one collapsed side and its swirling red and orange colors like a maple tree in autumn.

Modern girls didn't go weak-kneed kissing boys they'd known all their lives.

She pushed away. "I need to go." Her breathlessness embarrassed her, and it would certainly give Henry the wrong idea. "Have a little fun while I'm gone, won't you?" She gave his chest a playful swat.

He cleared his throat, but if he'd planned to say anything, it didn't come out.

"Goodbye, Henry. Write to me if you'd like." She turned and waved over her shoulder like she'd seen Clara Bow do in a film. She found herself annoyed that Henry wasn't walking away. He was ruining her exit. Would he really stand there as she got into her father's car and they drove away? Just stand there and watch her go?

As she stepped over the bluebells, she heard Henry say something. He kept it mostly under his breath, but it could have been "I'll make you proud." Or it might have been "I'll break the plow," so she decided to ignore it. She climbed into the front seat and squeezed the horn.

"Daddy, let's go," she called, determined not to look back at Henry.

Her father slid into the car beside her and tugged his hat lower on his forehead. "You're sure you're ready to go, then?"

"Oh, Daddy. I feel like I've always been ready for this." She leaned over and hugged his arm. "New York City, here I come."

Driving to the train station, her father made very little conversation, which was just how Margie liked it. When they reached the platform, he lifted her cases out of the car and put them on the ground.

He took her by the shoulders and smiled down into her eyes. "Oh, Margie, Margie girl. Look at you." He brought a hand to the side of her face, and she could see him searching her features for the little girl she'd been. Or maybe for signs of the lady she was becoming.

"You don't need to remind me to be careful or to be smart or to write to Mama or to look before I cross a street. I'm ready. It's time for me to go." She leaned up and kissed his cheek, blinking away something that prickled behind her eyes.

The train whistle blew, and she stepped aboard, hands full of cases and heart full of hope. This, she thought, is really what it means to be modern.

Two

Macy's was the largest department store in the world. All of the newspapers were talking about it. The articles gave details about square feet that made Margie's head spin. All she knew was that she was terribly glad she had a job here. She glanced at her nametag, a hard plastic rectangle that read "Betty." When she'd finished her training and they'd given her the tag, she'd asked about the name.

"In a few months, if everything goes well, you'll get a name tag of your own," her trainer had said. "Until then, you'll wear the one every new girl wears. Congratulations, Betty."

Somehow, she knew she should be offended. At least a little hurt. But she couldn't manage feeling anything but excited. She was a Macy's Betty, selling gloves to the rich and famous, or at least that was her plan.

She waved across the sales floor at the girl with the chestnut-colored bob. The girl glanced around, saw that they were alone, and left her counter.

"Hi," Margie said, admiring the girl's short hair. "I'm Margie."

"Betty."

"No, it's just my new nametag."

"Not you. Me. I'm Betty."

Margie laughed. "Betty really?"

"You've got it. I'm Betty-Betty. We all get to wear the tags, but I've never met another sales girl who can wear it like I do. I'm sure that at one time, there were at least a couple of girls who were really named Betty. I mean, they have the nametags. But for me, it so happened to be accurate."

Margie loved this girl's breathless, continuous talking. Even if it was nonsense, it felt free and passionate and completely modern.

"They've just moved me up from belts and suspenders. I think I'm going to like the change." Betty patted Margie's arm and grinned.

A woman walked into the department, dripping with strands of beads. Her skirt swished above her knees. Her hair was more than bobbed; it was shingled. Black slashes lined her eyes. She seemed to follow her hips across the floor. Margie and Betty watched her, slack-jawed.

"I need a scarf," she breathed. Her voice, low and deep, carried across the sales floor like a wave on the wind.

Betty reacted first. "A scarf. Of course. Come with me, please." She scrambled back to her counter.

The woman stood at a diagonal, one leg out to the side and her opposite hand on her hip. She looked like a drawing from *Harper's*. Everything about her looked stylish, from her hair to her dress, all the way down to her cunning little shoes.

Margie could now wear the skirt that only almost covered her knees without shame, but if she really wanted to embrace the flapper life, she'd have to get rid of her curls.

Her perfect Gibson Girl hair was, unfortunately, a decade too late. She could have been the height of fashion ten years ago, but who needed to be the height of fashion at the age of nine? She fingered her hair.

"I'm doing it," Margie murmured.

"Doing what?"

Margie startled at the voice and turned to see a young man standing very near the glove counter. She straightened and put on what she hoped was a professional smile rather than an embarrassed grin.

"How can I help you, sir?" She remembered to make eye contact and give the customer her full attention.

"I'm not sure what I came looking for, but I'll let you know if I find it." He smiled, running his very clean fingers over the seams in a pair of driving gloves. When he looked from the gloves to her, Margie wasn't at all sure he was talking about buying anything.

"You're new here, aren't you?" he asked, again looking from the gloves to Margie as if somehow he knew how it magnified his dark, thick eyelashes when he looked through them.

"I am," she replied, trying to manage the proper balance of aloof and flirtatious they'd taught her in training. "Do you spend a great deal of time in the glove department? Enough to know one sales girl from another?"

"I'd remember you," he said.

She blushed and smiled and tried to decide if she was more pleased or more embarrassed. Before she could formulate a response, he spoke again.

"Nobody in the city has hair like that anymore."

She turned to lift a pair of gloves off the shelf behind her, but really to recompose her face. Had he just said what she thought he did? Was he trying to offend her? Or trying to help her fit in?

"Now that I know where to find you, I'll be around," he said. "We'll get to know each other very well." He drummed his perfect, clean hands on the glass counter. He seemed to be leaving.

"You buy a lot of gloves?" What was she doing? She was embarrassed, wasn't she? She wanted him to go. But she wasn't so sure she wanted him to go. Maybe she needed someone in her life who would tell her how to be a New Yorker.

He leaned over the counter and lowered his voice. "I'm a courier. I help shoppers with packages," he pointed to the elegant lady at Betty's counter. "Shoppers such as this lovely woman, who will buy a small package she could probably fit into her purse, but she'll pay me to carry it to her waiting car or deliver it to her apartment."

"Sounds exciting," Margie said.

"No such thing. But it has its perks." He winked at her. "I'm Leo. Leo Spinelli."

"It's a pleasure, Mr. Spinelli."

"And you?" he asked, leaning even farther over the counter.

"You can call me Betty." She smiled, tapping her fingernail against her name tag. "Have a nice day."

He laughed and stepped away, pretending to tip the hat he wasn't wearing. Margie hugged her arms around her waist, holding in a laugh. She'd just flirted with a stranger. She'd behaved like a modern girl. She'd bantered. And she'd left him wanting more.

Well, she told herself. *That was fun.*

Three

Several sweltering summer weeks passed, and Margie found herself competent at her job. It gave her a daily thrill to step inside the giant store and know she belonged there.

Margie crossed the quiet sales floor and stood fingering the fringe on a blue and gold scarf. "Betty, I need some help."

"Sure, kid. What is it?"

"Will you let me take you out for lunch tomorrow?" Margie asked.

Betty laughed. "That hardly sounds like my helping you."

"Well, I need to make a stop first," Margie said, twining a curl around her finger. "I need to make a change."

The next day, the two girls slipped into a salon on their lunch break.

Margie stared at her reflection, which was about to change drastically. Maybe. Or maybe not. "This is a bad idea. I shouldn't do this today. Maybe next week?" She looked at Betty in the mirror. Betty shook her head.

A woman in a black dress stepped into the reflection. She reeked of cigarette smoke. "Ready to say goodbye to all this hair?"

"She is," Betty insisted.

"I am." Margie didn't sound so sure.

"Perfect." The woman picked up a pair of shears from the counter and snapped off a good percentage of Margie's hair. "Now nobody can change her mind. As it happens, I've done this before." Almost smiling, she chopped off another chunk of Margie's hair, and it fell to the ground with an audible swish. "Don't worry. You'll love it."

Margie stared at the floor, watching the pile of hair grow. Mere moments later, the woman said, "All right, then. You're done."

Now Margie looked into the mirror, tipped her chin from side to side, and felt a smile bloom over her face. "I look like a modern."

"You do. You are." The woman didn't even pretend to smile as she shooed Margie out of the chair, ready to bring another emerging modern in.

The girls ran from the salon, laughing. Margie stared into every window they passed, surprising herself with her reflection. "My mother will press her lips together. Then she'll look away. My father will probably cry right in front of me. He loves my curls. Henry will . . ." She wasn't sure how to finish that.

What would Henry say? What would he think?

"Henry?" Betty asked, sniffing out a story. "Who is Henry?"

"He's a boy from home. A boy I've known all my life."

"Is he handsome?"

Margie shrugged. "He's no Valentino." If only he were

suave and smooth like the men in pictures. If only he had elegant fingers. If only he had a little romance in his heart instead of work on his mind.

Even when he wasn't working, he was working. Evenings she'd often found him in his grandfather's old shed, fiddling around with the ancient glass-blowing tools the old man had left Henry. Over the past couple of years, his attempts at handmade vases had both alarmed and amused her.

"He climbs trees and fishes in streams. He eats a lot. He loses at checkers." What she didn't say about him filled her mind.

His strong arms wrap me up like I'm in the safest place in the world. His kisses make me forget how to speak. He works too hard and doesn't play enough.

He promised he'd write.

Four

Margie knew life was hard for people. She understood that her parents worked hard, that Henry's family practically never rested. She recognized that work meant long hours, body-punishing labor, and little reward. And she knew that nobody could be as lucky as she was with her job.

This department store work was hard on neither her body nor her mind. She woke up mornings and grinned at the thought of going to work. She loved the speed of the subway. She loved the streets of New York. She loved the variety of people she saw all day and every day. Occasionally she thought she should pinch herself to be certain she wasn't dreaming.

And then, in the evenings, she'd returned to her apartment, and the dream would fade to glossless reality. It took months of entering the building's front door for the wall of odor to assemble itself into distinct scents, and as soon as it did, she wished to un-know what she knew. It was all the worst of food and pet smells, combined with mysteries of the city that had never rolled across the hills to Pennsylvania. The three flights of steps got more daunting. Dark corners and muffled sounds behind closed doors felt more like a scary film plot than a real home

And with Felicity added to the formula, the apartment took on a new layer of mystique.

When she'd answered Felicity's newspaper advertisement for a "young, professional, female roommate," Margie had been thrilled to find a walkup apartment so near a subway entrance. But a more accurate ad might have mentioned odd hours, terrible housekeeping habits, and frequent parties.

"An apartment is a place to sleep," Margie reminded herself on an almost daily basis. She was thrilled to have a room of her own, especially because it was only big enough to hold her bed and a tiny armoire, which she couldn't open fully. The shelf above her bed held her three favorite novels and the crooked orange-and-red vase Henry had made her for her last birthday. A mirror hung on the wall, and she thought she might wear it out staring at her bobbed hair.

She hadn't managed to tell anyone back home about cutting off her hair. But it was a hit in the city. Leo the courier certainly seemed to like it.

"Good afternoon, Betty," he said, sweeping a foppish bow over the glove counter. He produced a flower, only a little worse for wear, from his lapel. She allowed herself to notice a tingle of electricity when their fingers touched.

"It's very kind of you to keep bringing me flowers," Margie said, tucking this one behind her ear.

He didn't reply beyond a self-depreciating nod. "I have heard talk," he said, "of a grand plan for next month."

Margie clapped her hands. "Do you mean for Thanksgiving? Isn't it the most perfect idea? A giant

Christmas parade." She produced some combination of a sigh and a giggle, which made her seem younger than she was. "I've never even seen a parade, much less been in one."

Leo laughed. "I'd imagine those would be quite different experiences."

"I'll walk in this one and watch the next one," Margie said, trying to sound a little more like an adult.

"So you're not going home for the holiday, I presume."

"No. But that's all right. I know exactly what everyone will wear, eat, and say at home. I'm perfectly happy to stay in the city and experience something new."

"You and me and a few thousand other young professionals," he said.

Margie looked around for customers but didn't find any. She leaned against her counter. "Will you be walking in the parade?"

He shook his head. "I'm not technically an employee of Macy's. I'm an independent contractor."

"Does that mean you don't get a paycheck? You just work for tips?" She hoped her voice carried the proper casual tone. She'd hate to seem too interested in Leo's financial status.

"You might be surprised how well the tips work out, Betty," he said. "The ladies love me."

"Of course. That doesn't surprise me in the least. I'm certain you do very well for yourself." She thought of the regular stream of lapel flowers, the offers for coffee and sodas. He must do fairly well. He was certainly charming enough to solicit tips from wealthy female shoppers.

"If you're not marching in the parade, what will you do for Thanksgiving day?"

"Is this an invitation?" He touched the flower behind Margie's ear. Her entire left side shivered. Why did his touch feel so personal? He'd only made contact with the flower. But there was something about those fingers, long and clean and manicured, that made Margie a little giddy.

"If you'd like to consider it an invitation, please consider it one to join all the Macy's Bettys at the parade." She dropped a little curtsey and winked.

It was getting easier, this casual flirting. She no longer looked over her shoulder for Henry every time she winked at a man. She rarely thought of his reaction to her hair when she saw herself in the mirror. She didn't turn to look for him when she heard a man's deep laugh.

Just like she'd hoped, she was letting go her silly girlhood and living a real life in the real city.

Five

Dear Margie,
    I walked past your house today, like I do every day. And still, every day, I feel sad that I don't see you. I don't catch sight of you pinning laundry to the line. You're not cutting flowers. Nobody's sitting with your grandma in your favorite rocking chair.
    How can it surprise me that you're not there? I know you're not there. With every single breath, I know how far away you are. But somehow, it still pulls at the rip in my heart that only you can mend.
    Love,
    Henry

    She tucked the letter back into her sleeve. Her face, heavy with pancake makeup, felt as if it would crack in the lines of her grin. When she placed the cone-shaped cap on her head, it slid down around her ears. The other girls grinned and giggled in the mirrors, shaking the oversized sleeves of their striped costumes. Margie stepped away from the mirrors, wiggling her legs. Striped trousers shimmied along them. Maybe she could arrange to travel home for Christmas in this clown costume. At least that way, Mother wouldn't fret about her knees showing. No, she'd have entirely different things to fret about.

Still grinning, Margie slid the conical clown hat up her brow and pushed through the other clowns and cowboys to her place in the lineup.

"Betty! Hey, Betty!"

A dozen heads in cone-shaped hats turned toward the voice. Cowboys, who spent their days as shoe salesmen, burst out laughing. The salesgirl clowns pretended to be offended at the teasing. Margie let her laugh break loose. At one time, all of these young women had worn a Betty tag, and now they got to spend their Thanksgiving morning walking the city streets, parading from Harlem to Herald Square. Margie was delighted. She was a Macy's Betty. She couldn't imagine the excitement ever wearing out.

Even the punishing city wind didn't feel too cold as the girls stepped out, into the morning sunlight. Margie grinned and waved at people standing on the sidewalks.

The elephants had been here.

Elephants walking the city streets—that was something Margie hadn't ever experienced in Pennsylvania. The Central Park Zoo animals led this parade, including lions and tigers and a camel, and they left their mark all over the avenue. Even with that unwelcome addition, the morning grew brighter and more exciting. Margie felt a little dizzy from glancing down at the pavement to avoid ruining her shoes, then up at the buildings soaring over the street, then across at the crowds lining the blocks, walking alongside the parade. Betty laughed and clutched her arm, swinging bright balloons over her head.

As the parade moved downtown, Margie listened to the

chattering and laughing of the salesgirls. She could hear and see and occasionally smell evidence of the zoo animals that accompanied the parade. The cold wind and the sunlight made her eyes water, but she wouldn't dare wipe at her clown makeup.

A few more blocks along, Margie and Betty noticed a group of men jeering and calling out ungentlemanly suggestions to some of the clowns. Ignoring the impolite element, the girls focused on the children. Dozens, maybe hundreds of children, and as her legs grew tired and sore, as her face creased into permanent grin lines, Margie knew this was a day she'd remember forever.

"Hey, glove girl!"

Her heart thudded. She was glove girl. So that was him. Leo. It had to be. He was watching the parade. But how could he know who she was? How could he tell her from any of the other clowns? It hardly mattered, anyway. She'd be past this block in a few minutes, and he'd go back home, or to his lady friend's house for dinner, or wherever young men went on national holidays.

As it happened, young men followed parades.

He shouted again at 103rd and 96th. When she hadn't heard him holler for several blocks, she started turning around to look for him. This left Betty with no choice but to hold her arm and yank her away from any and all elephant leavings.

"Margie, pay attention. You're going to wreck your shoes." Betty giggled, understanding that shoes were the least of Margie's concerns today.

Other Bettys noticed Margie's distraction. "Maybe he went to work."

"Maybe he got hungry." Another clown nodded her cone hat.

The girl walking beside her agreed. "Maybe he's cold and went inside. Maybe he's tired of this parade. I know I am."

"We've been walking for hours. Miles. This is mad."

Mr. Macaulay, the sales manager, rode a bicycle through the rank of clowns, handing out more balloons. "Smile, ladies. This is not about you. It's about customers."

Turning to look for Leo again at 65th, Margie caught sight of what should have been the end of the parade. An enormous crowd of people, cheering, shouting and marching along with the cowboys and Christmas Tree Ladies surged through the street.

"Look at this, Betty. We're really part of something."

"Glove girl!"

Her face went hot under the cracking pancake makeup. She clutched Betty's hand. Almost before she thought about it, she turned directly toward the shouting man and waved. If her mother had any inkling...

He pushed his way to the edge of the crowd. "There you are," he shouted. "I thought I'd never catch up with you again. Are you hungry?"

"What?"

"Are you hungry?" he yelled louder.

She laughed. "I heard you before. I just wasn't sure what you were talking about. I'm a bit busy here, see?" She made a general gesture toward the large parade marching down the street.

"I bought you half a sandwich." He looked at the paper-wrapped package in his hand, and his face fell. He apologized as he stumbled through the crowd at the parade's side. "I guess the timing isn't perfect, is it?"

"Not perfect," she laughed.

"Not bad, though," Betty muttered in Margie's ear.

"Later?" He asked, holding up the sandwich, grinning hopefully. "Lunch?"

"Sure." She warmed again to see his happy smile.

He didn't say goodbye. He didn't need to. He simply turned, faced downtown, and marched alongside the clowns at the edge of the parade.

"Get over there," Betty hissed. "Go on. Walk beside him."

"Someone will tell me to get back in my place."

"If that happens, then deal with it when it does. Meanwhile, go over there."

"I'll look like a floozy."

Betty's laugh blasted out of her mouth. "You're dressed as a circus clown. Hardly loose-morals material, sugar." She bumped Margie with her hip.

It only took one city block and three white lies for Margie to make her way to the outside of the line of clowns. "It's warmer in the center," she said to each of the Bettys wringing their frozen fingers. They gladly made way for her.

When she reached the outside of the crowd, she pretended to notice him for the first time. "Oh, hello, sir," she said, waving her striped arm in his face. "Enjoying the parade?"

"I sure am now. Great costume."

"How did you know it was me? We all look exactly the same."

He shrugged, his coat collar touching the edges of his hat. "Not exactly the same."

What did he mean by that? What might he mean? Was there something strange about her costume? Did she have some kind of mark on her? Had she sat in something?

"You don't all walk the same," he said, practically speaking to the sidewalk under his feet.

Her fists found her hips. "Mister Spinelli, are you telling me that you recognized me by the way I walked? I'm not sure that's complimentary."

He caught her eye. Grinned. Winked. "Oh, it is."

Six

Margie stepped inside the back door, pulling off the clown hat as she sagged against the wall. "Six miles. Whose big idea was that?"

The other Bettys responded with a variety of groans and giggles, depending on their current dispositions. The staff room was crowded with piles of costumes. As she pulled off her shoes, Margie felt rebellious, deliciously dangerous, at the prospect of walking through Macy's department store barefoot.

"Let's go see the decorations," Betty said, tugging on Margie's elbow. "We'll be the first New Yorkers to get a look."

"Don't you want to change out of these first?" Margie pretended to scorn the striped clown suit, but she couldn't deny that she'd grown used to it. She could certainly be talked into wearing trousers every day.

"Change later; explore now. How often does a girl get to wander all of Macy's without bowing and scraping to crabby customers?" Betty grabbed Margie's arm and pulled her into the store proper.

Margie gasped. Giant sparkling trees filled every corner. The scent of pine mingled with perfumes and colognes. Lights in the window displays twinkled against the paper-covered glass, ready to be revealed to the public in the morning. The girls ran toward the front doors. Margie couldn't hold in a laugh of joy. Two trees towered over the main entrance, glittering with clear glass balls.

"It's heaven," Betty sighed.

"It smells like Pennsylvania," Margie said, then giggled at her silly sentimentalism. "But look at these decorations," she said with a sigh, reaching for a clear glass ball the size of her fist. Swirls in the glass caught and splayed the light from the tree bulbs and the ceiling, making the ball glimmer like ice on a sunny winter day.

What if Henry could learn to make a beautiful thing like this? That would certainly be something.

She spun the glass ball in her hand, noticing the smooth sides and the collection of tiny bubbles at the base. The little globe was connected to the tree with a precious little wire hook shaped into a heart. Margie poked through the giant tree and found dozens of perfect glass balls, each holding onto the tree with a distinctive heart-shaped hook.

The girls ran from section to section, dodging the workers on ladders and those milling through the store. They tried to sneak glances at the window displays but could see nothing through the barrier coverings. They rode the wooden escalators up and up, into each department, made magical by glittering glass and electric bulbs.

The girls finally wandered into the employee room, where Betty grabbed a cardboard cup from the stack. She filled it with hot water from the coffee machine but didn't add anything to it.

"What are you doing? That doesn't even taste good." Margie laughed.

Betty's eyebrows arched in the way she'd deliberately designed them to. "It doesn't taste any better when you add that," she said, motioning to the coffee powder packets in the dispenser. "And this is free."

She wrapped both hands around the cup and held the steaming water near her face. "A portable heater, compliments of Mister Macy." She lifted the cup toward Margie in a salute, or maybe a toast.

"I don't even feel cold," Margie said. "I could parade from Harlem to Herald Square every day."

"Then come back here and sell record numbers of gloves, of course." Betty laughed. "The only reason you're not lying on the floor exhausted is that you don't have to work anymore today."

"You may be perfectly right, Miss Betty," Margie said with a grin. "But I'll continue to believe that every day should be parade day."

"Especially if that dashing Leo Spinelli walks the miles beside you?" Betty elbowed Margie, who blushed and stammered.

"The parade would have been just fine even without him," she managed.

Seven

That afternoon, as Margie stepped through her building's entry door, what she'd come to know as Apartment Aroma wafted around her on the warm air: cabbage and spiced meats and past-prime fruit mixed with something distinctly feline. She turned her key in the rusty mail flap, then sighed as she found, once again, nothing in the box.

She reached into her coat pocket for the letter Henry had sent weeks ago. She'd been so surprised by its eloquence that she'd kept it close. She didn't want to find that she'd imagined it, so she looked at it every day. Several times. Squeezing the envelope between her fingers, she whispered, "You are probably the only letter in all of New York City to have just marched in a parade. Happy Thanksgiving."

Habit dictated that she count the steps on each flight. Muttering under her breath about the design defects of nineteen steps per floor, she had occasion, once again, to feel grateful that the toe-pinching horror of these delightful little shoes was much worse going downstairs than up.

"Three flights. Fifty-seven steps. Who plans a staircase with nineteen steps? How much harder would it have been to just add the twentieth?" Margie's muttering got quieter at the top of the second flight. She feared that she was earning a reputation as the flapper who talked to herself. Sure enough, two boys, maybe ten or twelve years old, sat outside an apartment, playing some kind of game with a couple of metal nails. They watched her walk around the corner, and she made sure to swing her hips as she rounded the bannister rail.

I'll give them a little thrill, she thought, as her skirt swished the backs of her knees.

Pride mixed with shame as it always did when she acted that way. She was delighted to live in the city, thrilled to have a job at Macy's department store, giddy to live life as a modern young woman, but she couldn't give herself over fully to the flapper style. She held fast to her stockings and everything else that went on beneath her knee-length dress.

Felicity, her roommate, was another story.

Nineteen stairs later, Margie stepped to the doorway of apartment 3C, crammed the key into the rattling lock, and whispered a prayer to the god of doorknobs that the ridiculous thing would open tonight. Half a turn to the right, a quarter turn back to the left, and a minor curse—because Felicity promised that swearing helped—and . . .

No such luck.

With a repeat of the minor curse, she removed the key and sort of spat on it. Not enough to carry actual moisture; just enough to relieve some frustration. She stuck the key back into the lock and whispered, "Please open, honey. I'm hungry, and my feet are killing me."

Right, then left, a jiggle of the knob, and success. She threw the door open, grinning at her victory, and walked into her tiny living room, to find it stuffed full of people. A dozen young men and women—at least—perched on every surface and leaned against every wall.

Felicity half-ran, half-glided across the crowded room to the door. "Mimi, darling. You're home!"

Mimi? Darling?

Felicity clutched Margie's shoulders and kissed the air beside her cheeks. Putting her face close to Margie's ear, she whispered, "Play along, won't you? My first petting party will be nothing, absolutely nothing, without you."

Margie felt her eyes widen to the point that they might have turned inside out. Then she caught hold of her spinning mind. "Gee, thanks, Felicity."

"Fifi," she corrected under her breath.

"Right. Fifi. Thanks ever so much for the invitation, but I have to . . ." Margie nodded toward her bedroom and possible escape.

Felicity's eyebrows contracted for a second, then arched again in all their lined glory. She turned to the crowd and shouted over their conversations, "Gang, this is my darling roommate Mimi! Everyone say, 'Hello, Mimi.'"

Obediently, if not energetically, Felicity's friends said hello.

"She's completely bushed from a long day of work. You'll have to excuse her." Felicity pushed her toward her room, and Margie waved a limp hand while trying to mimic the bored expressions of the guests. Had any of them watched her in the parade? Had any of them done anything today that they'd remember for the rest of their lives?

Once inside her tiny bedroom, she let out the breath she'd been holding and laughed. She felt her cheeks dimple as she grinned at the sheer unbelievability of what was happening on the other side of the door. A petting party. She'd heard about those. Scandalous. And now one was happening inches away. She couldn't decide if she was more amused or embarrassed. Flopping onto her bed, she heard a papery crunch. She rolled over and retrieved a brown envelope.

Another letter from Henry. Felicity must have brought it up from the box.

How unexpectedly thoughtful of her.

Holding it in her hands, Margie imagined what it might say. She traced the letters of her name with an index finger. His handwriting was strong and upright, much like Henry himself.

He would be appalled at what was happening on the other side of that door. She giggled again. At least, she *thought* he would be appalled. When it came right down to it, she wasn't sure exactly what was going on out there.

What precisely did happen at a petting party? She blushed as she pictured Felicity sitting on some boy's lap, looking at him from under painted eyelids. That was as far as she was willing and able to imagine.

She held the brown envelope close to her nose, breathing in, trying to catch the scent of the western Pennsylvania woods. Instead, the envelope smelled depressingly like the entryway of the brownstone.

Dear Margie,

All the leaves are off the trees. It's sad and dreary around here. Sure would brighten things up if you could come for a visit.

Your family is doing well. Your mother has lots of dress orders, so she's staying busy. Everyone's asking your father for hams and geese and turkeys for Christmas. I stopped by to visit your grandma. Her ankle is healing nicely. She showed me the scars where the dog bit her. Lifted her skirt right up and showed me. Isn't she a scandal? She has beautiful ankles for an old woman. I told her so. She pretended to be offended for about one second, but she couldn't stop laughing. We shared an apple pie my mother made for her. I ate most of it. She said she didn't mind.

It was good to visit your family. It made you seem closer, somehow.

Please don't stay away too long. I have a surprise I want to show you.

Love,
Henry

Oh, Henry. Margie sighed. If only he oiled his hair and wore gorgeous tailored suits. But even if he did, he just didn't have the presence of a city boy. He was too big, too bulky. He was not exactly romantic. Nothing like modern. His father was a coke stoker. His grandfather had been a coke stoker. Henry worked hard, and she recognized that as an admirable trait and all, but he had black marks around his fingernails and in the skin of his knuckles.

Sure, he hated the smoke and fire that blackened the air around the ovens and poisoned the trees in the surrounding woods. But the job paid well, and it was stable. Nobody was suggesting that western Pennsylvania would run out of coal.

If only Henry were an artist. He'd tried. She looked up at the warped, leaning glass vase on her shelf. It listed dangerously to the left, but it was perfect for holding his letters. And it meant that the colors of Pennsylvania autumn were in front of her eyes every day. She admitted it to herself again—he'd tried.

He knew she wanted an artist, and he'd given it a shot, making her a series of awkward glass creations that no one could mistake for art. So maybe artist was out. He could be a musician, or a writer, or even an accountant. If he were a man with a romantic job, a girl could find herself in some danger of falling for him. If, that is, a girl had an eye for the large, muscled type. Margie preferred the slim, elegant city boys who had manicured hands and oiled hair. Boys who looked like Leo.

Margie wasn't in any real danger of falling in love with Henry. He'd been her playmate for years. They'd sort of fallen into a habit of spending all their time together. In a small town like Mt. Pleasant, it was easy to fall into such habits.

And it was certainly nice to fall into the kissing. That had happened quite by accident one day when Henry had been at her home for dinner. He'd thanked her parents for a lovely meal, politely as ever, and had taken Margie's hand as she'd walked him to the front porch.

"Dinner was nice," he'd said, still holding her hand. "You're nice." His fingers had tightened on her hand, and he'd smiled sideways.

Unused to even tiny flirtations, she'd grinned and blushed and hidden behind her curls. He'd reached his other hand over and brushed it across her hair, tucking the curls behind her ear. His touch was so gentle, so soft, that she'd looked up to make sure it was really him.

Their eyes had met for the thousandth time, but to her, it felt like the first. She'd tilted her chin up as he leaned down, and she'd had only seconds to wonder if kissing was something you needed to learn how to do. Then it had happened, and she'd felt like at least Henry seemed to understand the art of kissing. He'd smiled at her and said goodbye, and she'd stood on the porch wishing he'd come back and do it all again.

She couldn't deny now that she missed him, nearly as much as she missed her grandmother. She pulled the letter close and reread the part about Grandma's dog-bit ankle. Poor Grandma. She loved that stupid, angry dog past all reason. When it attacked her ankle, she didn't even kick back. She just apologized for getting in its way.

And Henry was there, eating pie with Grandma and making Margie think about him in a silly, old-fashioned way. She had to remind herself, again and again, that Henry was part of her past, not her future. The whole fact of him, from his generations of family in the Pennsylvania woods, to his coal job, to his muscle-bound arms, stood in opposition to her chosen modern lifestyle. She folded the letter back into its envelope and placed it with the others in the crooked glass vase.

Through the wall, Margie could hear Felicity's Victrola winding up.

Here we go, she thought. *Another round of "Carolina in the Morning."*

Felicity loved being the Southern-Belle-turned-City-Flapper. She played the Carolina song at the least provocation. Felicity's tinny, tight voice crooned along with the record.

"Wishing is good time wasted,
Still it's a habit they say;
Wishing for sweets I've tasted,
That's all I do all day."

Some of her guests must have gotten up to dance, because the sounds changed. There was a second, maybe two, when Margie thought she should open the door and join the party. Dancing would be nice. She made it as far as the two steps over to the door. Her fingers brushed the doorknob. But no. She couldn't go out there. She climbed onto her bed and knelt there, staring at the door.

When Felicity's song ended, Margie sat up, pulled a book off the tiny shelf above her bed, and opened it to the marked page. Only after she realized she'd read the same paragraph about thirty times did she give up. She reached into the vase and pulled out Henry's letters again. He missed her. That was obvious.

It was nice to be missed. But Henry had *intentions*. Who wanted intentions these days? Intentions meant decisions. Formality. Permanence. Margie wanted to toss her cares away, just like she'd tossed her long curls in favor of this bob. She fingered the ends of the curl that looped up her cheek. What would Henry say about it? She'd definitely neglected to mention the hair in any of her letters.

This was Margie's time to really live. To explore and to

flirt and to enjoy the elegance of the times.

And what were Henry's intentions, anyway? Nothing exciting. Nothing like living in the city. Nothing that sparkled

"I just want my life to sparkle for a while. Is that such a bad thing?" Margie said the words and wondered why they made her feel so rotten.

Eight

Dear Henry,
    Everything here is glorious. Working in the city is still as perfect as I could ever imagine it being. The whole city looks like a Christmas party, but nowhere is as beautiful as Macy's. Every floor glows with trees and tinsel and the most delightful blown-glass ornaments. They hang from every tree and look like balls of ice. Each one dangles from a perfect little heart-shaped hook, and each one holds the promise of a dreamy Christmas.
    And now you know the truth. I have become the kind of person who writes home about something you couldn't possibly care about.
    It turns out that I won't be able to come home for Christmas this year. But I'll have some time off in the spring, so I hope I can make it in time for the lilacs.
    What do you want for Christmas? I thought I didn't need or want anything, but it turns out that I wish for a little piece

of western Pennsylvania wrapped up in a box and delivered to New York. Do you know someone who can make that happen?
   Love,
   Margie

   Betty leaned across her display, intent on helping a tiny old woman match a scarf to her worn but clean coat. Mr. Macaulay, the floor manager, continued to clear his throat and beckon with a long finger. Brow lowered, he made the frown lines deeper. He stood in the doorway, trying not to show his limp. One of his legs was shorter than the other, and his crooked walk seemed to affect his mood. Never in a good way.
   Margie scuttled across the floor and stopped in front of him. "Can I help you with something, sir?" she said in her best Macy's Betty voice.
   "Don't flirt with me, Betty," Mr. Macaulay grumbled. He handed her a man's shirt, folded into a crisp and perfect rectangle. "Take this to the service booth closest to the front door. And make it quick. A very important customer is waiting."
   She patted the shirt. "All our customers are important, sir." She smiled, lowering her eyes in her best Demure Salesperson attitude.
   As soon as he turned his back, she hustled to the escalator and rode down three flights to the main floor. She handed the shirt to the silent, elegant woman working the main lobby register. The woman's nod almost acknowledged Margie but managed to leave her without a doubt about the woman's distinction and position.
   Ready to return to the gloves, she glanced at the doorway glimmering and flanked by the two huge trees. A woman stood there, dripping with pearls and laughing at a young man. The woman must have known the same trick the cashier did because, while flirting with the boy, she left no doubt that she was doing him a favor. The condescension

was obvious, but he didn't seem to mind. Margie could only see his back, but she could tell his posture was eager. Servile. The woman reached up and pulled a flower from behind the upturned edge of her cloche and tucked it into his lapel. He bowed and kissed her hand. The moment was somehow adorable and pathetic at the same time. The woman was so clearly above him. Whether he knew it or didn't, he didn't seem bothered by the difference

He turned. Leo. It was Leo. She felt a rush of shame for him, and for herself.

He was a momentary plaything for that woman, a lark. As the woman turned to leave, she waggled her fingers at Leo exactly how Margie might have waved at a baby or a puppy.

She watched him for a half second as he scrabbled for the door. Margie turned before he could see her.

She bumped into Betty, who put her arm over Margie's shoulders and gave her a squeeze. "Poor kid."

"You saw that?" Margie felt grateful. Embarrassed. Conspiratorial. They moved toward the escalators.

"I see that all the time," Betty said. "It's a little cycle. She gets the flower from a man who doesn't really care about her. Somehow she knows it, so she gives it to a boy she doesn't care about. He'll turn around and find someone, somewhere, who can look up to his lowly station. Someone will be grateful for his little gift. Poor kid."

Margie wondered whom Betty meant. Was Leo the poor kid because it would be difficult for him to find someone below him to pass the wilting flower to? Or was that next someone the poor kid?

Did she mean Margie? How had Margie let herself get all fluttery over used hothouse flowers in December?

She gripped the wood railing of the escalator and wiped an escaping tear as she stared at the ankles of the woman ahead of her. Betty pretended not to see the tear, instead whispering a little commentary about the crooked seam in the woman's stocking.

Grateful, Margie asked, "How are mine?" and kicked up her leg behind her.

Betty pretended to inspect. "Enviable."

"I'll take it." She blinked her eyes clear and smiled.

As they passed the shimmering tree at the corner of the sales floor, Margie put her hand out to touch one of the perfect, lovely glass balls. She fingered the sweet heart-shaped hook and breathed in resolve. She'd not be pathetic. She'd not fall at Leo's feet.

She did not need his third-hand castoff flowers. She'd not swoon at his gentlemanly smoothness. Manicured fingers did not make a man.

Hmm, she thought. She should needlepoint that on a pillow and put it on her bed. If only she knew how to sew.

The glove counter was quiet, as if it had waited for Margie's return. She moved a few pairs around the display and smiled at the heads of strangers who actively ignored her.

And then she saw him coming. He turned the corner, his roguish grin preceding him. Her heart thudded, and she was helpless to stop it. Even though she understood now that she was only part of a game, a piece of her heart was grateful to be a part of anything.

She busied herself with a box under the counter.

He leaned on the glass, humming something jazzy.

She took a fortifying breath and straightened up. "Good afternoon, sir. How may I help you?"

"Maybe you could join a starving man for dinner."

"I rather doubt any of the men shopping for leather goods today are starving."

Whether it was the reserve in her voice, or the lack of lean-in in her posture, or the glint of understanding in her eyes, he seemed to notice something. He straightened and pulled on the hem of his jacket.

"Now. Is there anything you're interested in here?" She

gestured to the gloves in the case so there could be no mistaking her meaning, even for him.

"Maybe I'd better get back to my post." He grinned awkwardly. "It's a busy day out there."

"Thank you for sharing a moment of it with me," Margie said, her voice formal, but sincere.

"You've made it beautiful," he said, reaching for the lily in his lapel.

She put up her hand. "Keep it," she said. "It looks just right where you have it."

He started to protest.

"I insist," she said. "I think I've developed an allergy. Goodbye." Turning away, she felt a strange combination of sadness and pride, as if in that little moment of growing up, she had left something sweet behind.

Nine

The apartment was a disaster. Unless she was planning a party, Felicity was a lazy cleaner at best. Sometimes the mess made Margie crazy, but generally she understood. A long day at work, followed by the monumental trek up the flights of narrow, steep stairs could kill anyone's desire to do housework.

A pile of dirty clothes and linens grew in the corner outside Felicity's bedroom door. Wilting flowers in cheap vases and jars cluttered the tiny kitchen table. The smallest bunch, the only bouquet that was Margie's, needed to be thrown out soon, but she couldn't part with it quite yet. Knowing she'd likely never receive another lapel flower from Leo made even these third-hand castoffs precious. She picked up the dented tin-can vase and held the flowers' stems as she poured out the murky water and replaced it with fresh.

She held the drooping flowers to her nose, craving a summer smell in this frigid winter. It was like magic, she thought, how someone could grow carnations in this season. Too bad carnations didn't smell like lilacs. She slid one of Felicity's vases over, sending petals scattering.

Then she noticed a tattered brown paper parcel. The box slouched on the table, one corner crushed in. Even so, nothing had ever looked more beautiful, because there, printed in Henry's careful block letters, was her name.

She squealed and giggled and hugged the box to her chest. Then she pulled it away. A box from Henry shouldn't make her so silly. But it was a box at Christmastime. She hugged it again. It weighed almost nothing. Her mind spun around all the possibilities. A gift, obviously, but why so light? Why so small? What could it be? She turned the box on its side and listened for clues, but all she heard was a tiny rustling, like paper. Or sand. Could Henry have sent her sand? She shook her head. Even for Henry, that would be odd.

What was inside?

Wait, she commanded herself. Why did she care? She didn't, not really.

Maybe she cared a little bit.

She tore one taped corner open, ready to ransack the box and get inside. But after only a second, she knew she needed to savor the moment. Her parents weren't likely to send her a gift; the money they'd already sent had probably strapped them more than they'd ever admit. Grandma would send something, but probably only a letter. Henry might be the only one to send her a gift at all. She should make it last a few days.

She set the box on the table and walked around the kitchen, putting a few crusted dishes in the sink. She moved back to the table. Touching a corner of the crushed box, she picked at the tape.

"No," she told herself. "Wait."

She brushed a pile of table crumbs into her hand and then into the waste basket. She kept her back to the table, trying to ignore the delicious secrets inside the box. What could be so light? What could make such a precious tinkling noise? Jewelry? Hair dressings? She pictured a hair clip dripping with tiny cascading gems, clinking every time she turned her head. She'd never be able to hold still wearing such a thing, she knew it.

Pacing the tiny kitchen, she realized that her feet were getting stuck to the same spot each time and decided that sweeping up would distract her. When she found herself humming and dancing with the broom, she gave up the waiting as a bad job.

She carried the box tightly against her chest. As she stepped around the couch to her bedroom, the front door opened, and Felicity tumbled inside, followed by a pile of greenery and two young men.

"Merry Christmas, Mimi darling," Felicity squealed. "I've brought us a tree." She pointed to the pile of wilting branches in the arms of an eager boy, all oiled hair and crooked grin.

"Where would you like it?" he asked Felicity, gazing at her with unhidden adoration.

She sauntered over to the tiny table wedged between the couches. After tossing a stack of her *Life* magazines to the floor, she brushed dust off the table with her hands. "Here. Put it here."

He hurried to the corner to obey, but when he got there, he stood looking nervous and uncomfortable. Felicity stood, hand on hip, head cocked, waiting for him to do something. Margie felt sorry for the boy.

He blushed and grinned and stared, then finally held out the green mound to Felicity. She pointed to the table, clearly waiting for him to produce a Christmas miracle.

Margie reached over and took the thing out of his arms. It resembled nothing so much as the discarded tip of a too-tall tree. Someone must have cut it off when their apartment turned out too short for it. Margie turned it, finding the trunk, then shook the mangled branches to restore some treelike quality.

"How would you like to display it?" she asked. She tried for a neutral tone, but even clueless Felicity may have heard her desperation. This was not a Christmas tree.

Felicity breathed out an impatient sigh. "I'm not an expert. Just put it on the table."

Margie placed the lump of greenery on the table, but it rolled onto the floor. "Did you bring a stand for it?"

Pouting, Felicity said, "You don't ever appreciate the things I do." She snuggled up next to the other boy, who obediently put his arm around her.

"Let me get a bowl," Margie said, waiting until she was in the kitchen to roll her eyes.

She pulled a dented tin bowl from the top of the cupboard. Wrapping her arms around the lip of the blue bowl, she steeled herself to finish this conversation.

Be pleasant, she told herself. *Be sweet. Felicity isn't trying to be trying. She's showing a kindness. She bought us a Christmas tree. In a manner of speaking.*

Margie brought the bowl back to the front room and set it on the little table. The brown-haired boy leaped over and placed the tree parts inside it.

"I think you've put it in upside down," Margie said, moving over to help. She righted the mass of needles so the pointy part was near the top, but the whole thing instantly fell out of the bowl. As she caught it, Margie grinned at the boy. "Actually, I'm wrong. You had it perfect." She shoved what might once have been the top of the tree in the dented bowl and let the rest cascade halfheartedly over the rim.

"This is going to be the most perfect Christmas tree in New York," Margie said. By the time she turned to face Felicity, she managed a nearly sincere smile. "Thank you for bringing it home. Merry Christmas." She stepped over the legs of the blonde boy and leaned over to kiss Felicity on the cheek.

Felicity managed to convey both pleasure and pouting at the same instant; Margie knew it was time to disappear. Waving to the boys, neither of whom seemed to notice, she picked up her box and slipped into her room.

"All right, Henry. What have you got for me?" She held the box up to her face, first with the crushed side toward her, then with the opened corner right in front of her eyes. She tipped it sideways and again listened to the tinkling rustle. Maybe jeweled hairpins were too much to expect. She shouldn't let her hopes rise. At least it didn't feel like a box full of coal. Or another heavy, warped vase.

She put it down and walked the perimeter of her tiny room, stepping onto the bed to move around two walls. She put her back to the box as she hung up a dress in the wardrobe. Dusting off her second pair of shoes, she snuck glances at the package out of the corner of her eye.

I should wait until Christmas. I should. It's going to be a discouraging day if all I have to look forward to is a gift from Felicity.

She climbed onto her bed and sat with her legs folded under her. Staring at the box wasn't helping to convince her that she should leave it alone. Maybe, she thought, she should put it on the tiny table under the tree-like thing in the bowl. But surely it would fall out of the bowl again and ruin her only gift.

Fine. Fine. I'll wait. From her knees, she popped up and lifted the box from the bed to the wardrobe. She leaned to place it on the top shelf by her black cloche hat. As it tilted, she heard it again, that magical jingling. It was the sound of Christmas, she decided. Right there in the box. Maybe not jeweled hairpins at all. Maybe a tiny set of silver bells to pin to her coat, bells that would make that precious tinkling sound when she walked.

Silver bells like those ought to be worn before Christmas, too, she thought as she snatched the box back out of the wardrobe and tore off the paper. *It's how Henry would want it.*

There it sat, on her bed in front of her, a rectangular cardboard box with a crushed corner, holding a Christmas dream. Once the idea of silver bells took up residence in her mind, she couldn't let it go. The sound of perfect evenings spent in sleigh rides, snuggled under Henry's heavy wool blanket, and his strong arm, and she could carry that sound wherever she went.

"Oh, Henry. This is perfect." She whispered the words as if writing him a letter. "Thank you for the bells. Each time I wear them, I'll remember the evenings we spent last winter driving around town. I'll remember the way you kissed me, just like in the movies. I'll remember how eager I was to get out of this tiny life and into the big city."

Why were her cheeks wet? Why in the world would this make her cry? She was where she wanted to be. She loved New York. She adored her job at Macy's. She was learning to manage Felicity. Life was nearly perfect, and she'd learned that *nearly perfect* was a great deal better than what she had any right to expect.

She lifted the lid and pulled out a piece of crumpled newspaper. Then the tears came in force. All along the bottom of the box—not a silver bell in sight—were tiny, clear glass shards, and three distinctive heart-shaped hooks. The ruins of a Christmas dream she hadn't dared expect.

The lovely ornaments would have been perfect for her Christmas. Perfect and beautiful and exactly what she needed.

"Oh, Henry," she whispered again, this time followed by a shuddering, indrawn breath. The only thing she could imagine bringing comfort was sinking into Henry's arms.

The realization came as clear as glass. Henry—exactly what she needed.

"What am I doing?"

Ten

Even as she put on her coat and walked out of the apartment, she knew she should go back. She was behaving thoughtlessly, but she was helpless to stop herself. Down the stairs she went, taking only sips of air. At the bottom, she pushed the door open, then practically ran down the block, passing the deli that was closed, the bakery that was closed, and the jewelry shop that was still holding on to shoppers. She rounded the corner to the post and telegraph office.

A harried man behind the desk caught her eye and nodded, possibly confirming that, indeed, the line was growing longer. Margie counted six people ahead of herself. She picked up a form from a table beside her and wrote in perfect block capitals. She didn't pore over each word; she simply let her thoughts fall onto the page.

HENRY YOUR GIFT ARRIVED AND YOU FOUND JUST WHAT I WANTED STOP SHOULD

BE HAPPIEST GIRL IN NYC BUT I AM HEARTBROKEN STOP BOX CRUSHED BULBS SHATTERED THE PRETTIEST THING I OWN A PILE OF SHARDS STOP NOT WHAT CHRISTMAS WAS SUPPOSED TO BE AND MAYBE I WAS WRONG ABOUT EVERYTHING STOP

"Next," the man called, and Margie handed over her form. He licked the tip of his pencil, counted the letters, and then looked up at her. She hurried to wipe the tears from her eyes. He tried to smile, but his exhaustion showed through. He nodded instead, as though he understood how she felt.

She handed over coins and nodded back. She wanted to touch his hand or reach over the counter to hug him, or something. He looked as disappointed with Christmas as she felt.

"It'll get better, kid," he said. "Merry Christmas."

As she walked away from the telegraph office, she wondered what she'd just done. What would Henry think when he opened that message? Would he understand? Would he think she was complaining? Of course he would. She was, in fact, complaining. Hot tears left trails on her cheeks that the cold wind instantly chilled.

Eleven

The next morning's walk from the subway station to the employees' door at Macy's was the longest on record, and it had never felt so cold. Margie's feet dragged along the slushy sidewalk. The usually welcome steam from the street grates disgusted her with its underground smells and its impotent puff of tepid air. The sun would surely never shine past this horrible curtain of steely cloud. Everyone in New York City selfishly hurried to their jobs or their shopping without caring that Margie was all alone on Christmas Eve.

She caught a glimpse of her face in a coffee shop window and nearly cried, then nearly laughed. She stopped and faced her reflection.

"Good morning, sullen," she said. "Lovely Christmas spirit you've got there." When she grinned at her reflection, she began to thaw.

Then she saw a man through the window, sitting in a tall stool, staring back at her through the window. He was at least as old as her father, with a drooping mustache and very little hair. His mug of coffee tilted a little as he ignored his newspaper and stared, open-mouthed, at Margie.

She tossed him what she hoped was a saucy little wave and turned again toward Herald Square. Her grin and flush remained as she rounded the corner.

Silly, she thought. *You're in New York City on Christmas Eve. Enjoy it.*

The tiny sandwich shop outside Macy's glowed with Christmas baubles and colored lights. As always, she stared up, taking in the cornices and pediments, which nobody could see from inside.

The world's biggest department store, and it couldn't possibly run without me.

Approaching the employee entrance, she hugged herself. *It's going to be a great day*, she repeated in her mind over and over. *A great day. A great day.* She'd already given that coffee-shop man a thrill. Maybe he'd accidentally show up in the glove department and spend a hundred dollars. Maybe Mr. Macaulay would see what a brilliant saleswoman she was and give her a fat raise.

Margie slipped inside the employee entrance's warm doorway. Hanging her coat in the cloakroom, she checked the clock and then warmed her hands around a cup of hot water from the coffee station.

Employees tumbled inside, wrapped to their noses in scarves and mufflers. She smiled at them as they unwound and unwrapped, not in a hurry to be the first Betty on the floor.

When the clock told her it was time, she poured out her now-lukewarm water and rode the escalator up to her floor. The polished wood soaked in the colored lights on each floor. As she rounded the corners of each level, she waved to the other salespeople. Her "Merry Christmas" was sometimes met with a grin and a wave, and at other times with a scowl of impatience, but she was sure that if she kept up the happy attitude, she'd mean it. All day she'd mean it. Until she finished work for the day and went back to her apartment to spend Christmas alone.

At every floor, she avoided searching out the decorated trees, but once she reached her floor, she could not help seeing the utter glorious perfection of the glass bulbs. They caught each sparkling light and turned it, spun it, then spread it across the tree. Every ball hung from its heart-shaped hook like a promise. Try as she might to hold onto her smile, she just couldn't. Those heart-held promises were for someone else.

She fingered the hook she'd put in her skirt pocket that morning. At least Henry had tried. He'd taken the hint that she'd loved the Macy's Christmas decorations. Somehow he'd found out what they were. He'd bought some. And he'd sent them to her. Even if they'd not arrived intact. In her head she knew the gift was all extremely romantic and wonderful. But all her heart held onto was the sound of shattered glass in the bottom of the box.

That shattered sound—just like her broken heart. She sighed. Then she laughed. How much drama could one modern girl generate? She squeezed the heart-shaped hook one more time and stepped over to her station. Time to work.

Mr. Macaulay rumbled onto the sales floor, his shorter leg slapping the ground with every other step. As always, Margie pictured his personal raincloud hovering over his balding head.

He stopped at the glove counter. "Good morning, sir," Margie said, forcing a formal smile. Mr. Macaulay didn't merit the flirty smile. He wouldn't be earning her a commission.

"Morning." He cleared his throat as though he was preparing a speech, but then he handed over a small cardboard box, barely big enough to cover the palm of her hand.

She had to stop herself from imagining pictures of all the lovely things the box could contain. Last night had taught her a lesson.

"Go on," he blustered, pushing the little box toward her.

She pulled the top off. Resting on a little rectangle of cotton lay a real Macy's name tag, with her name on it. She gasped a little thrilled breath.

"Oh, Mr. Macaulay, thank you. This is wonderful." She ran her fingers over the letters: M-A-R-G-A-R-T.

Margart? What was that supposed to mean?

He limped away, and Margie called after him. "Sir? This tag . . ." She wasn't sure how to say it without sounding ungrateful. "It's beautiful, but"—she pointed to the letters—"it's missing an E."

He continued to move away from her. He brushed off her comment with a sideways swipe of his hand. "Nobody will ever notice. And you can always go back to being Betty if you'd prefer."

She stood there, holding her prize, another thing she'd set her heart upon. Was this what it meant to be a modern girl? Was this what growing up was all about? Getting the things you think you want but then discovering their cracks, their flaws, their damage?

Margie tucked a curl behind her ear and straightened up. *If this is what it means to be a modern*, she thought, *I'll take it. With all its cracks.* Maybe modern life wasn't perfect, but it was hers. She unpinned her Betty tag and put it in her pocket. She placed her new tag over her heart. So it was spelled wrong. But it was *her* name spelled wrong. She spread both hands over the warm glass and grinned out onto the empty sales floor.

"Come on, Christmas shoppers. I'll make your day perfect."

Twelve

"Merry Christmas," she said for what felt like the thousandth time, stepping around the counter to hand the customer his purchase. Her cheeks hurt from keeping a smile on all day. She squeezed her shoulders around her ears and released them, sending away a portion of the day's tension. Her fingers found the heart-shaped hook in her pocket. She concentrated on breathing in and out for a few seconds, clutching the metal heart.

Betty slipped out from behind her glass counter and came to stand beside Margie. "Wow. What a day. This would have been a great day to keep count of sales. If we'd bet who sold more merchandise, you would owe me a coffee, a slice of cake, and a steak dinner."

Margie grinned. "Day's not over yet," she said and pointed to the back of a man in a woolen work coat, bent over a display case.

Betty leaped across the room as if she were starting a race. Margie smiled. If he wanted gloves, he'd come her way.

"Merry Christmas. Help you find what you're looking for?" Betty had perfected the flirty invitation combined with elegant gestures. She was certainly good at her job.

Whatever the man's reply, it made Betty laugh. "I'm not sure we can help you with that here, sir, but if you'd like to look at a scarf or gloves, you're in the right place."

"Gloves," he said as he turned toward Margie's counter.

She felt her mouth flap open, and then she let out a squeak befitting neither a Macy's Betty nor a modern girl.

"Henry!" she squealed, running across the sales floor. "Is it really you?" She jumped into his arms, and he picked her up off the ground in the hug she'd not known she missed so much.

"It's really me." He leaned down and snuck a kiss on her cheek. Flushed, she smiled up at him. He smoothed the front of his coat. "I had some business here in the city."

Business in the city? What a strange thing for a coal worker to say. But what a lovely set of words. A girl could definitely fall for a man with work in the city.

He leaned closer. "And I got a surprise telegram last night that I couldn't ignore." His hand cupped the entire side of her face. "Margie, look at you. You're so beautiful." He touched the curl on her cheek.

Her breath rushed through her, and her heart pounded. She couldn't tell if she was more likely to laugh or cry. Maybe she'd simply explode. She took a step back to look at him.

"I can't believe you're here," she whispered.

Before he could answer, Margie heard the distinctive displeased throat-clearing of Mr. Macaulay. She stepped a little farther from Henry. Straightening her skirt, she asked Henry, "What can I help you with today, sir?"

"Um, well, I . . . gloves." He glanced over his shoulder at Mr. Macaulay, who apparently still stood watching them. "I need a pair of gloves for my mother."

"That will make a lovely Christmas gift. Please, allow me to show you our selection." She stepped behind her case and leaned against the glass, grateful for the support for her suddenly shaking knees.

Henry kept sneaking glances toward the corner where Mr. Macaulay stood watch.

"Here is a pair perfectly suited for an elegant, modern lady."

Henry leaned close and shook his head. "You clearly don't know my mother." He spoke low, so only she could hear.

What was this? Henry was flirting. Henry. Flirting.

Margie swallowed a laugh and pointed out another pair. "These are wonderfully warm."

"Is this what's keeping your hands warm here in the city?" he whispered. "Or have you discovered better ways?"

She leaned across the counter to meet him in the middle. "What's happening with you? I'd hardly know you're the one speaking."

He shrugged. "Cold and serious didn't serve me well. I thought I'd try warm and witty."

"You're very good at it," she said. "Had much practice?"

Laughing, he said, "Who do you think I'd practice on?" He straightened and picked up a glove. Looking from it to Margie, he couldn't seem to suppress a smile. "Are you, by any chance, jealous?"

She pulled another pair from the case. "Let's call it curious."

He didn't answer. He picked up glove after glove and placed each one back on the counter. "Can you take a break or something? A walk?"

She looked at her wristwatch. "I have forty minutes until the store closes. Do you think you could amuse yourself around here for that long?" She pictured him trying out his newfound flirting skills with the sales force. "There are lovely curtains one flight up, and the dearest old man can help you find what you need."

He checked over his shoulder again for Mr. Macaulay and whispered, "Curtains sound nice, but I know what I need." He reached into his pocket and pulled out a small package. Then he smiled and slipped it into her hand. "I'll meet you by the front door in thirty-nine minutes. Just in case, I'll be there in thirty-eight."

As he turned and walked away, she stammered, "Thank you, sir. Merry Christmas." Since when had he become eloquent? And since when had she been speechless?

Mr. Macaulay finally, *finally* left his lookout in the corner and limped toward the escalators. Betty rushed over.

"Who was that? *What* was that? You've got a story to tell."

Margie felt her face flaming. Her heart pounded in her throat. "That was my . . . That was Henry. From home."

"Henry? The coal worker?" Betty shook her head. "The Henry you talk about is a boy. That's no boy, sister."

"I've known him all . . . we used to . . . when we were . . ." Margie couldn't seem to hold a thought. "You're right. He's not a boy." She clutched the little box.

Betty noticed. "What is it?"

"A Christmas present, I guess."

"Open it."

Margie turned the box in her hand. "Maybe he wants me to wait and open it when he's here."

Betty shook her head. "He handed it to you and walked away. Open it."

The tape holding the brown paper folded over a black fingerprint, and Margie stifled a frown. Poor Henry; those fingers would never be clean. But what could she expect? He was a coke stoker. She sighed.

Her fingernail slipped under the tape. Betty tapped her fingers against the glass but said nothing.

Margie smiled and tore through the paper. Inside was a small wooden box, no bigger than two inches square, hinged with gold. A tiny catch that pressed over a tiny post was all that stood between Margie and whatever Henry had brought her.

What if it was something horrible? Could she pretend she loved it?

What if it was something amazing? Could she let herself be swept into it?

What if it was a ring?

What if it wasn't?

What if Henry was making a declaration?

And what if he wasn't?

She was going to drive herself distracted. She took a deep breath. Touching the tiny peg, she got a little shock but couldn't tell if it was electricity or anticipation.

Prying back the lid, she realized she was looking at the ceiling. She forced her eyes to the box, but they drifted to the gloves under the glass counter. She shook herself, forced her gaze to the box and to a tiny gold chain. She pinched it between her fingers and lifted it. Dangling from the end was a distinctive heart-shaped hook. The heart from the glass balls. The heart that had captured her fancy and her imagination. The heart she'd set her Christmas dreams around was here, in her hand, delivered to her by Henry.

Thoughts tumbled through her head. How had he found this necklace? How had he known this was the part of the ornaments she loved best? When had he had it made?

Betty leaned over and clasped the chain around Margie's neck. The heart settled in the hollow of her throat as though it had been made specifically for her.

She lifted the tiny wooden box. On the bottom she saw the design for the glass blowing shop, Penn Woods Glass. But there was more: Henry Edwards, Penn Woods Glass.

No. She had to be dreaming this. It was simply not possible.

She read it again. The words were the same—Henry's name, connected to the symbol of her modern New York Christmas. Was it possible? Could it be? Had Henry made the bulbs? Henry, who'd made clunky, bulky, misshapen vases? Henry, her Henry, had created the magical, perfect ornaments that Macy's had used to transform the biggest department store in the world into a Christmas wonderland.

When a customer walked to Margie's counter, she snatched the box and stuffed it in her pocket. Her "Merry Christmas" was as sincere as her smile. Between customers, she rechecked her wristwatch. The minutes were behaving so oddly: speeding up and then slowing down.

When it was exactly six o'clock, she resisted the urge to turn off her display lights and lock up the cabinet. Even at closing time on Christmas Eve, a Macy's Betty would never press a customer to leave.

"How can I help you?" she asked a young woman clutching a ragged cloth handbag.

"Oh, I'm not sure I can afford anything," the woman said, putting on a brave face. Margie could see the tremble of her chin, the shine in her eyes.

"Is there someone special you're shopping for?"

"My . . . he's my, well, friend." She looked a dizzying combination of proud and nervous.

"Does he wear ties? Cuff links?" Margie glanced in the direction of the escalators, wondering if Henry would be upset that she was late.

Keep your focus on the customer, Betty.

The girl shook her head with a little laugh. "He's an artist."

A tiny ripple of envy rising in Margie's heart made her sad, then made her laugh. What she'd wanted for years was what she had right here—a working man with an artist's touch: Henry, the artist. Henry, the creator.

Henry, the man she'd discounted. The man she might have lost.

My Modern Girl

She glanced again toward the escalator and saw him standing there, near enough to watch her work, but far enough to be out of her way. She shivered with the happy thought that he'd come back to wait for her.

"I know exactly the thing," she said. "This Christmas, Macy's is decorated with the most beautiful blown glass ornaments. They're perfectly lovely, and the balls are suspended from the most charming hooks shaped like little hearts. Have you seen them?"

The young woman nodded and pointed to the tree in the corner.

"I happen to know the artist who created them. He's a young man with a great future ahead of him." Margie forced her eyes to stay on the customer. "What if you bought your friend one of those ornaments? Nothing would tell him you love him better than a gift from your heart." She aimed her words to the young woman but knew Henry was hearing every word.

The girl nodded, and Margie directed her to the proper floor. As she guided her toward the escalators and wished her a Merry Christmas, Margie caught Henry's eye. She looked down, suddenly nervous. She held up a finger to ask him to wait as she closed up her counter for the holiday.

He stepped over to her. "It's time to go," he whispered. "It's Christmastime." He drew his finger along the tiny gold chain resting over her collarbone.

She reached up and took his hand in hers. "Oh, Henry. I love the necklace. I love it so much." She squeezed his fingers. "How did you do it?"

He laughed softly. "Which part?"

"Did you really make all of those ornaments? When would you have time for that? How did you sell them to the store? How did you get them here? "How come you never told me?"

He tucked her curl behind her ear. "That was the really hard part," he said. "I wanted to tell you. You can't imagine how often. After you left, I couldn't write to you for a month because I was sure I wouldn't keep the secret. When Macy's made an order, I wanted to drive the package here myself. I wanted you to see me delivering it. I wanted so much for you to be proud of me. To do something that could make me worthy of you."

"Oh, Henry. I *am* proud. So proud. I've been such a dummy. I thought I needed . . . I thought I knew . . . It's all tumbled up in my head."

He took her hand and led her out the front doors. "You can't always count on your head to tell you what's best."

She laughed. This was the Henry she'd known—and, she realized, loved—for all her life. "I'm terribly glad you came." Her words came out clouded in puffs of frozen air.

"I could have stood there watching you work all day." He let go of her hand and put his arm over her shoulders. Her cheeks flushed warm in the cold evening.

"I love it here," Margie said. "I do. It's almost everything I wanted—but not the most important thing." She leaned her head closer to his shoulder. "You must think I've been so silly."

His arm tightened around her shoulders. "Not silly. The city is perfect for you. You're a modern girl." He stopped walking and turned on the crowded sidewalk to face her. "You're *my* modern girl."

She took in his confidence, his posture, his forthrightness. "You've changed."

"So have you," he said. "More than the haircut."

"What are the chances we've both changed in the exact way to become perfect for each other?"

"That sounds like a pretty tall order," he said with a smile. "Like a Christmas wish."

With her hands on his giant shoulders, she leaned up and whispered, "It's all I have left to wish for this Christmas. You've made everything else come true."

My Modern Girl

He fingered the heart on the chain. "You're wearing my heart. That's all I've ever wished for."

ABOUT BECCA WILHITE

Becca Wilhite loves books—reading and writing them. She also loves lots of other things: her near-perfect husband and four brilliant kids, buttery foods, movies, walks, blogging, planning exotic vacations to places she can't spell, teaching high school English, Juicy Pear Jelly Belly candy, waking up early, the wooden escalators in the New York City Macy's department store, and singing along to cheesy Broadway musicals. Her published books include *Bright Blue Miracle* and *My Ridiculous Romantic Obsessions*.

You can get inside her head (in a completely benign way) at www.BeccaWilhite.com

Dear Timeless Romance Anthology Reader,

Thank you for reading this anthology. We hoped you loved the sweet romance novellas! Heather B. Moore, Annette Lyon, and Sarah M. Eden have been indie publishing this series since 2012 through the Mirror Press imprint. For each anthology, we carefully select three guest authors. Our goal is to offer a way for our readers to discover new, favorite authors by reading these romance novellas written exclusively for our anthologies . . . all for one great price.

If you enjoyed this anthology, please consider leaving a review on Goodreads or Amazon or any other e-book store you purchase through. Reviews and word of mouth is what helps us continue this fun project.

Also, if you're interested in become a regular reviewer of the anthologies and would like access to advance copies, please email Heather Moore: heather@hbmoore.com

Thank you!

The Timeless Romance Authors

MORE TIMELESS ROMANCE ANTHOLOGIES

For the latest updates on our anthologies visit our blog:
TimelessRomanceAnthologies.blogspot.com

www.ingramcontent.com/pod-product-compliance
Lightning Source LLC
LaVergne TN
LVHW021757060526
838201LV00058B/3131